INSPECTOR WITHERSPOON ALWAYS TRIUMPHS . . .
HOW DOES HE DO IT?

Even the Inspector himself doesn't know—because his secret
weapon is as ladylike as she is clever. She's Mrs. Jeffries—the
determined, delightful detective who stars in this unique
Victorian mystery series. Be sure to read them all . . .

The Inspector and Mrs. Jeffries
A doctor is found dead in his own office—and Mrs. Jeffries
must scour the premises to find the prescription for murder.

Mrs. Jeffries Dusts for Clues
One case is solved and another is opened when the Inspector
finds a missing brooch—pinned to a dead woman's gown. But
Mrs. Jeffries never cleans a room without dusting under the
bed—and never gives up on a case before every loose end is
tightly tied . . .

The Ghost and Mrs. Jeffries
Death is unpredictable . . . but the murder of Mrs. Hodges was
foreseen at a spooky séance. The practical-minded housekeeper
may not be able to see the future—but she can look into the
past and put things in order to solve this haunting crime.

Mrs. Jeffries Takes Stock
A businessman has been murdered—and it could be because
he cheated his stockholders. The housekeeper's interest is
piqued . . .and when it comes to catching killers, the smart
money's on Mrs. Jeffries.

continued . . .

Mrs. Jeffries Reveals Her Art
Mrs. Jeffries has to work double-time to find a missing model *and* a killer. And she'll have to get her whole staff involved—before someone else becomes the next subject . . .

Mrs. Jeffries Takes the Cake
The evidence was all there: a dead body, two dessert plates, and a gun. As if Mr. Ashbury had been sharing cake with his own killer. Now Mrs. Jeffries will have to do some snooping around—to dish up clues . . .

Mrs. Jeffries Rocks the Boat
Mirabelle had traveled by boat all the way from Australia to visit her sister—only to wind up murdered. Now Mrs. Jeffries must solve the case—and it's sink or swim . . .

Mrs. Jeffries Weeds the Plot
Three attempts have been made on Annabeth Gentry's life. Is it due to her recent inheritance, or was it because her bloodhound dug up the body of a murdered thief? Mrs. Jeffries will have to sniff out some clues before the plot thickens . . .

Mrs. Jeffries Pinches the Post
Harrison Nye may have been involved in some dubious business dealings, but no one ever expected him to be murdered. Now, Mrs. Jeffries and her staff must root through the sins of his past to discover which one caught up with him . . .

Berkley Prime Crime titles by Emily Brightwell

Anthologies

MRS. JEFFRIES
PLEADS HER CASE

EMILY BRIGHTWELL

BERKLEY PRIME CRIME, NEW YORK

MRS. JEFFRIES PLEADS HER CASE

A Berkley Prime Crime Book / published by arrangement with
the author

PRINTING HISTORY
Berkley Prime Crime mass-market edition / April 2003

ISBN: 978-0-425-18947-4

Berkley Prime Crime Books are published
by The Berkley Publishing Group,
a division of Penguin Putnam Inc.,
375 Hudson Street, New York, New York 10014.
The name BERKLEY PRIME CRIME and the
BERKLEY PRIME CRIME design
are trademarks belonging to Penguin Putnam Inc.

PRINTED IN THE UNITED STATES OF AMERICA

10   9   8   7   6   5

CHAPTER 1

"They won't get away with it," Harlan Westover muttered to himself as he charged into his flat and slammed his door shut. He winced at the noise and then remembered that Mrs. Lynch, his landlady, was out of town and wouldn't be bothered by his fit of temper.

Harlan tossed his overcoat onto the settee and stalked across the room to the desk in the corner. Yanking out a chair, he sat down, pulled out a piece of paper from the stack in the top cubicle, and grabbed his pen off of the brass inkstand.

He froze for a moment, frowning at the pristine white page and then shrugged. It didn't matter how he wrote the affair up, it only mattered that he got the facts correct.

For ten minutes the only sound in the quiet room was the scratch of his pen across the page. He paused, read what he'd written and then nodded in satisfaction. The prose wasn't elegant, but it told the tale well enough.

A knock sounded on his door, and he started in surprise. The nib of the pen slapped against his fingers, smearing the tips with ink. The knock came again, and without realizing it, he jerked and his stained fingers brushed against his shirt collar. He shoved the paper into the dictionary lying on the edge of his desk, put the pen back in the stand, got to his feet, and crossed the room.

Harlan opened the door. "What on earth are you doing here? Oh, I suppose you'd best come in . . ." he motioned for his visitor to step inside. "If you think to dissuade me from my course, you've wasted your time. There's nothing anyone can say that will stop me from doing what's right."

His visitor said nothing.

Confused by the silence, Harlan frowned. "Perhaps we'd best sit down," he started toward the settee. "Let me move my coat . . ." his voice trailed off, a strangled gasp escaped from his throat, and he toppled onto the plump cushions. A splatter of blood seeped out from the now-bleeding gash on the side of his head and dripped onto the dark paisley fabric of the overstuffed arm of the settee. Then his eyes closed and he lapsed into unconsciousness.

The visitor moved quickly and efficiently. It took only moments to rearrange Harlan's body. As he'd fallen awkwardly, the visitor found it easiest to prop Westover up at the other end of the settee. It was important to set the scene correctly. No one must suspect the truth.

Harlan Westover's visitor pressed a revolver into the unconscious man's hand and then positioned his arm so that the weapon was aimed at the bleeding gash where he'd been struck. The weapon fired once and he slumped to one side, his arm dangling over the end of the settee. The gun was strategically placed on the carpet, just below the man's fingers. It had to look like he'd dropped the revolver himself.

The guest smiled in satisfaction. Harlan Westover was most definitely dead. He wouldn't be telling anyone anything.

The household of Inspector Gerald Witherspoon was gathered around the table in the kitchen for their morning tea.

"I suppose it's just as well that we don't have a case, what with Luty and Hatchet being gone," Mrs. Goodge, the cook, said. She was an older woman with gray hair, wire rimmed spectacles, and a rather portly frame. She'd cooked in some

of the finest houses in England but counted herself lucky to
have ended up working for Gerald Witherspoon.

"Why'd they want to go off in the dead of winter?" Wiggins, the footman, asked. He was a handsome, brown-haired
lad of twenty. He helped himself to a slice of bread and then
reached for the butter pot. "Seems to me January is a miserable time to be crossing the Atlantic."

"They didn't have much choice," Mrs. Jeffries, the housekeeper, replied. "Luty's American lawyers insisted on the
meeting. Apparently, she's got to make a number of important decisions regarding her properties in that country. She
still has a number of investments in her native land."

Mrs. Jeffries was a short, vibrant woman of late middle
age. She had auburn hair liberally sprinkled with gray, sharp
brown eyes, a ready smile, and a mind like a steel trap.

Betsy, the pretty, blond-haired maid, tossed a quick glance
at her fiancé, Smythe. He was a large, rather brutal looking
man with dark hair, heavy features, and the kindest brown
eyes in the world. He was also Inspector Witherspoon's
coachman. Betsy and Smythe had been engaged for several
months now and were devoted to one another.

Mrs. Jeffries ducked her head to hide a smile as she saw
the quick, rather furtive glance the maid darted at her beloved. No doubt the two of them felt just a bit guilty when
the subject of "investments" came up. Betsy, being Smythe's
fiancée, knew the truth about him. So did Mrs. Jeffries. She
was well aware of the fact that Smythe wasn't just a mere
coachman, he was a very rich man with a legion of investments of his own. Every time the subject of money came up,
these two squirmed like a couple of guilty puppies. Well,
that was to be expected. Keeping secrets was often very uncomfortable, especially for such naturally honest souls as
these two.

Smythe, interpreting Betsy's expression correctly, decided
to steer the conversation to more comfortable waters. "Did
they know 'ow long they'd be gone?"

"Luty hoped they'd be home by the end of the month.
They'd like to come home at the end of the month on the
Corinthian."

"That's a bit quick isn't it?" Smythe reached for a slice of bread. "What's the 'urry. You'd think they'd want to stay a bit. Doesn't Luty ever get homesick?"

"She's scared if they stay too long she'll miss a murder," Mrs. Goodge said bluntly. "Besides, Luty's lived in London for so many years, I don't think that she's got any reason to prolong a visit to America. She doesn't have any family there."

"Funny, isn't it, how so many of us don't 'ave much family," Wiggins said, his expression wistful, but then he looked up and grinned. "It's right that we've got each other, then, isn't it?"

"Indeed it is," Mrs. Jeffries said calmly. But the lad's remark had hit very close to home, she thought. She gazed around the table. Thank goodness they did have each other. They'd come together several years ago when Gerald Witherspoon inherited this house and a sizable fortune from his late Aunt Euphemia.

Smythe and Wiggins were already here, having worked for Euphemia Witherspoon in the capacities of coachman and footman. Even though the inspector had no need for a coachman and was far too informal to use a footman properly, he'd been too kindhearted to turn them out. Gerald Witherspoon had had no idea how to run a large house, so he'd hired Mrs. Jeffries as his housekeeper. Mrs. Goodge, who'd lost her last position as a cook because she was getting old, had come along and finally, Betsy, half-starved and half-frozen had landed on their doorstep. Though Betsy had no proper training, once she'd regained her strength, the inspector had insisted on hiring her as a maid. They'd been together ever since.

"It's too bad we don't have a case," Betsy muttered. "It seems like a long time since we were out snooping about. It's getting a bit boring." And her beloved was beginning to pressure her to set a wedding date as well. Smythe was a wonderful man, and she loved him with all her heart, but when they weren't actively trying to catch a killer, he tended to forget they'd agreed to wait a bit for marriage. When they were in the midst of a case, he understood how important their investigations were to both of them.

"We just had one," Mrs. Jeffries pointed out. But the truth was, she rather agreed with the maid. Life was boring when they weren't on the hunt, so to speak. However, she did feel it was her duty to remind everyone that murder wasn't really the sort of thing one ought to wish for, regardless of how bored one was.

"That was months ago," Wiggins interjected.

"It was October," the cook said. "And it's wrong to wish someone would die just so we'd have a murder to sort out." Like the housekeeper, she felt morally obligated to defend the sanctity of law and order. But she did love their cases.

"I'm not wishing someone would die," Betsy protested. "I'm just sayin' life is more interesing when we're on a case."

"Of course it is," Mrs. Jeffries agreed. "But according to the inspector there's absolutely nothing on the horizon. He's spent the last week working on an alledged fraud against an insurance company. The only corpses that have turned up have been an elderly man freezing to death on a church porch and a suicide over on Charter Street off Brook Green."

"Someone froze to death outside a church?" Smythe shook his head. "That's disgustin'. Why didn't they do something for the poor old fellow?"

"Perhaps they didn't know he was there until it was too late," Mrs. Jeffries shrugged sympathetically. "The inspector didn't have many details, but there certainly wasn't any suspicion of foul play."

"How about the suicide?" Betsy asked eagerly.

"According to the papers, there was no indication of foul play there either, I'm afraid," Mrs. Jeffries sighed. "More's the pity."

"But you just said it were wrong to wish someone dead just so we'd 'ave us a murder to investigate," Wiggins said, his expression confused.

"I wasn't wishing this unfortunate person dead," she explained, "I was simply hoping it was murder. Suicide is such an ugly circumstance for a death. It's so difficult for the family and friends."

"And he'd be much better off if he'd been murdered," Mrs. Goodge added with a shake of her head, "at least then he'd not be roasting in hell."

Chief Inspector Barrows was a bit embarrassed. He didn't like having to be less than honest with one of his subordinates. But, of course, it wouldn't do to let his discomfort show. "So you see, Witherspoon, we'd best be very circumspect in this matter. Have a bit of a look around on the quiet, if you know what I mean."

"Actually, sir, I'm not sure that I do," Inspector Gerald Witherspoon admitted. "If the coroner's inquest has already ruled the man's death a suicide, I don't understand what it is you want me to do."

"We've some new evidence, Witherspoon. But it's evidence that can be interpreted any number of ways." He could hardly admit that the new evidence consisted solely of the dead man's landlady being utterly convinced that the victim wouldn't ever have committed suicide. But as the landlady was Chief Inspector Barrows's old nanny, he'd promised her he'd have another look at the case.

"What kind of evidence, sir?" Witherspoon asked.

"It's Westover's landlady," Barrows spoke carefully, hoping this most brilliant of detectives would actually understand the delicate political situation they were facing. Magistrates didn't particularly like having their inquest verdicts questioned, especially on this sort of evidence. "She came to see me. She's utterly convinced the fellow wasn't suicidal."

"Westover is the victim's name?" the inspector clarified. He was still a bit confused. If they had new evidence, it was perfectly permissible to ignore the coroner's inquest and open an investigation, mind you, some magistrates got a tad irritated when this happened, but justice had to be served. "I take it he's the fellow who shot himself in the head a couple of weeks ago?"

"Not according to his landlady. She's convinced he was murdered."

"On what evidence, sir?"

Barrows looked down at his desk and then back up at the inspector. "The only evidence she has is her knowledge of the man's character. She claims he wouldn't have killed himself under any circumstances. Harlan Westover was a Roman Catholic. I believe they consider suicide a mortal sin."

As far as the inspector knew, most Christians considered suicide a sin, but he wouldn't debate the point with his superior. "Why didn't his landlady give evidence at the inquest if she knew this?"

"She wasn't home," Barrows replied. "She only returned from the north yesterday evening. She was horrified when she found out her tenant had not only taken his own life, but that the inquest had already taken place and a verdict rendered."

Witherspoon nodded thoughtfully. "So the only new evidence we have is her assertion that he wouldn't have killed himself for religious reasons."

Barrows winced inwardly. As evidence, it was decidedly weak. "That's why I wanted you to have a bit of a look around on the sly, so to speak."

"I think that can be done, sir," Witherspoon nodded. "I'll be very discreet. There's no point in upsetting the apple cart at this stage, sir."

"It's not very good evidence, I'm afraid," Barrows said.

"I wouldn't say that, sir," the inspector replied. "Obviously, the victim's landlady felt strongly enough about it to come and see you. It could well be that she's absolutely correct." But she probably wasn't. Roman Catholic or not, the physical evidence at the scene had indicated suicide to the investigating officers. Still, Witherspoon felt he ought to keep an open mind. "What is the landlady's name?"

"Helen Lynch." Barrows's austere face broke into a smile. "Actually, she's my old nanny. She's expecting you this morning. You're in luck, Witherspoon, she's not touched the flat since she's been home, so the crime scene hasn't really been disturbed. I'll write out her address."

The inspector nodded and pushed his spectacles, which

had a tendency to slip down his nose, back into place. "West-over died two weeks ago, right?"

"Correct, the report says it was probably January sixth." Barrows looked up from his writing. "Nanny Lynch returned from Galway on Saturday evening. She came to see me last night."

"So the murder, if indeed murder is what we have here, is a fortnight old," the inspector frowned. "The trail's a bit cold . . ."

"I'm aware of that," Barrows laid down his pen. As all policemen knew, the longer it was between the crime and an investigation, the harder it was to catch the killer. Witnesses forgot pertinent information, important details were over-looked, and physical evidence was destroyed or mislaid. "Look, Inspector, I know we're at a distinct disadvantage here, if, as you noted, a murder has taken place. But as I've already told you, the crime scene's not been touched and as far as I know, Westover's solicitors haven't begun divvying up his property."

"Did he have any relations?" Witherspoon asked.

Barrows shrugged. "I don't know. Why don't you go along and have a chat with Nanny Lynch. Westover had been her tenant for the last three years. She can tell you all about him."

"Yes sir," he reached over and picked up the paper with Nanny Lynch's address on it. "I'll take Constable Barnes and pop along to see her straight away. Er . . . uh . . . how discreet do I need to be sir?"

Barrows stroked his chin thoughtfully. "I'll leave that up to you, Inspector."

"Right sir," Witherspoon nodded respectfully and then left. Barrows slumped in his chair. He had a moment of misgiving about this whole business. Witherspoon might be his most brilliant homicide investigator, but the fellow had the social acumen of a tree stump. Sometimes Barrows wondered if the fellow wasn't just a bit backwards, not stupid or anything that harsh, but a bit like one of those terribly sad defective individuals who couldn't tie their shoes but could do multi-plication and long division without any trouble at all. Barrows had attended a lecture last year about the subject. He shook himself to dislodge the thought. Witherspoon was the best homicide detective he'd ever seen and a decent chap to boot. But he did hope that the fellow had the good sense to keep a low profile on this investigation, at least until they got some conclusive evidence.

"Do you think there's anything to this, sir?" Constable Barnes asked as they rounded the corner off Shepherds Bush Road and started up Charter Street towards Helen Lynch's house.

The constable was a craggy-faced veteran of London's streets. He'd walked the beat for years before he'd joined up with Inspector Witherspoon. Under his policemen's helmet, his hair was iron gray and his mind as sharp as a razor.

"I don't know," Witherspoon sighed and pulled his heavy topcoat closer against the cold, winter wind. "From the report I read, there doesn't seem to be much in the way of clues."

"If you ask me, the report wasn't very thorough," Barnes complained. "Just a few pages of notes and no witness interviews at all. Here we are, sir." He opened the gate and started up the stone walkway to number 6.

Helen Lynch's house was a neat, two-story red brick affair with a small, enclosed front garden and white lace curtains at the bow front windows.

"The report wasn't very detailed," Witherspoon agreed as they reached the front door. "But then again, the officers were under the impression they were dealing with a suicide. The doors were all locked from the inside, and there was no indication of a struggle." But privately, Witherspoon thought the chief officer assigned to the case had done a very shoddy job.

Barnes reached over and banged the heavy brass knocker. A moment later, the door opened and an elderly, gray-haired woman peered out at them. "So you've finally arrived, have you? It's about time. I told Neddy to get right on this." She stepped back and gestured for them to step inside.

Witherspoon smiled at the idea that 'Neddy' was their austere Chief Inspector Barrows. "Good day, ma'am, I'm

Inspector Gerald Witherspoon and this is Constable Barnes."
They stepped inside to a small foyer crowded with a wooden
coat tree, a huge ceramic umbrella stand, and a trestle table
holding a giant potted fern. A staircase with thick, brown
carpet was next to the table. "I take it you're Mrs. Lynch?"

"That's correct," she nodded curtly. "Give me your coats
and hats, please." They shed their outer garments and handed
them to their hostess. Witherspoon noticed there were three
large umbrellas in the white and blue stand. He wondered if
one of them belonged to Harlan Westover.

"Come along then," Mrs. Lynch ordered, "let's go into the
sitting room. Mina will bring us tea. It's so cold outside. But
then again, it's the middle of winter so I suppose we can't
expect sunshine."

She led the way down a short hall and into a large, nicely
furnished sitting room. A fireplace and mantel were on the
far wall, and opposite was a rose-colored settee with white
antimacassars along the top. On each side of the settee was
a straight back chair, with maroon upholstering on the back-
rest and the seat. The wallpaper was a cheerful rose and
green paisley against a white background, and there was a
pale gray carpet on the floor. Two huge potted ferns, stood
on pedestals at each side of the door.

"Sit down, gentlemen," Helen Lynch gestured toward the
settee and the chairs. "I'm sure you've a lot of questions to
ask me. I didn't mean to be rude earlier, but I do want this
resolved as quickly as possible. Mr. Westover did not commit suicide. I can't imagine why anyone would think he did."

Witherspoon nodded and took one of the chairs. Barnes
took the other one, leaving the settee to their hostess. The
constable whipped out his little brown notebook. The inspector cleared his throat, but he wasn't quite sure where to
begin. Then he remembered something his housekeeper was
always saying, "You're so very clever, sir. You always go
right to the heart of the matter." Of course, that's where he
ought to start.

The door opened and the maid came in, pushing a tea
trolley. "Here you are, ma'am," she put the trolley in front
of Mrs. Lynch.

"Thank you, Mina." She dismissed the maid with a nod and then looked at the two policemen. "How do you take your tea?"

"Sugar and milk for both of us," Barnes answered quickly. Despite the fire, he was feeling the cold.

She nodded, poured and handed them their cups.

Witherspoon took a quick sip of the warming brew. "Thank you, this is wonderful. Mrs. Lynch, why are you so convinced that Mr. Westover didn't commit suicide?"

She sighed impatiently and put her own cup down on the trolley. "I've already told Neddy . . ."

"Yes, I know that," he replied, "but if you don't mind, I'd like to hear it from you. Learning information secondhand, so to speak, isn't as efficient as hearing it directly from a witness."

She raised an eyebrow. "Is that what I am, then? A witness."

"A very important one, Mrs. Lynch," Constable Barnes interjected. "So far, you're the only one who's come forward with any information at all about this case . . ."

Mrs. Lynch interrupted him with a loud snort. "Seems to me if the police had done their job properly, there'd have been any number of witnesses that could have told you plenty. That's what I told Neddy, too. You've left it a bit late now, and you'll be lucky if anyone can remember seeing or hearing anything about poor Mr. Westover's murder."

Witherspoon rather agreed with her, but he could hardly admit it. "Uh, Mrs. Lynch . . ."

"I know, I know," she waved him off impatiently. "You're still waiting to hear why I'm so convinced it was murder. To begin with, right before I went off, Mr. Westover told me he was going on holiday next month. People who are planning on killing themselves don't make plans to go on holiday."

"Mr. Westover was going on holiday?" Barnes looked up from his notebook. "At this time of year?"

She nodded eagerly. "He was going to go to Sicily. He said it was warm there and he needed to get away from his work. He'd been working dreadfully hard. Some days he'd leave before dawn and not get home till late in the night. I believe he'd actually booked his tickets."

"Do you know where he booked them?" Barnes asked.

Mrs. Lynch shook her head. "I never thought to ask. Why? Is it important?"

"It could be," the constable looked back down at his notebook.

"What kind of work did Mr. Westover do?" Witherspoon asked. He knew from his quick look at the report that he'd been employed at an engineering firm somewhere nearby.

"He was an engineer," Mrs. Lynch replied. "Quite a clever one too. He worked for a firm off the Kensington High Street. Donovan, Melcher, and Horrocks."

"Did Mr. Westover have any family?" Constable Barnes asked. "There wasn't mention of anyone in the corner's file or the police report."

"He really hadn't anyone," Mrs. Lynch smiled sadly. "He never married, and both his parents were dead. There are a couple of cousins in Bristol, but he hadn't had any contact with them in years."

"No brothers or sisters?" Witherspoon pressed. Like the constable, the inspector wanted to have some idea about who might be likely to benefit from Mr. Westover's death. Generally, the person who benefited the most was someone near and dear to the deceased.

"No, Inspector. As I've said. He was quite alone in the world. It's sad. He was a very nice man. He would have made some woman a good husband. But he was one of those men who are married to their work. Honestly, there were times when he'd be poring over those funny papers of his, and I swear, he'd not hear a word I'd say."

"Funny papers?" Witherspoon wondered what on earth she meant.

"Oh, you know, these funny papers with drawings of all sorts of newfangled nonsense on them," she retorted. "I asked him once what they were, and he told me they were his designs for some sort of engine. Proud of it, he was. He spent a good half hour explaining how the ruddy thing worked, and I had to stand there and pretend to understand what he was going on about." She broke off and looked away. "I wish now I had understood. He was so proud of that silly engine, and all I wanted to do was to get back to my kitchen and have a cup of tea." She sniffed and swiped at her cheeks with her hand.

The inspector cringed inwardly. She was crying. He was hopeless at dealing with weeping women. He'd no idea what to do.

"Mrs. Lynch," Barnes said softly, "don't take it so hard. You weren't to know he was going to die."

She drew a long, deep breath and straightened her spine. "You're right. Of course I didn't know, and he could go on and on about his work."

"Was that the only thing he ever spoke about?" Witherspoon asked. He was grateful that Barnes had gotten her to stop crying.

"Of course not, Inspector. He was devoted to his work, but he read the newspapers. He could talk about what was going on in the world. I miss him very much and not just because he always paid his rent on time and took care to be considerate."

"I take it you and Mr. Westover were quite . . . er . . . friendly," the inspector stumbled over the last few words. He didn't want to imply anything that might offend the lady. She was, after all, his chief inspector's old nanny.

Mrs. Lynch laughed. "Of course we were friends. He was lonely. He spent many an evening in my front parlor chatting with me in front of the fire." She shook her head and smiled wistfully. "I shall miss him. I guess you could say, we were both a bit lonely."

"Was Mr. Westover your only tenant?" Witherspoon asked.

"No, Mr. Baker has the rooms on the top floor. But he's not here very often, he travels for his work. So usually, it was just Mr. Westover and me. He took all of his meals here. Mind you, recently, he'd missed supper a good deal of the time because he'd been working so hard." She stopped and seemed to shake herself. "So tell me, Inspector, what are you going to do about his murder?"

"Ah, Mrs. Lynch, I'm not quite sure . . . uh, so far the only evidence you've given us that the poor fellow was murdered is that he was planning on going on holiday . . ."

"That's not all," she interrupted. "There's a bit more than that. I know Mr. Westover didn't kill himself. He couldn't. He didn't own a gun. So how did he come to blow his brains out then? Answer me that!"

"The inspector's a bit late this evening," Betsy said as she came to stand next to the housekeeper in the front parlor. "I wonder what's keeping him." Neither woman would ever admit it, but they did worry just a little when he was delayed. He was, after all, a policeman, and that wasn't the safest occupation in London.

The housekeeper cocked her head toward the window. "I believe I hear a hansom pulling up outside." She stepped close and yanked the heavy velvet curtain to one side. "Oh good, it's the inspector. He's finally home."

"Should I pop down and get his dinner tray?" Betsy asked as she started toward the door.

Mrs. Jeffries hesitated. "Wait here for a few moments, let's see if he's hungry." Because he was a good hour and a half late, she suspected something might be in the wind. If that was the case, her dear inspector might want a glass of sherry and a nice chat before he had his meal.

The front door opened and Witherspoon stepped inside. His narrow face brightened. "Good evening, Mrs. Jeffries, Betsy."

"Good evening, sir," she held out her hand for his hat. "You're a bit late, sir. Was the traffic terrible?"

He gave her his bowler and started to unbutton his heavy black overcoat. "Traffic was bad," he sighed, as he slipped the garment off his shoulder, "but no worse than usual. I'm afraid I'm late because . . . well, I'm not quite sure how to put this, but I think there might have been a murder."

Behind the inspector's back, the two women exchanged glances. "Shall I go down and get your dinner tray, sir?" Betsy asked.

"I believe I'll have a sherry first," Witherspoon replied. "It has been a very tiring day."

Mrs. Jeffries took his coat and hung it just below his hat. "Come along into the drawing room, sir. A sherry is just what you need. Betsy, why don't you bring up the inspector's tray in about fifteen minutes."

"That'll be perfect," Witherspoon replied. Betsy nodded and hurried off toward the backstairs. Mrs. Jeffries knew that the moment the maid got to the kitchen she'd tell the others to be "at the ready," so to speak.

She led the inspector the short distance down the hall and into the drawing room. He immediately went to his favorite armchair and sat. She moved to the sideboard, pulled a bottle of *Harvey's* out of the bottom cupboard and poured him a glass.

"Do pour one for yourself as well," he called to the house-keeper. "You've probably had a tiring day too."

"Thank you, sir." She poured another for herself, picked up the glasses, and made her way across the room. Handing him his drink, she said, "Now sir, what's all this about a possible murder?"

Witherspoon sighed and took a sip of his sherry. "It's all the chief inspector's doing. It seems his old nanny came to him this morning all in a dither about stories that one of her tenants had taken his own life."

"The suicide," Mrs. Jeffries murmured aloud as she thought back to the conversation she'd had with the others earlier in the day.

"The suicide," the inspector repeated her words. "How did you hear about it?"

Mrs. Jeffries caught herself. "Oh, I didn't really, sir. It's just that the only thing that's been in the papers the last few weeks is a suicide and an accidental death." She held her breath, praying he wouldn't realize how closely she and the others watched the papers. She couldn't have him suspecting she'd been nosing about, trying to see if he had anything interesting on his plate. "I'm sorry, please do go on."

"You're right. It was the suicide." He took another quick sip. "The chief inspector had me go around and have a quick look-see because he didn't wish to disappoint his old nanny."

"His old nanny?"

"It was her tenant that supposedly took his own life. But honestly, Mrs. Jeffries, I think Mrs. Lynch is right."

"You mean you think her, er . . . lodger was murdered?" She forced her face to stay blank and her tone calm. But inside, her spirits soared.

"Well," he hesitated. "I can't be sure. But she did make a rather interesting point. A few days before Mr. Westover's allegeded suicide, Mrs. Lynch thinks he booked tickets for a long holiday. As Mrs. Lynch pointed out, one doesn't spend all that money for a trip to Italy and then kill oneself."

"Was that her only reason for thinking his death was murder?" She wanted to make sure she got all of the details out of the inspector.

Witherspoon pursed his lips. "No, she claimed that Westover didn't own a gun and therefore, couldn't have killed himself with one. I didn't want to upset the dear lady by pointing out that revolvers are quite easy to acquire."

"But as far as she knew, he didn't have a weapon," Mrs. Jeffries said thoughtfully.

"Correct," the inspector's brows drew together. "She also insisted that Westover wasn't in the least depressed about anything and that he was positively looking forward to the future."

"What, precisely, were the circumstances of the death?" Mrs. Jeffries took another sip of her sherry.

"Actually, I uh, didn't read the file very carefully. I didn't have much time, you see." Witherspoon was so embarrassed he fibbed just a bit. He'd read every word of the file, but he didn't want to admit to anyone, even Mrs. Jeffries, how little information the investigating officer had obtained. "But the long and short of it is, Harlan Westover died of a gunshot wound to his head. The gun was found lying on the carpet right under his fingertips. This happened almost a fortnight ago."

"A fortnight!" She hadn't realized it had been quite that far back. The newspaper account had only appeared last week.

"My sentiments precisely," the inspector shook his head. "The trail, if indeed there has been a murder, is exceedingly cold. But it couldn't be helped. Mrs. Lynch only arrived home herself a couple of days ago. She was quite shocked when she realized that not only had her lodger died, but the coroner had already made a ruling and the case was considered closed."

"Who discovered the body?" Mrs. Jeffries asked. The case had just begun, and it was already a bit muddled.

"A man named James Horrocks, he's the general manager of Westover's firm. When he didn't arrive at work the next day and didn't send a message, they got concerned and went around to his rooms."

"How'd they get in if the landlady was gone?"

Witherspoon's brow furrowed. "You know, I'm not sure. I don't think the report mentioned how Mr. Horrocks got inside. I shall make a note to follow up on that question. However, be that as it may, the fellow got inside, saw what had happened, and then fetched the police. You know what happens after that. The coroner's inquest ruled the death a suicide, and the case was closed."

"Does Mr. Westover have any family?" Mrs. Jeffries asked.

"Just some distant cousins. From what I gathered from Mrs. Lynch, he didn't stay in contact with them. According to her, he was quite alone in the world. Of course, Mrs. Lynch might not know the extent of his relations."

"Does he have an estate, sir?" Might as well get that aspect out into the open, she thought. People who stood to inherit were frequently those who most had reason to want someone dead. "Even if he's no family to speak of, someone's got to inherit his things."

Again, the inspector frowned. "I don't really know. I suppose I ought to go around to his rooms and see if I can find the name of his solictor." He sighed and tossed back the last of his sherry. "I do hope it isn't a murder, because if it is, the case is already a bit of a mess. Frankly, Mrs. Jeffries, I've not a clue about what's the best way to go about this investigation. The fellow died two weeks ago. Any witnesses there might have been have disappeared. The crime scene has been mucked about, and we don't even know if anyone heard the gunshot that killed the poor man. Where does one begin?"

Mrs. Jeffries understood her employer's dilemma. At the best of times, he wasn't overly burdened with self-confidence. Trying to track down a possible murderer under these circumstances would be a daunting task for anyone.

But she knew what he needed. "You begin where you always do, sir," she said briskly. "With the victim. Learn the victim, and you'll find the killer, that's what you've always said, sir."

"Really?" He sounded genuinely surprised. "I said that?"

He'd said no such thing, of course. But it was sound advice. "Of course you did, sir. You mustn't let a little thing like a delayed investigation make you feel you're not up to the task. Why you know you're absolutely brilliant at catching killers, even killers that think they've gotten away with it." And that would be the case now. If Harlan Westover had been murdered, his killer wouldn't be expecting an investigation at this stage of events. That might just work to their advantage.

She stopped, aware that she was already thinking of the case as a murder. She mustn't do that. Not yet. Not until they knew for certain one way or the other.

"Thank you, Mrs. Jeffries," he brightened immediately and got to his feet. Talking his cases over with his housekeeper always made him feel so much better. She was such a good listener. "I'm flattered by your confidence in me and shall do my best to live up to it."

"But of course you will, sir." She led the way toward the dining room. "Now, sir. Why don't you have your dinner? I'm sure you'll feel much better with something in your stomach."

CHAPTER 2

Mrs. Jeffries questioned the inspector further as he ate his roast beef and mashed potatoes. When he'd finished off his treacle tart and retired to his rooms, she dashed down to the kitchen. Betsy and the others were ready for her. Within minutes, they had the dining room cleared and the dishes done. Then they took their usual places at the kitchen table.

"All right then, have we got us a murder or not?" Mrs. Goodge asked as she lowered herself to her chair. She was eager to begin. She'd helped with the cleanup, even though the others had protested. She might be getting old, but she could still do her fair share.

"It's a bit difficult to say," Mrs. Jeffries hated to dash their hopes, but she had to be truthful. "How much has Betsy told you?"

"Just that the inspector said 'e might 'ave a murder," Wiggins replied.

"So do we or don't we?" the cook persisted.

"I'm not sure," the housekeeper said quickly. "Do you remember that suicide we talked about earlier today? It turns out that perhaps it might have been a murder after all. Chief Inspector Barrows has asked our inspector to have another look at the matter."

"But I thought the papers said that there weren't any signs of foul play," Smythe reminded her.

"Apparently, the papers might have been wrong," Mrs. Jeffries nodded, "and it appears the coroner's inquest may have been a bit hasty in their verdict as well. Therefore, I suggest we assume we've a murder investigation to conduct. The inspector didn't know much at this stage, but I did learn a few facts." She leaned back in her chair, took a deep breath, and gave them a full report.

When she'd finished, the room fell silent as they thought about what they'd just heard. Wiggins shook his head. "Seems to me there ain't no doubt. Fellow was murdered all right."

"Don't say 'ain't'," Betsy told him absently. Like the others, she was thinking of all the questions that needed to be answered.

"I don't know that I like this one," Mrs. Goodge muttered darkly. "Murder or suicide, it's been two weeks . . ."

"The inspector's concerned about that as well," the housekeeper said. "But that certainly shouldn't stop us. We've worked on cases like this before. Providing that is, that everyone wants to give it a good try." She'd bet the next quarter's household money that everyone would want to have a go at it.

"But what if it was a suicide?" Smythe complained. "We don't want to be runnin' about wastin' our time over nothin'."

"As I said, I think we ought to go on the assumption that it's murder. Although he wouldn't come right out and admit it, I think Inspector Witherspoon believes the police investigation wasn't very thorough."

"And his landlady felt so strongly that there'd been a gross miscarriage of justice, that she went to the police," Betsy said firmly. "That's good enough for me."

"Me too," Wiggins added. "This Mrs. Lynch went to the trouble to make a bit of a fuss. The least we can do is snoop about a bit and see what's what. Besides, it's not as if we've got anythin' else on our plates."

Smythe laughed and threw up his hands in mock defeat.

"All right, all right, I wasn't sayin' we oughn't to put our oar in, I was just thinkin' we might try and get a few more facts before we make up our minds for sure."

"I agree," Mrs. Jeffries said.

"What do you want us to do first?" he asked her. "This one's goin' to be a bit 'arder. The trail's probably cold as a banker's heart."

Mrs. Jeffries thought for a moment. "This case does have a rather unique set of circumstances, but we mustn't let that assume too much importance in how we proceed. I think we ought to do precisely what we've always done in the past."

"Concentrate on the victim," Mrs. Goodge nodded in agreement.

"Right then," Smythe got to his feet. "I'll get along to the local pubs and see what I can learn about Westover."

"Wouldn't it be better if you started with the hansom drivers?" Betsy asked. "Seems to me that the more time that goes by, the dimmer memories are going to get. Whoever did the killing had to get to the Lynch house that night. Maybe they took a hansom."

He gave her a lazy grin. "I can do both. You just don't want me hangin' about in pubs flirtin' with the pretty barmaids."

"Don't be daft," she gave him a saucy grin of her own. She knew her beloved hadn't even looked at another woman since their engagement. "You do better with hansom drivers than you do with pretty barmaids. They're too busy pulling beer to have time to talk."

"I'll pop along to the Lynch neighborhood and see what I can learn," Wiggins volunteered. "Maybe someone's maid or footman saw something the night he died."

"We don't know that he was killed at night," Mrs. Jeffries pointed out. "His body wasn't found until the next day when he didn't show up at work. Westover might have been killed the previous day."

"This isn't going to be an easy one," the cook frowned ominously. "I can feel it in my bones."

"To be fair, Mrs. Goodge, none of 'em are ever easy," Smythe said dryly.

"True, but on the others we've generally known whether it was murder or not. Or when they were killed or that they had a whole pack of scheming relatives who wanted them six feet under. But this Westover fellow doesn't even have that, just a couple of cousins in Bristol. Where do we start? That's what I want to know."

Mrs. Jeffries could understand Mrs. Goodge's frustration. The cook did her investigating in a far different manner than the rest of them. She needed names. Lots of them. A veritable army of informants trooped through her kitchen. Give the cook the suspects' names and she could pry every last morsel of gossip there was to be had about any of them. Rag and bones men, chimney sweeps, laundrymen, delivery boys, and even street arabs could all be found eating buns, drinking tea, and talking their heads off in Mrs. Goodge's kitchen.

The cook also had a vast network of old colleagues and associates she could call upon when needed. She'd worked in a number of places in her many years of service.

"Why don't you see what you can find out about James Horrocks," Mrs. Jeffries suggested.

"You mean the one that found the body?" The cook's frown deepened. "But he was just Westover's employer. Why would he want him dead? Seems to me if he didn't like the fellow it would be much easier just to sack him."

Everyone laughed.

"You're right, of course," Mrs. Jeffries said. "But according to what Mrs. Lynch told the inspector, Westover spent most of his time at work. Besides, it's as good a place to start as any."

"I'll go along with Wiggins tomorrow and have a word with the local shopkeepers," Betsy said.

"And I'll have a word with Dr. Bosworth," Mrs. Jeffries told them. "Perhaps he'll be able to give us a bit more information about the circumstances of the victim's death."

Wiggins got up. Fred, the black and brown mongrel dog who'd been lying on a rug by the door to the hall, leaped up as well. He trotted over and nuzzled the footman's hand. "All right, fella, we'll go for a walk now." He grinned at the others. "If this does turn out to be murder, Luty and Hatchet'll 'ave a fit that they missed it."

The offices of Donovan, Melcher, and Horrocks were located on the first floor of a three-story white stone building on the Kensington High Street. Inspector Witherspoon and Constable Barnes sat in the reception area of the outer office. They shared the room with three clerks who were sitting at desks behind a low counter. The clerks sat hunched over ledgers and papers, but they couldn't have been getting much work done, they kept sneaking glances at the two policemen.

"I'm sure someone will be right with you," the lad nearest to the inspector muttered. "I told Mr. Horrocks's private secretary that you're here."

On the far side of the room a door opened and a dark-haired man, with a huge handle bar mustache, stuck his head out. He stared coldly at Witherspoon and Barnes. "You may come in now, Mr. Horrocks will see you."

Annoyed at the fellow's tone, Barnes gave him a good frown, but the inspector simply nodded. They followed the secretary down a long hall and past the open doors of the other offices, all of which were empty. They came to the door at the end, and the secretary knocked once, opened the door, and led them inside.

They entered a large office with pale green walls, brown carpet, and three narrow windows looking out on the High Street. At the far end of the room there was a round table with a map of England on the wall. A mahogany desk with two straight-back chairs in front of it was opposite the door. Sitting behind the desk was a bald man with narrow shoulders and a long nose. "I'm James Horrocks," he said.

"I'm Inspector Gerald Witherspoon, and this is Constable Barnes," he said as they went toward the desk.

Horrocks motioned for them to sit down and then looked at his secretary. "This oughtn't to take long, but do see that I'm not disturbed."

"Yes sir," he withdrew, closing the door quietly behind him.

"Why have you come?" Horrocks asked bluntly.

The inspector decided to be just as blunt. "We're here to ask you some questions regarding Mr. Harlan Westover."

"Westover?" Horrocks frowned. "I gave testimony at the coroner's inquest. Dreadful business, but I told them everything I know. Westover's death was a suicide, so I don't understand what questions you could possibly need to ask now."

"Well, uh . . ." Witherspoon knew he had to be careful. There was no need to stir up sentiments against the police if one could avoid doing so. "There are a few areas that weren't covered quite as well as they should have been." Drat, what made him say that? He certainly didn't want to imply that the police had been lax in their initial investigation. Even if it were true.

"What things? The police asked me all sorts of questions when it happened."

"Of course they did, sir," Barnes interjected. "But additional evidence has come to light, and we would be remiss in our duty if we didn't investigate further."

"What additional evidence?" Horrocks leaned halfway across his desk. "What are you talking about? What evidence?"

"We're not really at liberty to say," Witherspoon replied, he shot his constable a grateful look. "But we do hope we can count on your cooperation."

"Cooperation. I never said I wouldn't cooperate," Horrocks blustered. "This is a dreadful business. Dreadful I tell you. Most upsetting for all of us."

"I'm sure it has been, sir." The inspector took a quick, deep breath and tried to remember the questions he needed to ask. "How long has Westover worked for your firm?" Egads, that wasn't what he'd meant to ask.

"Three years," Horrocks replied. He pursed his lips and looked out the window. "He came to us from a small firm in Birmingham. He was our chief engineer."

"What sort of things do you make here?" Barnes asked.

"We don't make anything here," Horrocks said. "This is just our offices. But we've a small factory on Watling Street in Stepney. We make engines. Mainly used in mining operations."

"Did Mr. Westover have any enemies?" Witherspoon asked. That was always a good question.

"No, of course not. He worked hard, got along well with his staff, and minded his own business."

"Can you tell us how you came to go to his rooms the day you discovered the body." That was another good one.

Horrocks shrugged his narrow shoulders. "I got concerned when he didn't show up that morning. Westover was a very punctual man—hard worker. When it went half past ten and we'd heard nothing from him, I knew something was wrong, so I went to his rooms in Brook Green and . . ." his voice trailed off and he looked out the window. "You know what I found."

"How did you get into the house?" Barnes asked softly. "His landlady wasn't home."

"The door was unlocked," Horrocks admitted. "I knocked and when no one answered, I went inside and up the stairs to his rooms."

Witherspoon's brows drew together as he tried to recall what the original report had said. "Was the door to his rooms locked?"

"Oh yes, but the key was right there, so when he didn't respond to my knock, I unlocked the door and went inside."

Barnes looked up from his notebook. "Where, exactly was this key?"

"On the floor," Horrocks replied. "It was just lying there on the carpet. Almost as if someone had dropped it."

"What did you do when you found the body?" Witherspoon wanted to get the sequence of events just right. He wasn't sure why it was important, but he knew it was, and he'd learned to trust his instincts in these matters. As his housekeeper frequently told him, "Let your inner voice guide you sir, it's never wrong."

"What did I do? I went for the police, of course. I'm no expert on these matters, sir, but even I could see that something dreadful had happened and Harlan was dead." Horrocks dropped his gaze to the desk. "It was quite shocking, Inspector."

"When was the last time you'd seen Mr. Westover?" Witherspoon asked.

"Alive?"

"Uh, yes."

"It was the day before he died. He was in his office, working." Horrocks cleared his throat. "Is that all? I do hate to be rude, but I've a very important meeting scheduled . . ." he looked up as the door opened. "Yes, Jackson, what is it?"

"It's Mrs. Arkwright, sir, she's here."

"Then go get Mr. Arkwright," Horrocks ordered.

The secretary winced. "He's gone to Birmingham, sir. Remember, he went to see about the strivets. Mrs. Arkwright is a bit upset, sir. She insists that Mr. Arkwright was supposed to meet her here. I, uh, don't really know what to do with her."

"I suppose she's causing a commotion," Horrocks sighed. "Send her in here, then. I don't want her upsetting the staff. God knows there's been enough turmoil about the place lately."

"Yes, sir," Jackson disappeared and Horrocks smiled apologetically at the two policemen. "I'm sorry, but I shall have to deal with Mrs. Arkwright. She's the wife of one of our general partners. I expect she's gotten a bit muddled about something . . ."

The door opened and a tall, attractive middle-aged woman stepped into the office. She paused just inside the doorway and surveyed the scene out of a pair of dark brown eyes. Beneath an elegant hunter green veiled hat, her hair was the same dark color as her eyes. Her full lips curved into a half-smile. "Oh dear, it appears I'm interrupting something important. I'm sorry."

James Horrocks had risen from behind his desk. "Not at all, dear lady. Not at all, it's always a delight to see you. These gentlemen were just leaving."

Witherspoon shot a quick look at Barnes. The constable shrugged. The inspector realized they probably weren't going to get much more out of Horrocks, so he got to his feet.

"Actually, Mr. Horrocks, we do have a few more questions for you, but we'll be happy to speak to you a bit later. Right now I'd like a word with the rest of the staff."

Horrocks, who'd been coming out from behind the desk, stopped in his tracks. "The staff? Why do you want to speak to the staff?"

"It's routine, sir," Barnes assured him. "We've just a few general questions."

"Oh dear," Mrs. Arkwright said. "Are these gentlemen here about that dreadful business with Mr. Westover?"

"I'm afraid so," Horrocks said as he continued toward Mrs. Arkwright. "I'd hoped that was all behind us."

Witherspoon turned to Mrs. Arkwright. "I'm Inspector Gerald Witherspoon, and this is Constable Barnes. You didn't, by any chance, happen to see Mr. Westover on the day he died, did you?"

It was a silly question, and the inspector regretted asking it as soon as the words were out of his mouth.

"Now see here, Inspector," Horrocks blustered. "Mrs. Arkwright barely knew the man . . ."

"It's all right, James," she soothed. She gave the two policemen a dazzling smile. "Actually, I did see Mr. Westover that day. I'd come to have luncheon with my husband. He was going to take me to Wentworths after the board meeting. We saw Mr. Westover as we were getting a hansom downstairs. I must say, he looked quite angry about something."

Witherspoon jerked his head toward Horrocks. "You had a board meeting? Was Mr. Westover in attendance?" He'd no idea what prompted him to ask the question, but ask it he did.

Horrocks scowled. "I don't think we're obligated to make the police privy to our internal company affairs. But yes, we did have a meeting, and yes, Mr. Westover was in attendance. As I told you, he was our chief engineer."

"What was the meeting about?" Barnes queried.

Horrocks gaped at them. "What was it about? I don't really see that it's any business of the police . . ."

"It's our duty to investigate suspicious deaths, sir," the inspector replied. "And everything about Mr. Westover's day

might be important." Drat, he thought, that was hardly being
subtle. But gracious, it was difficult to be subtle and still get
any information out of anyone. Besides, he was getting a
feeling about this case. There was something about this "suicide" that simply didn't feel right. As his housekeeper was
always telling him, he must have faith in his feelings and
instincts. She seemed to think the whole mysterious process
was really just his mind gathering information and prodding
him along a certain path. He'd no idea what caused him to
get these "ideas" when he was on a case, but he'd learned
to trust them.

"I'd hardly call Harlan Westover's suicide a suspicious
death," Horrocks snapped. "The man blew his brains out in
a locked room."

"With a key found just outside the door," Barnes added.
"A key that could have been used and then dropped by anyone."

Mrs. Jeffries smiled sweetly at the tall, red-haired man coming out the side door of St. Thomas's Hospital. He caught
sight of her and immediately turned in her direction.

"Mrs. Jeffries, how very delightful to see you. I do hope
you've come to see me," Dr. Bosworth said.

"Of course I've come to see you," she replied. The good
doctor had helped on several of their cases. There was no
need to be coy with him. "But if this is an inconvenient time,
I can come back later."

"That won't be necessary. My last appointment didn't
show up, and I've a bit of free time." He laughed in delight,
took her arm, and started off. "There's a tea shop up the
road. Let's go have a cuppa, and we can have a nice chat
about why you've sought me out."

They crossed the Lambeth Palace Road to a small café
tucked around the corner on Crosier Street. Dr. Bosworth
pulled open the door to the café, ushered her inside, and
seated her at a table by the window. A few moments later,
he was back bearing two cups of steaming tea. Placing one
in front of her, he sat down and smiled at her. "What's this
all about? Another murder?"

Mrs. Jeffries sighed. "I think so, but to be honest, we're not sure."

"Not sure?" Bosworth repeated. "Goodness, this is intriguing."

"You see, the coroner's inquest ruled the death a suicide."

"There's already been an inquest?" Bosworth interrupted.

"I'm afraid so."

"So there isn't a body . . ."

"It's already been buried," she said. She knew why he'd asked the question. In several of their other cases, Dr. Bosworth had been able to examine the victim before the autopsy and before the coroner's inquest. Bosworth had spent several years working in America. He had some rather revolutionary ideas about how close observation of the wounds could give one information about the cause of death. He was of the opinion that one could ascertain from the wound what kind of weapon had been used to do the killing, and sometimes even the precise time of death could be known. Dr. Bosworth had come to his conclusions after working for two years under a doctor in San Francisco. Apparently, there were plenty of gunshot, knife, and bludgeoning victims in that part of the world. "But we're hoping you'll be able to read the autopsy report and give us your opinion."

He raised an eyebrow. "I'm flattered by your faith in my abilities, Mrs. Jeffries. But a report isn't the same as an actual examination. How did the death occur?"

"He used a gun."

Bosworth frowned. "Messy business, guns. What's the victim's name?"

Mrs. Jeffries gave the doctor all the information she'd learned from the inspector. Bosworth listened carefully, occasionally stopping her to ask a question. When she finished, she leaned back in her chair. "Well, what do you think? Is there any chance you might be able to find out anything useful from the police surgeon's report."

"That depends on how thorough the surgeon was," Bosworth shrugged. "Do you know who it was?"

"I'm afraid I don't, but the victim died at home and he

lived in Brook Green near Shepherds Bush. Is that of any use?"

"That means the body was probably taken to West London Hospital on King Street for the postmortem. I've a good friend that works there, he can probably get me a copy of the report. I'll tell you what, I'll have a go at it today and see what I can find out." He finished off his tea and rose to his feet.

Mrs. Jeffries did the same. "Shall I call around to see you later in the week?"

"That won't be necessary," he grinned. "I'll contact you straightaway if I've got any useful information."

"Thank you doctor, I don't know what we'd do without you," she replied gratefully.

He laughed. "Oh, I've no doubt you'd do very well, Mrs. Jeffries. Very well indeed."

Wiggins drew his heavy coat closed and then reached down and patted Fred on the head. "You doin' all right, fella? I know it's cold out 'ere, but we've got to 'ang about a bit longer if we're goin' to find us someone to talk to."

Fred wagged his tail and pranced about on the cold footpath. Wiggins sighed and looked up at the row of houses on Charter Street opposite Brook Green. So far, no one had so much as stuck their heads out this morning. Cor blimey, he thought, you'd think someone along the street had to do a bit of shopping or something . . . but no, he'd been here almost an hour, and he'd not seen hide nor hair of anyone. If this kept up, he'd not have anything to report this afternoon at their meeting.

In the house directly opposite him, the curtain in the front window jerked to one side. "Oh blast, Fred," Wiggins muttered. "That bloomin' curtain is twitchin' again. Maybe we ought to get movin'." Nonchalantly, he tried to edge further onto the green. "I don't want anyone rememberin' we was 'ere." Like the others, Wiggins knew the importance of being discreet when he was out investigating one of the inspector's cases.

Keeping his eye on the curtain, he and Fred headed across

the footpath. He wished he'd brought Fred's ball along. Playing with the dog would have looked less suspicious than just hanging about.

He breathed a bit easier as he and Fred reached a bench in the center of the green. At least now no one could see him from the street. He decided to have a sit down and think what to do next.

"You're wastin' your time, you know. She's gone home." The cheery voice came from behind him.

Startled, he whirled around and saw a young girl gazing at him. She wore a thin overcoat and a wool hat that had definitely seen better days. The strands of hair escaping from the hat were dark brown, her skin was pale and spotty and her eyes were hazel. "What's the matter," she challenged, "has the cat got your tongue."

"I beg your pardon, miss," he replied. He wondered if she'd mistaken him for someone else. "But I don't know what you're on about."

"Oh who do you think you're foolin'?" she laughed. "Louise said you'd be comin' around. Mind you, it took you long enough. She went home last Thursday on account of her gran takin' ill. We expected you to come 'round the back, though, not hang about in front of the house for the whole world to see. The missus will have a fit if she finds out, but I expect you know that."

Wiggins hadn't a clue what to do. On the one hand, the girl was out here talking to him. On the other hand, it was clear she had mistaken him for Louise's young man. Wiggins decided to go along with the charade for a bit longer. Inquisitive girls like this one were just the right sort to have seen something that might be of interest to him. "Sorry, I guess I should 'ave gone around the back, but, uh, I didn't want to run into the mistress."

"There'd be no chance of that. The missus don't poke her nose into the kitchen before noon. But it's just as well you didn't. That nosy Olga's been hanging about all morning. Anyway, I've got to get a move on, I've got to get to the butcher's."

"Can I walk along with ya?" He asked quickly.

"Why?" She looked at him suspiciously. "There's no more that I can tell you. Louise has gone back to Wales. We don't know if she's even comin' back. The missus knows, but she'll not lower herself to tell us." She started off down the footpath.

"I've got to get back to work myself," he began as he fell into step next to her.

"You've got a position, then?" the girl asked eagerly.

"Uh, yes."

"What kind of a position is it? Oh, it's too bad that Louise isn't here. She'd be ever so thrilled you finally got work."

Blast a Spaniard, Wiggins thought, now he had to keep on lying. Maybe he ought to just wash his hands of this. It was getting a bit messy. "Well, actually . . ."

"Did you get that job down at the rubber factory, then?" she continued. "Louise said you were trying to get on there."

"Uh, no, I got another one." He had an idea. "I got it a couple of weeks back . . ."

She stopped and stared at him. "Louise didn't say anythin' about you having a job before she went home."

"She didn't know," he replied. "I tried to tell her, but she were so full of her own news I never got a word in edgewise."

The girl looked doubtful. "What news? Nothin's happened to Louise acceptin' her granny gettin' sick."

"News don't have to be just what happens to you," he forced himself to laugh. "She told me all about that neighbor of yours that blew his brains out."

"Oh that." The girl pursed her lips. "I don't see why Louise would be excited about tellin' that. Fellow did a suicide."

"That's not what Louise heard," Wiggins fervently hoped Louise stayed in Wales, he was about to use her name shamelessly. "She said she'd 'eard it were murder, not suicide."

"Murder," the girl repeated. "She must have been havin' you on. Even the police said it were a suicide. I know, because Louise told me she heard the gun go off herself and she never said anything about a murder."

"Louise never said anything to me about hearin' a gunshot.

If she heard so much, why didn't she go fetch a policeman?"
Wiggins countered. He'd no idea how the events surrounding
the death had unfolded, but that didn't stop him. He had the
girl talking and that was all that mattered.

"Fetch a policeman? Not bloomin' likely. She's not one
for stickin' her nose in other people's business," the girl said
defensively.

"Cor blimey, she hears a gun go off, and she thinks she'd
be a nosy parker if she went for the police," Wiggins shook
his head in disbelief.

"She thought it was them lads over on Dunsany Road settin' off some explodin' bon-bons left over from Guy Fawkes.
It's happened before, so she claimed she didn't take much
notice until the next day when she saw the coppers comin'
and goin' about Mrs. Lynch's house."

"About what time did she 'ear this gunshot?" Wiggins
pressed.

The girl stopped and gave him another long, suspicious
look. "What's your name?" she asked abruptly.

"What do ya mean, what's my name . . ." he sputtered. Cor
blimey, what a time for the lass to start asking questions.

"I didn't stutter," she shot back. "Now tell me, what's your
bloomin' name? I don't think you're Louise's feller at all. I
think you're just some stranger hangin' about the green and
havin' me on."

"I wasn't 'avin' you on, I'll admit I was 'angin' about as
you put it," he protested, "but well, uh . . . the truth is I've
been wantin' to meet you. When you come out and thought
I was this 'ere Louise's feller, well, I uh just went along with
it." Cor blimey, he was lying through his teeth. He held his
breath, hoping she'd believe him. He knew he wasn't a bad
looking lad, but he didn't value himself so highly as to think
every young woman he met found him attractive. Still, it was
all he could come up with on the spur of the moment.

Her expression softened. "You've been wantin' to meet
me," she repeated. "Why?"

"Uh, I saw you the other day walking down the street, and
I thought you looked ever so nice," he shrugged. "But if you
want me to leave you in peace, I'll be off . . ." he picked up

his pace and shot ahead of her. "I'll not stay where I'm not wanted."

"Wait," she called. "Wait please. Uh, I don't mind if you walk with me."

Blast a Spaniard, he thought, he'd been half-hoping she'd let him go on about his business. His conscience had apparently jumped out of its matchbox and was now poking at him uncomfortably. He had no right to lead this poor girl on just to get information. But this was about a murder, he argued with himself. Killers didn't have the right to go unpunished. He stopped, turned, and looked at her. She smiled hopefully, and he felt like a worm. "Are ya sure? I don't want to be forward . . ."

Her smile widened. "It's all right, you look like a nice lad, and I'd like the company. What's your name?"

For a split second he considered lying. "Wiggins." He couldn't do it. "What's yours?"

"Marion." They started walking again. "Marion Miller. Uh, do you live 'round here?"

He hesitated. "I work over near Holland Park," he finally admitted. "I'm a footman. 'Ow about you?"

"I'm a maid," she replied. "I work for the Cuthberts. They've got the biggest house on the street. There was four of us worked there, me, Louise, Olga, and cook. Now there's just me and Olga doing all the maid work. Cook's lazy, she won't get off her arse and do anything but prepare meals." She clamped a hand to her mouth. "Oh, that sounded awful, I didn't mean to be coarse . . ."

Wiggins laughed. "Not to worry, I don't think you're coarse. I know what you mean, though. Lots of households work a body to death. Where's the butcher shop?"

"Up on Shepherds Bush Road," she replied. "It's only a few minutes walk."

"I know that area," he said. "There's a café on the corner. Have you got time to stop for tea and a bun?" Wiggins had plenty of coin on him. It was odd, too. He always kept a bit of change in his top drawer, but no matter how often he dipped into it, the pile never seemed to get any smaller. Truth was, it seemed to grow a bit everytime he looked at it. Maybe he ought to mention it to Mrs. Jeffries. But then again, maybe he was just being fanciful.

"I'd like that," Marion's eyes brightened. "I like buns. We don't have them much at the Cuthberts's house. I can't stay too long, though. I've got to get the chops back to cook before luncheon, but they'll not miss me for half an hour or so."

"Sorry, but I can't 'elp ya. I don't remember takin' any fares to Charter Street or Brook Green." The driver untied the horse's reins from the railing of the cabmen's shelter. He shrugged apologetically at Smythe and mounted the cab. "Try talkin' with Danny Leets. He was workin' that night too. He might remember something."

"Where can I find 'im?" Smythe asked.

"Hang about a bit, and he'll be along soon."

"Thanks," he called as the cabbie pulled out into the traffic. Smythe looked around the busy neighborhood. This shelter was just across from Shepherds Bush station, at least a half a mile away from the Lynch House, but it was the closest one. He leaned against the lamppost and peered down the road, hoping to see a cab headed his way. There were omnibuses, carts, water-wagons, broughams, and four-wheelers, but not a hansom in sight. Blast a Spaniard, he didn't want to hang about here much longer, but he'd not had any luck at the pubs around Brook Green either. He was meeting the others in an hour, and he was sure they would have plenty of information. He didn't want to be the only one to show up empty-handed. Just then, a hansom pulled by a huge bay came around the corner. Maybe it was Danny Leets, and maybe, just maybe, he remembered taking a fare to Westover's rooms on the day of the murder.

The cab pulled up at the shelter and a big, burly fellow with a ruddy, pockmarked complexion climbed down.

"Are you Danny Leets?" the coachman asked.

The man's blue eyes narrowed suspiciously. "Who wants to know?"

"Me. I'm not a copper or a crook. I just want to ask ya a couple of questions." He reached into his pocket and pulled out a wad of pound notes. "I'll make it worth yer while."

The cabman's eyes cut to the cash. "I'm Danny Leets. What can I do for ya."

Mrs. Goodge hummed as she set a plate of brown bread in the middle of the table. She couldn't wait for the others to get here. She glanced at the clock and saw that it was almost four. They ought to be coming in soon. She put the butter next to the plate of bread, checked that the roast was cooking properly in the oven, and then put the kettle on the burner.

She'd been so depressed after the others had gone out this morning. She'd been sure she wouldn't find out anything about the murdered man. But goodness, as luck would have it, she'd struck gold on her first try. She glanced at the laundry hamper by the hall door. Thank goodness for delivery boys, especially ones that did deliveries to the same neighborhood where the murder'd been committed. Mrs. Goodge hummed as she flicked a crumb of bread off the tabletop. Oh yes, she simply couldn't wait till the rest of them got here.

CHAPTER 3

The last one to arrive for their meeting was Mrs. Jeffries. She dashed into the kitchen, taking off her hat and coat as she walked. "I'm so sorry to be late, but there was an accident at the upper end of Holland Park, and it tied up traffic for ages." She tossed her outer garments onto the coat tree and took her usual place at the table.

"We've not been waiting long," Mrs. Goodge said as she poured a cup of tea for the housekeeper. "Wiggins has only just got back himself."

Wiggins nodded in agreement. "I was late too, Mrs. Jeffries, and the silly thing about it is I've not found out a thing about our Mr. Harlan Westover. Cor blimey, it were 'ard enough tryin' to find someone to talk to about the bloke, and when I finally did, she didn't know a bloomin' thing about the poor feller." He'd been bitterly disappointed. He'd thought from what she'd told him that he'd learn the time of death. But closer questioning had revealed that the absent Louise hadn't mentioned anything useful to Marion Miller.

"Don't take it to heart, lad," Smythe said. "I've not 'ad much luck either."

"It's still early days yet," Mrs. Jeffries said stoutly. In

truth, she'd not learned anything useful either, and from the comments Dr. Bosworth made about police reports, she suspected that even when he'd read the thing, she still wouldn't know much. She cast a quick look around the table as she sipped at her tea. Betsy was frowning at the tabletop, Smythe looked irritable, and Wiggins was slumped in his chair. The only one who looked at all chipper was the cook. "From your faces, I don't think any of us have had much luck except, perhaps, Mrs. Goodge."

"I've learned a thing or two," the cook replied. She pushed the plate of brown bread toward the housekeeper. "I don't know how useful it is, but at least it's a bit of a start."

"That's better than I've done," Betsy muttered. "I talked to every shopkeeper in Shepherds Bush and Brook Green. I didn't hear anything about Westover. No one had heard of the man until he died. Mrs. Lynch does all the shopping for that household. He's not so much as bought a tin of tobacco."

"Don't fret, lass," Smythe smiled at his fiancée. "We'll find out what we need to know. As I said, I didn't find out anythin' either. Westover doesn't seem to 'ave ever set foot in the local pubs."

"Did you have a chance to speak to any hansom drivers?" Mrs. Jeffries asked. Whoever murdered Westover had to have gotten there on some means of conveyance.

"I spoke to a couple of 'em," he admitted, "but no one remembered takin' a fare to Westover's neighborhood on the day 'e died. Maybe our killer walked to the house." His chat with Danny Leets had been useless. The bloke had taken his cash and then not known a ruddy thing.

"That's possible. I take it you're going to keep trying," Mrs. Jeffries reached for a slice of bread.

"There's a couple of drivers I didn't get a chance to talk to. I'll 'ave another go at 'em tomorrow."

Mrs. Jeffries smeared butter on her bread. "Mrs. Goodge, you're the only one who doesn't have a long face. Would you like to share what you've learned?"

"Oh, it's not all that much," Mrs. Goodge said modestly. "But I'll give it a go. Actually, it was almost an accident that I found out anything. I was sitting right here trying to get something out of George Wilkes, you know him, he's the one who delivers the heating fuel. Well, he'd nothing to say at all. He just sat here, stuffing his face with my treacle tarts, when the laundry lad brought back our sheets. The lad overheard me asking George about the 'suicide' over on Brook Green. Luckily, Henry's got no manners . . ."

"Is Henry the laundry boy?" Betsy interrupted.

"That's right, he overheard what I was asking George, and he jumped right into the conversation." The cook laughed. "He said he'd seen Westover on the day it must have happened. He remembered because he was dragging out a huge hamper from the house next door to Mrs. Lynch's when Westover came charging past and almost knocked poor Henry on his backside."

"So all he did was see the man?" Smythe asked.

"Give me a minute," she retorted. "I'm getting to the interesting part." She took a quick sip of tea. "Harlan Westover came charging down the street so hard he barged right into the hamper. Henry didn't see him coming, and he was ever so surprised when all of a sudden a man comes flying over the top of the lid."

"He actually flew over the hamper?" Wiggins asked. He glanced at the household hamper, which was still by the door leading to the back stairs. "Cor blimey, that thing's as big as a trunk. That must 'ave 'urt."

"I expect it did. But when Henry tried to help him up, Westover brushed him off and said for him not to worry, that it was Westover's fault for not paying attention to what he was doing. Then he took off towards his house." The cook looked around the table expectantly, but all she saw was blank stares. "Well, don't you understand? That proves it was murder."

No one said anything. Finally, Mrs. Jeffries said, "I don't quite follow you . . ."

Mrs. Goodge sighed. "Maybe I'm not saying this right, but Henry said he was sure that the man was angry about something . . ."

"He were angry about takin' a tumble over a silly laundry basket," Smythe suggested. "His pride were smartin'."

"No, no," the cook protested. "Hold on, now. Give me a minute so I can get this right. You know how you can get impressions of how people are feeling without actually having them say anything." She paused. "Well, Henry was sure that Westover was boiling mad about something, and it were something that had him so rattled he wasn't watching where he was going. That's why he banged into the hamper in the first place. Because he was so furious, he wasn't payin' attention to his surroundings."

"But why does that make you think he didn't kill 'imself?" Wiggins asked.

"Because he was angry that day, not despairing," she replied. She smiled smugly. "That proves he wouldn't have taken his own life. Angry people don't kill themselves."

Mrs. Jeffries wasn't so sure about that, but she didn't want to quell the cook's enthusiasm. This case could use as much enthusiasm as it could get. "That's a very interesting point of view, Mrs. Goodge. Do you happen to know what time all this took place?"

"Around two o'clock. Henry remembered, because by rights, he shouldn't have been there at all that time of day. Usually he dropped off clean laundry early of a morning. But there'd been a problem and they'd not done their deliveries until the afternoon. That's why he remembered, they was watching the time real close so they could get done by nightfall."

"How did he know it was Westover?" Betsy asked. "Had he met him before?"

"Saw him every week when he delivered the laundry to the Lynch household," Mrs. Goodge replied. "Henry said Mr. Westover was a nice man, always greeted him kindly and had a word or two with the lad."

Mrs. Jeffries thought for a moment. "Why didn't Henry come forward at the inquest and tell them what he knew?"

The cook shrugged. "I didn't think to ask him. But I imagine Henry's the sort who didn't give the incident another thought until he heard me talking about the coroner's verdict in the newspapers. By then it was too late. Besides, he's not the sort to go running to the police unless he had to."

"You're right, that was a silly question. Of course he wouldn't have gone to the inquest." Mrs. Jeffries said. She knew most of London's poor and working class had a real distrust of the police and the courts. Often, they had good reason for their misgivings. "Do you have anything else for us?"

"No, but now that I know Westover was hopping mad, I've got my feelers out."

"For what?" Wiggins asked.

"For whatever had happened at his office," the cook replied. She saw that the others were listening intently.

"How do you know something happened at the office?" Betsy asked. "Maybe something happened to make him angry on his way home."

"I don't know what happened where," the cook retorted. She reached for the teapot. "But I've got to start somewhere, and considerin' the state Westover was in when he went barreling into the laundry hamper, I'm willing to bet that it wasn't something like missing the omnibus that had him in a right old state."

"Do you have any names?" Mrs. Jeffries didn't beat about the bush. "Because if you don't, I should be able to get the names of his work colleagues out of the inspector."

"I've just got the one—you know, Horrocks, the man who found Westover. But it's a place to start."

"I agree," the housekeeper replied. "I expect that's where the rest of us ought to put our efforts as well. Let's have a quick meeting tomorrow morning before we get out and about. By then I'll have spoken with the inspector and we ought to have a few names to track down."

Betsy frowned. "You don't want us to concentrate on Westover's neighborhood?"

"You haven't had much luck with the local shopkeepers," Mrs. Jeffries pointed out.

"I know," the maid admitted. "But he was killed in his rooms, not his office."

All of a sudden, Fred leapt up, barked once, and charged down the hall toward the back door. Wiggins dashed after him. "What's got into you, boy?" he called. "Cor blimey, there's someone at the door." They heard the back door open. "Hello, we've not seen you in awhile. When did you get home?"

They heard the low murmur of voices and the sound of footsteps. A moment later, Wiggins and a blond-haired, middle-aged woman came into the kitchen, Fred trotted at their heels, his tail wagging furiously as he paid his respects to one of his favorite people, Lady Cannonberry.

"Good gracious," Mrs. Jeffries rose to her feet. "Ruth, it's so good to see you. Do come in and have tea with us."

"I hope I'm not interrupting," she replied. "I only got home an hour ago. I simply had to come over and say hello. It's been ages since I've seen you."

Lady Ruth Cannonberry was the widow of a peer of the realm and their neighbor. She was also the daughter of a minister and had a highly developed social conscience as well as a politically radical point of view. Though titled and wealthy, she insisted all the Witherspoon household call her by her Christian name of Ruth. She and Inspector Witherspoon had been developing a very special relationship. Unfortunately, family duty had called her out of town frequently in the past two years, so her and the inspector's friendship hadn't progressed very far.

"Indeed it has," Mrs. Jeffries agreed, "but we're glad you're back. Are you in town for long?"

"I'll get another cup and plate," Betsy smiled and got to her feet.

"Sit right 'ere next to me," Wiggins patted the empty chair to his left. "We've missed you, you know. Are you goin' to stay about for a bit now that you're back?"

Ruth laughed and sat down. "I hope so. Uncle Edgar is on the mend, so I think I'm at home for the foreseeable future. Unless, of course, someone else in the family thinks it's their turn to take ill."

"You've 'ad a spate of bad luck, that's for sure." Smythe said. He liked the lady very much and hoped she'd hang about long enough for her and the inspector to renew their friendship. Now that he and Betsy had their understanding, he was convinced that the rest of the world would be much happier if paired off properly.

"Thank you," Ruth said as she took a cup of tea from Betsy. "I know I should have given you some warning instead of just popping around, but I did so want to see what you've all been up to lately. Have you had any good murders?"

Unfortunately, Ruth, like several others of their acquaintance, had also guessed that the staff had been helping the inspector. When she was in town, she frequently volunteered her services. The others, however, were wary of involving her too closely. It wasn't that they didn't trust her, that wasn't the case at all. They simply didn't want to do anything to harm the budding (albeit slowly) relationship between her and the inspector. Sneaking about behind his back asking questions about his cases could most definitely be considered a hindrance to a harmonious friendship.

Before Mrs. Jeffries could give a nice, noncommittal reply, Wiggins blurted out. "We've got us one now, but we don't know 'ow good it's goin' to be. So far, we've 'ad the piker's worst luck on findin' out anythin'."

"How exciting." Ruth's smile widened. "I got back just in time. I can help you."

"That's very kind of you," Mrs. Jeffries said quickly. "But we don't want to put you to any trouble, especially as you've just got back. You must have much to do in your own household."

"And there's all your social obligations," Mrs. Goodge added.

Ruth waved them off. "I've nothing to do, the butler makes sure everything works properly whether I'm at home or not. As for my social obligations, why, that's the very best sort of places for one to start asking questions. Now, who got killed?"

Mrs. Jeffries was at the front door when the inspector arrived home. Within moments, she had him comfortably seated in his favorite chair in the drawing room. "Dinner will only be a few moments, sir," she said as she handed him a glass of sherry.

He took a sip and closed his eyes. "Oh, this is very nice. Aren't you having one?"

"I believe I will, thank you." She poured one for herself and took the seat opposite him. "So, how did your day go?"

He sighed. "Not very well. So far, we know absolutely nothing except that the fellow is dead."

"Oh dear, I'm sure you must know more than that, sir. It's always this way at the beginning of an investigation."

"I suppose you're right," he took another sip. "But honestly, getting information out of people is very difficult. You'd think they'd want to help the police, not hinder them. Take for instance today, we went along to have an interview with James Horrocks. Frankly, the fellow could barely tear himself away from work long enough to even speak with us. Then, when we did start getting a bit of information out of him, we were interrupted by one of the partners' wives . . ."

"Which one," she interrupted.

"Which one," he repeated. "Oh, it was Mrs. Arkwright. She'd gotten a bit muddled about where she was to meet her husband. But that's beside the point, actually, now that I think of it, it was perhaps a good thing that Mrs. Arkwright interrupted us."

"How's that, sir?" Mrs. Jeffries prompted.

"If she'd not said something, we'd never have known that on the day Westover died he'd been at a board meeting." He sighed. "I don't think Mr. Horrocks would have volunteered that information on his own. Gracious, he didn't even want to tell us where he was on the afternoon of Westover's death. We were halfway out the door before we could get it out of the fellow." He shook his head. "Mind you, as alibis go, his is very weak."

"Really?"

"He says he went to lunch at a local pub and then went to look at some property he's thinking of buying near Shepherds Bush. It's an office building on the Goldhawk Road."

"Then the estate agent can vouch for his whereabouts," she ventured.

"I don't think so. He's already told us he only looked at the outside. Claims he didn't want anyone to know he was interested in purchasing the leasehold on it."

"What about the pub?"

"We'll send a lad to check it tomorrow. But pubs are dreadfully crowded that time of day. Besides, he eats there all the time, they'll not remember if he was there on any particular day."

"Which pub was it?" she asked. She'd make sure she got the name to Smythe at their next meeting.

"The Kings Head," he answered. "It's just around the corner from the office." He sighed. "This is going to be a very difficult case."

"Not at all. So far, you've been very astute, sir," Mrs. Jeffries said. Her mind worked furiously, and she took a quick sip from her glass to gather her thoughts.

Witherspoon stared at her, his expression confused. "I'm not sure I understand what you mean?" If he'd been astute, he wasn't aware of it.

She laughed. "Now don't tease me, sir. I'm on to your methods. You know perfectly good and well that you've learned something of great importance. Why, obviously this board meeting is pertinent to your case, because, as you've just pointed out, Mr. Horrocks quite deliberately didn't tell you about it."

"Er, uh, yes, you're right. He wouldn't have mentioned it at all if Mrs. Arkwright hadn't blurted it out." He nodded sagely. "As a matter of fact, once she did tell me about it, Mr. Horrocks became most unreasonable when I started asking questions about it. Most unreasonable, indeed." He went on to tell Mrs. Jeffries every little detail of his day. In the telling, he became more and more convinced that something was indeed amiss in Harlan Westover's death.

The next morning, she told the others what she'd learned from the inspector.

"Well, it's something, I suppose," Betsy said. "Do we know who all was in that board meeting?"

"Yes, we do," Mrs. Jeffries replied. "The entire board was

present. Oliver Arkwright, he's the general secretary, Harry Donovan, he's the chairman, and of course, the general manager, James Horrocks. There's another general partner, Lawrence Melcher. He doesn't have a title but he's on the board. The only other person present was Harlan Westover."

"How long did the meetin' last?" Wiggins asked. He'd no idea why he needed to know, but he felt it was important.

Mrs. Jeffries hesitated. In truth, she'd not thought to ask. "I don't know. I'll see if I can find out from the inspector."

"We ought to be able to find that out ourselves," Betsy said confidently. Now that she had a direction to go in, she felt much better.

"I'm glad you think so," Mrs. Goodge commented.

"It'll be easy. People work in the office, someone's bound to have noticed when the meeting started and stopped."

"That's an excellent place to start," Mrs. Jeffries nodded approvingly.

"Seems to me we'd best be worryin' about what went on in the meetin'," Smythe muttered. He was thinking hard. It would cost a lot to find out what went on behind the closed doors of a board meeting. Luckily, he had plenty to spend. After he'd paid a visit to the Kings Head pub in Kensington, he'd go along to the docks. This might be a job for Blimpey Groggins.

"Oh, I've no doubt we'll find out what went on in the meeting," Mrs. Jeffries replied. "It's been my experience that a closed door doesn't stop secrets from getting out."

"Did the chief inspector agree with you, sir?" Constable Barnes asked softly as he and Witherspoon went down the stairs of the station house.

Witherspoon frowned. "Actually, he seemed a bit annoyed when I told him I thought the case warranted further investigation. I've no idea why. You'd think he'd be pleased that his dear old nanny was right."

Barnes stifled an amused smile. Sometimes the inspector was so naive. Of course the chief inspector wasn't going to be pleased to find out that not only had a coroner's inquest given the wrong verdict, but that they'd apparently done so based on a very slip-shod investigation by the police. The force had barely started to recover from all that Ripper ruckus, it wouldn't look good when and if the press got hold of the fact they'd botched another investigation. Barnes cut a quick look at Witherspoon. He knew something that his inspector didn't, and he wasn't sure if he ought to mention it just yet.

"I do hope he's not going to be too hard on the lads that did the initial investigation," Witherspoon said as they stepped out the front door and started across the cobblestone courtyard. "On the face of it, the death did look like a suicide."

The constable decided to keep his secret for a while longer. In the near future, he might need a decent bargaining chip or two. They came to the curb and looked down the busy road for a hansom. Barnes spotted one discharging a fare down the block, and he waved at the driver. "Nonetheless, sir, they did rush to judgment. Even a cursory investigation would have revealed there was something odd about the death. A suicide can't leave a key on the other side of a locked door."

The cab pulled up, and Barnes reached for the handle. "Number 14 Sussex Villas, South Kensington," he called to the driver and then turned back to Witherspoon, "and all they'd have had to do to know that fact was to ask the right questions. Horrocks told us about the key straight away."

"I wonder why he didn't mention it to the constables when he was first questioned?" Witherspoon climbed into the hansom. "Perhaps I ought to ask him. It might be important."

"I agree sir," Barnes swung in next to the inspector. "But more importantly, we've got to find out how that key got on the other side of the door."

"Oh, that's easy," Witherspoon waved his hand. "The murderer dropped it."

They discussed the case the rest of the way to South Kensington. Barnes paid off the cab, and they made their way up a short walkway to a tall, brick house in the middle of a row of town houses. The steps were freshly painted, the brass door lamps polished to a high sheen, and there wasn't so much as a weed in the small patch of garden behind the ornate wrought-iron fence. Witherspoon banged the knocker, and a moment later the door opened. A short, plump woman wearing a black housekeeper's dress smiled out at them.

"Good day," the inspector said politely. "We'd like to see Mr. Oliver Arkwright, please. I'm Inspector Gerald Witherspoon, and this is Constable Barnes. I believe Mr. Arkwright might be expecting us."

"Please come in," she opened the door wider and ushered them in. "Wait here please, I'll see if Mr. Arkwright is receiving."

Barnes waited till she'd disappeared into the room at the end of the hall before he asked, "Why would Arkwright be expecting us, sir?"

"Because I'm quite sure that Mrs. Arkwright must have mentioned our visit to his office yesterday. I imagine he knows he'd be next on our list." Witherspoon replied. For some odd reason, he felt strangely confident about this case. Everything was going to fall into place, he simply knew it. He could feel it in his bones.

The housekeeper returned, "Mr. Arkwright will see you, sir. Please follow me."

They walked down the long hall, passing portraits of sour-faced individuals who were probably Arkwright ancestors. The housekeeper lead them through a set of double doors.

A man sat behind a huge desk on the far side of the room. He didn't bother to get up. He had brown hair with a few streaks of gray at the temple and a very disapproving expression on his narrow, thin-lipped face. "I'm Oliver Arkwright." He focused his gaze on the inspector. "I understand you'd like to speak to me."

"That's correct," Witherspoon replied. "This is Constable Barnes, and I'm Inspector Gerald Witherspoon. We'd like to ask you some questions about the death of Harlan Westover." He couldn't help noticing that there were pictures and portraits of Her Majesty, the Queen, on virtually every wall of the study.

Arkwright frowned slightly. "I should imagine the less

said about that unfortunate incident, the better. The man's dead and buried, he killed himself."

"We're not entirely sure of that," the inspector said. "That's why we've come. There is some evidence that perhaps Mr. Westover's death wasn't self-inflicted, in which case, it would be murder." He was deliberately blunt. It bothered him that Arkwright hadn't acknowledged the constable's presence by so much as a glance and that he'd not bothered to invite them to sit down. Then he got himself under control. He mustn't let his personal feelings influence his work. This wouldn't be the first time he'd questioned someone while standing up.

Arkwright's frowned deepened. "My wife mentioned that you were around at the firm yesterday asking questions. I supposed it was something to do with his insurance."

"The police do not investigate insurance claims," Barnes said softly. He'd taken out his notebook and pencil.

"I suppose you'd best have a seat," Arkwright motioned toward the two straight-backed chairs to the right of his desk, and the two policemen sat down. "Though I've no idea what you think I can tell you. I never saw Westover after he left the office that day."

"I understand there was a board meeting that day and that Westover was in attendance," Witherspoon said.

Arkwright started in surprise. "Who told you that?"

"Your wife. She mentioned it yesterday when we were talking to Mr. Horrocks. Why? Was there something amiss with Mr. Westover being at the meeting."

Arkwright's mouth thinned even further. "Of course not, I'm just surprised that you'd bother with anything my wife said. For goodness sakes, she's only met Westover a time or two. But that's neither here nor there. In answer to your question, Westover was at the meeting."

"Was that normal business practice?" Witherspoon's gaze was caught by an ornate silver picture frame on the desk. Again, it was a likeness of the queen—taken, he was certain, in celebration of her jubilee. Gracious, the man must be extremely patriotic.

"I'm afraid I don't quite follow you?" Arkwright replied.

"What do you mean, 'normal business practice'? Westover worked for the firm, he was there to give the board a report. That's all there was to it."

"What kind of report?" Barnes asked.

Arkwright's brows rose in surprise. "I don't see how our internal business affairs have any connection to his death."

"We've no idea why Mr. Westover was murdered," Witherspoon said quickly, "so any help you can give us will be invaluable."

Arkwright sighed. "He was there for the simplest of reasons. We've designed a new engine, you see, and Westover was in charge of the project. We've already sold one, and it's on a ship as we speak. It's being sent to Africa, to be used to run equipment in the gold mines. Westover was giving the board a report on how quickly more engines could be manufactured."

"Did anything unusual happen at the meeting?" Barnes asked.

"No." Arkwright shook his head. "He said his piece and then left. I didn't even know he'd left the office until the next day when he didn't come into work."

The study door opened, and Mrs. Arkwright stepped inside. "Oh dear, Oliver, I'm so sorry, I'd no idea you were busy." She smiled warmly at the two policemen. "How very nice to see you again."

"Did you want something, Penelope?" Arkwright asked irritably.

"Only to tell you that the others have arrived. Shall I have Mrs. Grebels show them in?"

Arkwright flushed. "Oh, no, that won't be necessary. Tell them I'll be available in a few minutes."

"I told them you're talking with the police," she retorted, "and that you might be tied up for quite some time."

"You oughtn't to have done that." His eyes flashed angrily. "What will they think?"

Mrs. Arkwright appeared unperturbed. "They'll think whatever they like. Oh for goodness' sake Oliver, it's just those nosy old fools from the London Architectural Committee."

Arkwright's neck turned bright red as he held himself in check. Finally, he glared at his wife and then turned to the policemen. "I serve on one of His Highness's civil committees."

"That's quite an honor, sir," Witherspoon murmured.

"I'm related to Her Majesty through my mother," Arkwright explained.

"Distantly related," Mrs. Arkwright added. She pulled open the study door and stepped out into the hall.

"I'll be with them in a few moments," he yelled as she moved away. "Have Mrs. Grebels take them into the study."

Witherspoon, who had been both repelled and fascinated by the exchange between husband and wife, knew they weren't going to get much more out of Oliver Arkwright. He glanced at Barnes, and they both rose to their feet.

"Thank you for your time, sir," Witherspoon said.

"Is that it, then?" Arkwright got up, started to extend his hand, but then thought better of it. He'd obviously decided that a police officer wasn't his social equal. "I take it you're finished with me?"

"For the present, sir," Barnes said softly. He'd noticed the aborted handshake and was angry on the inspector's behalf. "But do keep yourself available, sir. We may need to ask you more questions."

"I don't see why," Arkwright sputtered. "I've told you everything I know."

"I'm sure you think you have, sir. But one never knows, does one? Do tend to your guests, sir. We'll show ourselves out," Witherspoon said.

Betsy's feet hurt. She'd spent half the morning watching the front of the offices of Donovan, Melcher, and Horrocks before she realized that once the staff was inside for the day, they weren't likely to come outside again until the office closed at half past five. She frowned at the double-wide front door of the elegant building where the offices were housed. She couldn't face going home this early, and she'd no idea what to do next. Maybe she ought to try some of the shopkeepers on the Kensington High Street, maybe one of them knew something. Just then, the door she'd been watching opened and a young man carrying a large satchel stepped outside. Her spirits brightened. He worked for Westover's company. She'd seen him go inside the offices earlier.

He stopped, put the satchel on the pavement, and adjusted his scarf beneath his heavy coat. A moment later, he'd picked up his burden and was on his way. Betsy followed at a discreet distance until he turned the corner, then she took off at a fast clip. She rounded the corner just as her quarry crossed the road and stopped at an omnibus stand. Unfortunately for Betsy, the omnibus was practically in front of the fellow. Taking a deep breath, she flew across the busy road. Dodging hansoms, carts, four-wheelers, and pedestrians, she raced toward the omnibus. Her hand grabbed the front pole of the platform, and she swung onboard just as the horses pulled away.

She ploughed into the young man. He was still standing in the aisle, his satchel tucked under one arm while he dug in his pocket for coins with his other hand.

"Oops," Betsy exclaimed, "I'm ever so sorry. Are you all right?"

He blushed a deep hue. "Don't fret, miss. It's my fault, I oughtn't to be standing in the aisle . . ."

"Then why don't you sit down," the conductor ordered. He jerked his head toward two empty seats in the front row.

The young man blushed even redder. "I'd best sit down," he sputtered. He eased his lanky frame into the seat. Betsy plopped down in the empty space next to him. She ignored the disapproving look the middle-aged woman in the seat across the aisle gave her. Let the silly cow think Betsy was a forward hussy. She didn't care. There was a killer on the loose.

"Are you sure you're all right, then?" she said chattily. She smiled brightly. "I banged into you pretty hard."

"I'm fine, miss," he smiled shyly in return. "You've no need to apologize. It was my fault." His voice was just a bit on the loud side.

"I'm sure you were just in a bit of a hurry to get home,"

she soothed, saying anything to keep the fellow talking. She prayed he was going to the end of the line.

He laughed. But the sound seemed to pass through his nose rather than his mouth, and the end result was that he sounded a bit like a braying mule. "If only that were true. I'm on me way to take some papers to our factory over on Watling Street. Then I've got to get back to the office." His voice was even louder than before.

"What office do you work in, then?" she asked. She deliberately pitched her own voice very, very soft. Maybe he'd take the hint and the entire omnibus wouldn't be privy to their conversation.

"Donovan, Melcher, and Horrocks. I'm a clerk. My name's Gilbert Pratting. I'd normally never be settin' foot in the factory exceptin' that our chief engineer has passed away and I've got to get his notes and papers over to our Mr. Barker, he's the factory foreman. Not that he could make sense of them, Mr. Westover, he was our engineer, he was a downright genius. Designed the most remarkable new engine . . . it's so good that a company in Africa bought the first one, sight unseen. It's on a ship right now. I can't see that Mr. Barker will be able to make heads or tails of Mr. Westover's papers. But then again, that's not my problem." He laughed again.

"How sad," Betsy winced. His voice drowned out the loud, London street traffic. The entire omnibus was staring at them. "Was the poor man ill before he passed away?"

"Not as far as I know," he finally lowered his voice a bit. "But he must have had something wrong with him, he committed suicide."

She gasped in shock. "How dreadful."

"Leastways, that's what the coroner's inquest ruled, but now they're all having fits. We've had the police around, you see," he laughed again. "And they're askin' questions like they think it might be something more than suicide. They're acting like someone did poor Mr. Westover in. Murdered him."

Betsy gasped again. "How terrible that must be for you and the rest of the staff."

"It's not terrible for me, I'd no reason to kill him."

"Goodness, you make it sound as if someone else did!" Betsy risked a quick glance around the omnibus. Her heart sank. Everyone, including the conductor, was openly staring at them. She was hardly being discreet. She brushed the problem aside. Right now she had to concentrate on getting as much information as possible out of Gilbert Pratting.

"Not as far as I know," he replied. "Mr. Westover was a harmless sort of fellow. Nice enough and very polite, but like a lot of people, he could really be stubborn. Especially about anything to do with his designs. Had a right old fit when he found out Horrocks had bought cheaper struts than the one's he'd specified. They had a right old blowup about that." He leaned closer to Betsy. She tried hard not to cringe back. She wasn't afraid of Pratting, but she was concerned that if he didn't lower his voice her hearing would be permanently damaged.

"I can't think why Mr. Westover was surprised about them struts," Pratting continued, he shook his head. "Everyone knows how cheap the old man is. Why at our Christmas party last month, all we got was one tiny mince tart and a cup of tea. Can you fathom such a thing? If you're going to be so cheap and nasty about the whole matter, why bother to have a party in the first place?" He paused for a breath, and Betsy tried to think of a question. But she wasn't fast enough, and he continued on. "Mind you, we shouldn't have expected any better than what we got. Mr. Jorgens, he's one of the other clerks, he helps with the books, he claims that if we'd not sold poor Mr. Westover's engine when we did, none of us would even have a job. Oh look, here's my stop coming up. I've got to change to another line." He gave Betsy a smile as he rose to his feet. "You never did tell me your name."

She thought quickly. "It's Henrietta. Henrietta Baker."

CHAPTER 4

A hard, steady rain pelted the inspector and Barnes as they emerged from the hansom in front of the offices of Donovan, Melcher, and Horrocks. They dashed for the door and managed to reach the dim foyer without getting soaked completely through.

Barnes took off his helmet and shook off the water. The damp seemed to soak into him, causing his knees to throb. He frowned at the sliver of late afternoon light coming in through the transom over the doors. He hurt, but he wasn't about to complain. The inspector, kind-hearted fellow that he was, would send him home. Barnes wasn't having any of that. He was a copper, and if he had to stand on his aching knees until the cows came home, so be it. He'd do his duty. But he did hope that whomever they interviewed next would offer them a chair. "Which one do you want to see first?" he asked. "Donovan or Melcher?"

Witherspoon shook the last of the water off his bowler and put it back on his head. "I don't suppose it matters much. Let's see who is here."

"And let's hope we get more information than we got out of Mr. Arkwright." Barnes pulled open the door to the outer office, and they stepped inside.

The clerks looked up from their desks, and the one closest to them got to his feet. "May I help you, sir?"

"I'm Inspector Witherspoon, and this is Constable Barnes."

"Yes, sir, I know. You were here yesterday."

"We'd like to see Mr. Donovan or Mr. Melcher."

"Mr. Donovan isn't in as yet," the young man replied, he smiled faintly. "But Mr. Melcher's in his office. If you'll wait here, I'll announce you."

He hurried across the room and down the hall. A few moments later, a tall middle-aged man with thinning blond hair and dark circles around his eyes appeared at the end of the hallway. He stopped in the doorway and gazed at the two policemen. "I'm Melcher," he said bluntly. "What do you want?"

Witherspoon was taken aback. "We want to talk to you, sir. As I told Mr. Horrocks yesterday, I'm going to be speaking to everyone in the firm."

Melcher stared at them and then waved them across the room. "James did mention you'd been by to see him. Come along then, we'll go into my office." The clerk, who'd been standing behind Melcher, scurried back to his desk.

"Inspector," Barnes said softly. "If you don't mind, I'd like to have a word with the rest of the staff," he jerked his head to indicate the clerks.

Witherspoon frowned slightly. "Hasn't someone already spoken to them?"

"Yes sir," Barnes replied. "A couple of lads took statements yesterday, but if you don't mind, I'd like to have a go."

"Certainly," he replied. He trusted Barnes completely. If the constable wanted to have a word with the clerks, he must have a good reason.

"Come along, Inspector," Melcher called over his shoulder. "I've not got all day."

"Yes, just coming." Witherspoon hurried down the hall and into the first open door. Melcher was already behind his desk. He nodded toward one of the two empty chairs opposite him. "Have a seat, sir."

"Thank you." The inspector sat. He decided to get right to the heart of the matter. "As I'm sure you've heard, Mr. Melcher, we've reason to believe that Harlan Westover didn't commit suicide."

"James told me you think it's murder," Melcher snorted. "A bit late in the day to be poking about looking for a killer, isn't it?"

"Better late than never, sir," Witherspoon replied. "Now, if you'll just answer a few questions, sir. Can you tell me what happened at the board meeting on the day that Westover died?"

Melcher's eyebrows shot up in surprise. "Why on earth do you want to know about that? It was just a board meeting. What's it got to do with Westover's death?"

"He was there, wasn't he?"

"Yes, we'd invited him along to give a progress report on a new engine he'd designed. He gave us his report, and then he left the office."

"Was he upset about anything?" Witherspoon asked.

Melcher shrugged. "He didn't appear to be. Actually, I wasn't paying all that much attention to the man. I'd a lot on my mind."

"Were you here at the office for the remainder of the day?" Witherspoon asked.

Melcher frowned. "I'm not sure I understand the question."

"I'll try to be more precise." Witherspoon wondered how much clearer he could be. "What time did the meeting end?"

"Around a quarter past twelve. Just before luncheon."

"Did you continue working here in the office the rest of the day?"

Melcher shook his head. "No. I went to my club for lunch, and then I went home."

"What time did you arrive at your home, sir?" Witherspoon wasn't sure what good this line of questioning was, they weren't sure what time the murder had been committed, only that it had been done in the afternoon. Still, it never hurt to get as much information as possible.

"I don't know, Inspector. I wasn't looking at my watch."

He leaned forward somewhat aggressively, his expression darkening. "What is this, sir? Are you accusing me of having something to do with Westover's death?"

"Of course not," Witherspoon assured him. "These questions are very routine, sir. I had, of course, simply assumed you and the other board members had spent your afternoon working here. Now it appears that you weren't here at all."

"Neither were any of the others," Melcher snapped. "Arkwright and Donovan scarpered as soon as the meeting adjourned, and as I left, I heard Horrocks telling Jackson that he was in charge and to make sure to lock up properly, so he wasn't here either." He paused and took a deep breath. "I think, Inspector, that you'd best ask everyone where they were that day."

"I intend to do just that, sir," Witherspoon said. "So you went directly home from your club after luncheon?"

"That's right."

"Where do you live, sir, and where is your club?"

"I live on Argyll Road in Kensington. Number 19. My club is Jensens, it's just down the street here."

"I know the place," Witherspoon said.

Melcher nodded slightly in acknowledgment. "I was there until half past one. You can check if you like, dozens of people saw me."

"And from there you went home," the inspector pressed. "Did you take a hansom?"

"No, I walked. Traffic was a mess. A coopers van had overturned, and I thought I'd get home faster on foot than if I took a cab. It's not all that far."

"What time did you arrive at your home?"

Melcher shrugged. "I'm not absolutely sure, but I think it was close to two."

"Would your housekeeper recall the time?"

Melcher gave him a thin smile. "She might if she'd been there, but she wasn't. She was out, and before you ask, so was the rest of the staff." He leaned back in his chair and flicked a bit of lint off the sleeve of his brown tweed coat. "I'm a widower, Inspector. My household is small, just a housekeeper and two maids. None of them were home that afternoon. It was their afternoon off. I was home alone until half past six, when Mrs. Brown, my housekeeper, returned from visiting her sister in Colchester."

Witherspoon nodded. He really didn't know what to think. "So you have no one who can vouch for your whereabouts after you left your club?"

"That's correct," Melcher replied. "Frankly, it never occurred to me that I'd have to account for my whereabouts."

"You had no idea that Mr. Westover was upset about something?"

"None at all, Inspector. He seemed perfectly fine at the meeting."

"That's odd, we've already spoken to one witness that claims Mr. Westover appeared to be very angry when he left here."

Melcher snapped out of his languid posture and leaned aggressively across his desk. "There are a number of people around here who have very vivid imaginations, Inspector. I shouldn't take everyone seriously, if I were you."

"We always take witnesses seriously, sir." Witherspoon hoped he wasn't being too indiscreet at this point in the investigation, but his instincts were prodding him to dig just a bit deeper. After all, Mrs. Jeffries was always telling him to trust his "inner voice" and obviously, that voice was prompting him along a certain path. "Why did everyone leave the office after the board meeting? Was that your normal practice?"

"No," Melcher said. "Generally we all went back to work. I can't speak for the others, but I left because I had a headache. Now see here, sir. I don't mind cooperation . . ." he broke off as a clerk stuck his head in the door.

"Sorry to interrupt, Mr. Melcher, but there's a cable just arrived from Cape Town. Do you want me to bring it in?"

Melcher waved impatiently, "Bring it in, boy. Bring it in." He looked at Witherspoon. "I'm afraid we'll have to continue this later. Cables from our customers generally require a good deal of work on my part."

• • •

Mrs. Jeffries was reaching for her cloak and bonnet when there was a loud knock on the back door. The cook, who was sitting at the table peeling apples, started to get up. Mrs. Jeffries waved her back to her seat. "I'll get it," she said. "You finish with your apples."

"Thanks, I want to get this pie done and in the oven. I've half a dozen sources coming by this afternoon. They stay longer and talk easier with their bellies full of sweet pie and custard."

The knock came again, and Mrs. Jeffries hurried down the back hall. She flung open the door. "Dr. Bosworth, gracious, this is an unexpected pleasure."

"Sorry to barge in on you, but I've discovered some information that I thought might be useful."

"Do come in," she stepped back and opened the door wider. "You've gone to a lot of trouble, doctor. You should have sent me a message, and I'd have been quite happy to come to you. I didn't mean for you to be inconvenienced on our account."

Bosworth stepped inside. "Please don't fret, Mrs. Jeffries, I had to come over this way today for a meeting at St. Giles Hospital. That's just up the road a piece from here. I thought I'd take a chance on catching you in and kill two birds with one stone."

"That's very kind of you." She led the way down the hall and into the warm kitchen. "Do have a chair, and I'll get us some tea."

Mrs. Goodge had already put the kettle on. She nodded respectfully at their guest. "It's nice to see you, Doctor. We'll have tea ready in just a moment."

Bosworth took off his hat and coat and placed them on the coat tree. "It's good to see you, too, Mrs. Goodge. This kitchen smells wonderful . . ." he stopped and sniffed the air, smiling in pleasure at the scent of cinnamon and apple. "Reminds me of when I was a boy."

They spoke of trivial things until they were sitting comfortably at the kitchen table with tea in hand and a plate of treacle tarts in front of them. Dr. Bosworth helped himself to a pastry. "This is excellent," he nodded at the cook.

Mrs. Goodge smiled politely, but Mrs. Jeffries could tell by the tight set of her mouth that she was impatient to find out why the good doctor was here. She also wanted her kitchen free.

"We're very curious as to why you're here," the house-keeper said.

Bosworth laughed. "I'm sure you are. Actually, I don't know if my information will be useful or not. But I thought it best to let you make that decision." He took a quick sip from his cup. "I spoke to the doctor who did the postmortem on Harlan Westover. He's quite a competent chap, actually, from what I hear of the fellow, he's a bit more than competent."

"That's always good to know," Mrs. Jeffries replied. There were some doctors that did postmortems that weren't very good at all.

"He was a bit reticient at first, but after we'd chatted for a bit, he told me a very curious thing. He found an abnormality in Westover's brain."

"Abnormality? What does that mean?" Mrs. Jeffries didn't know much about the human brain, but she did know it was a mysterious and complex organ.

Bosworth paused. "An abnormality is a growth in the brain that shouldn't be there. In this case, your Mr. Westover had a small growth on his frontal lobe."

"Did the doctor mention this in his postmortem report?" Mrs. Jeffries asked.

"There was no reason to put it in the report. The post-mortem is only concerned with the cause of death. That was quite clear, Westover died from gunshot wounds to his head."

"So once he finds the cause of death, so to speak, the doctor doesn't care what else is in a body," Mrs. Goodge frowned.

"That's right." Bosworth took another bite of his tart.

"Then how did the doctor find this uh . . . uh abnormality if he weren't lookin' for the ruddy thing?" Mrs. Goodge asked.

He laughed. "According to him, it was hard to miss. It

was quite close to the bullet entry wound. Just above it, in fact. As far as medical science knows, the growth shouldn't have had much, if any, impact on Westover. But after the doctor and I got to discussing the case, he wondered if maybe there might have been more of them."

"More what?" Mrs. Goodge demanded.

"More growths in Westover's brain," Mrs. Jeffries said softly. "If there were, could these growths cause someone to act out of character?"

"Perhaps," Bosworth shrugged. "It's very possible, but neither I nor any other doctor can say for certain. There is simply too much about the brain that's still a mystery. For all we know the poor fellow's brain might have been peppered with the wretched things, and it wouldn't have had any impact on him at all. Or it might have caused him to behave in ways completely out of character. There's some interesting research being done in Scotland and on the continent, but we simply don't know for sure."

Mrs. Goodge frowned darkly. "Are you tellin' us that if he had these here growths, he might have actually picked up that gun and shot himself?"

He hesitated. "I don't know. But the possibility is there."

"So it might not have been murder after all," Mrs. Jeffries murmured. This was most disappointing news.

"We've a bit of a problem, you see," Bosworth continued. "As I said, Dr. Garner, he's the one who did the postmortem, didn't mention the first growth in his report. He thought it obvious the man had committed suicide. When the coroner agreed, Garner thought no more about the case and went about his business. But when he found out the police were now investigating Westover's death as a possible murder, he realized the information he'd left out of the report might be important."

"What difference could it make?" Mrs. Goodge asked. "You've already told us that doctors don't know if these here growths cause people to act strange."

"But it's still pertinent information. Even though we don't know for certain, many doctors, and I'm one of them, are of the opinion that a growth on the brain could cause someone to act very differently than he normally might."

"Why doesn't Dr. Garner simply tell the police what he knows?" Mrs. Jeffries suggested. "He wasn't negligent. He did ascertain the cause of death."

"Yes, I know, but still, it won't make him look very good, will it?" Bosworth replied. He looked definitely uncomfortable, "Garner's a good doctor, generally takes a great deal of care with his reports. But on that particular day, he was covering two districts. Right after Westover was brought in, he had two other postmortems at St. Bartholomew's to attend to, so he wasn't as detailed as he should have been."

Mrs. Jeffries thought she understood perfectly. "So you want us to make sure the inspector finds out about the growth. That way your friend will be able to keep both his position and his reputation."

"I'm not sure what I want you to do." Bosworth sighed heavily. "Dr. Garner is very worried. He's afraid that Westover's death really was suicide, not murder. He doesn't want to see an innocent person arrested and hung because he left a pertinent detail out of a P.M. report."

"Reassure Dr. Garner that an innocent won't be unfairly tried for this death," Mrs. Jeffries said firmly. "If it was a suicide, we'll find it out. But just because you found a growth in the man's brain doesn't mean it wasn't murder. As you said yourself, the growth may have had no effect on his behavior whatsoever, right?"

"Yes, of course you're correct." Relieved, he smiled. "And you're right to investigate these circumstances as a murder as well. But I did think you ought to know about this."

"Of course," Mrs. Jeffries replied. "It's now quite possible that Westover did take his own life. We must keep that in mind. But we will find out the truth."

"You always do." Bosworth grinned and popped the last of the tart into his mouth.

"Was there anything else, Doctor?" Mrs. Jeffries asked calmly, even though her mind was now racing with this new possibility.

"Not really. The only other thing Dr. Garner mentioned

about Westover was that he had inkstains on his fingers and an old bit of chicken pox scaring on his shoulders. I guess one could say that apart from the gunshot wounds and the growth, the fellow seemed to be in quite good health."

Smythe elbowed his way through the crowded public bar of the Dirty Duck. Smoke from the fireplace wafted through the room, helping to mask the stink of unwashed clothes and bodies. Along the walls, narrow benches were filled with men and women drinking beer or gin. Couples and small groups occupied the half a dozen rough-hewn tables scattered in front of the fire, and they were standing two-deep at the bar.

Smythe wedged his bulk between a post and a solitary drinker and caught the barman's eye. "What'll you 'ave, mate?" the publican called over the noise.

"Beer," Smythe yelled. He scanned the crowd, looking for a familiar pork pie hat and checked coat. Nothing. "Blimpey Groggins been around?" he asked, as the publican slapped a mug of beer in front of him. Smythe took care to lay down two shillings, far more than the cost of the beer. He shoved them toward the barman.

"You a friend of 'is?" he asked as he picked up the coins.

"More like a customer," Smythe replied. "And I need to see 'im right away. As a matter of fact, you could say I'm one of 'is best customers." He wanted to make it clear he meant Blimpey no harm. Groggins was a man who had many friends, but the nature of his work insured he had an equal number of enemies.

"Blimpey'll be 'ere in a few minutes, he's just gone to have a word with someone out the back."

Smythe nodded and sipped his beer. While he waited, he relaxed and studied the crowd. It was what you'd expect— dockworkers, day laborers, washerwomen, prostitutes, and probably more than one pickpocket in the lot.

"I thought I might be 'aving a visit from you," the familiar voice came from behind him.

"And how's that?" he asked as Blimpey Groggins stepped up to the spot just vacated by the solitary drinker.

Blimpey Groggins was a short, portly, ginger-haired fellow, wearing a pork pie hat and a dingy brown and white checked coat. A bright red scarf was draped about his neck. He'd once been a petty thief and a burglar. But circumstance had shown him that it was far safer to sell information than stolen goods. He was possessed of an incredible memory, a vast network of contacts, and enough brains to realize he was a lot less likely to hang for selling information than for housebreaking. He'd deliberately set about learning every scrap of information there was to be had about anyone and anything in London. People paid good money to know things, and Blimpey wasn't one to ask questions of his customers. If they wanted to know something, he'd find it out for them.

"I figured you'd be around as soon as I 'eard your in-. spector was havin' a nose about that Westover suicide." Blimpey grinned at the barman and jerked his head toward Smythe. "He's buyin' so I'll have a double whiskey."

Amazed, Smythe shook his head. He knew the man made his living buying and selling information, but the inspector had only got the case two days ago—and there was even some doubt that there was even a murder at all. "Is there anything in this town that you don't know about?"

"Not much, mate," Blimpey shrugged modestly. "That's my job now, init? I take it you'll be wantin' the usual?"

The publican gave Blimpey his whiskey. "Ta, George."

Startled, Smythe dropped his gaze and fumbled with his pockets. He dug out more coins. Cor blimey, he thought, was he such a regular now Blimpey knew what he'd be needin' as soon as he walked in the door? That took the wind out of his sails. "That's right, we need to know all we can about the victim."

"Harlan Westover," Blimpey shot back. "Worked for an engineering firm by the name of Donovan, Melcher, and Horrocks."

Smythe wasn't the least surprised by Blimpey's knowledge. "Doesn't look like Westover 'ad much of a life outside of his work."

"Don't you believe it, old boy," Blimpey laughed slyly.

"Everyone's got a life. It's those quiet, hardworkin' types that are usually full of the most surprises."

"You're right about that, mate," Smythe muttered. "Anyway, find out what you can about 'im, and find out about the people he worked for, too."

"The owners of the firm?" Blimpey asked.

"Right. Their names are James Horrocks, Harry Donovan, Oliver Arkwright, and Lawrence Melcher. I don't know that any of them 'ave anything to do with Westover's death, but we've got to start somewhere." He took another drink of his beer. "How much time do you think you'll need?"

"Give us a couple of days. I'll 'ave something for you by then." Blimpey cleared his throat.

"Right, then, I'll be back here the day after tomorrow."

"Mind you come in about this time."

Smythe drained the rest of his beer and pushed away from the bar.

"What's the rush, then?" Blimpey held up a hand. "I've not seen you in a bit. Stay and 'ave a bit of a natter."

Smythe's eyebrows rose in surprise. He'd known Blimpey for a goodly number of years, but they were more business acquaintances than friends. Still, he liked the fellow. For an ex-thief, Blimpey was a decent sort, and he'd done Smythe more than one favor over the years. For that matter, Smythe had done Blimpey a good turn every now and again, as well. "All right, I'm in no 'urry," he shrugged. "So what've you been up to lately?"

"Oh, the usual." Blimpey took another quick sip of whiskey and then took a deep breath. "There's somethin' I want to ask you, and I don't want you gettin' all shirty on me."

Curious, Smythe gave him a long, appraising look. Blimpey's face was flushed, and there was a tight, pinched look about his mouth. If Smythe hadn't known better, he'd have sworn that Blimpey looked nervous.

"Well, are ya goin' to hold your temper or not?" Blimpey swallowed hard. "You're generally an easy goin' sort, Smythe. But it wouldn't do to get on the wrong side of you. God knows more than one dockside tough has found that out the hard way. But to be honest, I'd not like to lose you as a customer because I've offended you. This is important though, and ... well, I need a bit of 'elp 'ere."

"That depends on what you're askin'," Smythe replied warily. "Look, why don't you just spit it out? I'm not that bad-tempered. Leastways I never thought of myself that way."

"You're not," Blimpey sighed. "But a man's got to be careful when he starts askin' personal questions." He raised his arm and signaled to the barman. "Another round over here, George. Put it on my bill."

"Cor blimey, this is a first," Smythe exclaimed. "You must be in a state, if you're goin' to pay."

"It's a measure of how desperate I am," Blimpey replied darkly.

Genuinely alarmed now, Smythe leaned closer to the smaller man. "What's wrong, Blimpey. Are you in some sort of trouble with the police?"

"Oh no, it's much worse than that. My solictors can handle the coppers." He paused as the barman brought them their drinks.

"Are you sick?" Smythe couldn't think of what else it could be.

"In a way," Blimpey tossed back the second whiskey like it was water. "Truth is, I need to ask your advice about a rather delicate matter. You're the only person I know who was in a bit of the same situation as I find myself in and you came out all right."

"What are you goin' on about?" Smythe couldn't think of anything they had in common. "What turned out for me?"

"The lass," Blimpey sputtered. "You got engaged to your lass."

"Engaged? You mean me and Betsy?"

"Unless you've gone and gotten engaged to another woman since I last saw you." Blimpey took another deep breath. "And that's why I wanted to have a word."

"You're wantin' to get married?" Smythe fought hard to keep from grinning.

"I am. I'm at the age when the idea of settling down and havin' a family begins to 'ave a bit of appeal," Blimpey nodded his head.

As Blimpey was pushing fifty at least, Smythe reckoned he was well past that age, but he kept his opinion to himself. "So if you want to get engaged, why don't you just ask the woman to marry you? I'm assumin' it's someone you've been courtin' regularly."

"That depends on what you mean by 'courtin'," Blimpey replied. "I see her every day, and I think she's got feelin's for me. But how the 'ell is a bloke to know?"

"Ask her," Smythe said flatly.

"But what if she says she don't want me," Blimpey cried. He shook his head. "I want 'er in my life. If I ask and she says 'no', she might not want me about."

"That's a risk you've got to take," Smythe said kindly.

"Easier said than done, my son," Blimpey shot back. "I mean, if I say nothin', then we can go on as we are. But if I ask and she says 'no', then it'd be awkward for us to be together after that. And I'd rather 'ave her as a friend than not at all."

"Then keep 'er as a friend," Smythe suggested. He knew exactly what Blimpey was going through. "But if you want more than friendship, you've got to go that next step."

Blimpey took a deep breath. "So you think I ought to just tell her straight out 'ow I feel?"

"That's right. Beatin' about the bush won't do you any good."

"Is that what you did with your Betsy, ask her straight out?"

That most definitely hadn't been what Smythe had done. He'd danced about Betsy for months before he'd worked up the courage to even hint about his feelings for her. And then he'd only had the courage to pursue her when she'd made it clear she'd had feelings for him. But he wasn't going to share that with Blimpey, the bloke was too close to giving up as it was. "That's exactly what I did. But then again, it were a bit different for me. I was livin' in the same 'ouse as the lass, so I saw 'er all the time."

"Did give ya a bit of an advantage, didn't it?" Blimpey sighed. "Well I guess there's not much else I can do. If I want to be livin' in connubial bliss come this time next year, I'll have to risk tellin' her how I feel."

Smythe nodded wisely. "You can do it, Blimpey. By the way, why'd you ask me for advice? Why not one of your other friends?"

Blimpey shrugged. "Cause you're the only person I know who was in the same sort of situation."

"What do you mean?"

"Just what I said. My lady's a bit younger than me." Blimpey grinned. "You know, just like you and your Betsy."

Smythe winced. He wished he hadn't asked. "There's not that much of an age difference between us."

Blimpey laughed. "There's a good fifteen years, mate. Just about what there is between me and my Nell."

Luckily for Inspector Witherspoon, just as he came into the outer office, Harry Donovan walked through the front door. He was a short, portly man, with dark hair highlighted by thick gray streaks at the temples. He was impeccably dressed in a dark black suit, paisley waistcoat, and white shirt with an old-fashioned collar.

He held out his hand in greeting when Witherspoon introduced himself. "Harry Donovan," he said, his blue eyes flicked toward the hall. "Chairman of the board. James said you'd been by. Come along into my office." He turned his head toward the clerk sitting a few feet away. "Where's Melcher?"

"Mr. Melcher's gone to the factory," the clerk replied. "He had a telegram from Capetown. He said he had to go and see the foreman about making the ship dates."

Donovan nodded. "When he gets back, tell him to come see me. Come along, Inspector, my office is this way."

Donovan's office was twice as large as the others and had a marble fireplace opposite the entry door. Above the fireplace was a huge portrait of an austere-looking gentleman in old-fashioned clothing. "That's my grandfather," Donovan said proudly. "He started the firm."

"That's a very nice portrait," Witherspoon replied. Actually, the fellow didn't look nice at all, but he could hardly say such a thing. Not waiting for an invitation to sit, he went to one of the two green paisley upholstered chairs in front of Donovan's huge mahogany desk.

"Thank you." Donovan sat down behind the desk. "I understand you're investigating our poor Mr. Westover's death as a murder."

"We're investigating the circumstances," Witherspoon replied.

Donovan's right eye twitched rapidly. "The coroner ruled the death a suicide."

"I know, but some additional evidence has turned up and so we must, of course, investigate. Now, I understand that on the day Mr. Westover died, he was present at your board meeting."

Donovan nodded slowly. "Yes, we asked him for a list of equipment requirements. He'd designed a new engine, and we'd shipped the first one off. We've gotten orders for more," he broke into a wide smile. "It's an excellent piece of engineering. Revolutionary, in fact."

Witherspoon no longer cared why Westover had been at the meeting. "Yes, yes, I understand all that. What I'd like to know is if you noticed anything odd or unusual about Mr. Westover that day?"

Donovan sat back in his chair and his right eye started twitching again. "I can't think of anything specifically. But I did notice he wasn't as cheerful as usual."

"Was he generally a cheerful fellow?" the inspector asked. He forced himself not to stare at Donovan's fluttering eyelid.

"He was always pleasant enough," Donovan frowned. "He wasn't of a naturally cheerful nature. I suppose what I ought to have said was that he was a bit more dour that day than usual." He smiled sadly. "I suppose I ought to have been a bit more solicitous of the fellow and asked him if there was anything wrong. I'd no idea he was in such despair that he'd take his own life."

"What did you do after the meeting?"

Donovan looked surprised by the question. "I continued working."

"Here?" the inspector pressed.

"Where else would I work, Inspector," Donovan replied. This time, his left eye twitched.

Witherspoon didn't particularly like calling people liars, but Melcher had already told him that everyone had left after the board meeting. "Are you sure, sir?"

"Sure?" Donovan exclaimed, "Of course I'm sure . . ." his voice trailed off as he realized that the police had already spoken to the others. "Oh dear, of course, of course. I didn't work that afternoon . . . yes, that's right. I've gotten my days mixed up. I left after the meeting." He gave Witherspoon a weak smile. "I'd quite forgotten. It's been several weeks ago that it all happened."

"Where did you go, sir?" Witherspoon prompted softly.

Donovan's bushy eyebrows drew together. "I don't know why I'm having such difficulty remembering. Perhaps it's because it turned into such a dreadful mess, what with poor Westover killing himself. I've quite put the whole day out of my mind."

"Nevertheless, we do need to know your whereabouts."

Both of Donovan's eyes jerked rapidly. The inspector tried not to stare, but it was impossible. The poor fellow's eyes were jerking faster than hummingbird wings.

Finally, after what seemed an age, Donovan sighed. "I took my wife for an early luncheon at Maitlands, and then I went for a walk."

"Did your wife accompany you on the walk?"

"No, she had some shopping to do, so I put her in a hansom for Regent Street."

"Did you happen to see anyone who you knew?" Witherspoon realized that this was quickly becoming a case where movement and timetables might be important. He made a mental note to himself to do up a nice timeline when he got home. Timelines had been most useful to him in the past.

"No, Inspector, I did not." Donovan stood up. "Now, sir, if you'll excuse me, I'm very busy."

It was obviously a dismissal. But the inspector had gotten quite a lot of information. "Of course you're busy, sir, so are the police. Would you mind giving me your address."

Donovan's jaw dropped at the same time both his eyes

began to twitch. "Why on earth do you need my address?"

The inspector did his best to ignore Donovan's contorting face. The poor fellow couldn't help his affliction. "We'd like to have a word with your wife, sir. She met you here, correct?" He was guessing, but sometimes he actually guessed right.

"She did," Donovan admitted, "but I don't see why you need to speak to her."

"She might have seen Mr. Westover, might have spoken to him. She might have observed something everyone else missed. I think women sometimes notice things that men don't." His housekeeper was always noticing things that escaped him, but he wasn't going to share that with Mr. Donovan.

"I very much doubt that," Donovan replied. "My wife barely knew Mr. Westover."

"She didn't see him at all?" Witherspoon pressed.

Donovan hesitated. "I . . . uh, well, I can't say for certain. She might have seen him."

"Perhaps even spoken to him . . ."

"All right, Inspector, you've made your point. I live in Mayfair. Number 7 Wywick Place."

"Thank you, sir."

"Please do me the courtesy of being as discreet as possible, Inspector. My grandfather built our house. We have a position to maintain. I shouldn't like my neighbors to notice you going in and out of my home."

CHAPTER 5

"It was terribly disconcerting," Witherspoon said to Barnes. "Everytime he answered a question, one of his eyes twitched. I didn't know whether to look away or simply pretend I didn't notice." The two policemen were in a hansom on their way to the Donovan house. The rain had finally stopped, but the day hadn't improved any. Though it was barely half past three, the afternoon light was fading fast and they still had interviews to do. It would be full dark by the time either of them got home.

"It's hereditary, sir," Barnes said. "Apparently Mr. Donovan's father and grandfather had twitchy eyes as well."

"Gracious, really? How dreadful for them," Witherspoon clucked sympathetically. "At least that proves he wasn't twitching because he was lying. Though, frankly, that had been my impression of the fellow."

"How did the interview go, sir? Was he forthcoming with information?"

"Not particularly. He took umbrage when I asked him to explain his movements the day Westover was killed," he sighed and told the constable everything he'd learned from Harry Donovan.

73

Barnes whipped out his little brown notebook and took careful notes. When the inspector finished, he looked up, his expression puzzled. "Donovan claimed that the board asked Westover to be there because of equipment requirements? That's odd, sir. One of the clerks told me that it was Westover who insisted on going to the board meeting. That's two of them now that's said the same thing."

"What do you mean?"

"Donovan and Melcher both implied that they'd asked Westover to be at the meeting to give a report," Barnes explained. "But that's not what the clerk said."

"Why, Barnes, how very clever of you to find that out. I hadn't even thought to ask that question. Once I heard Melcher's statement, I simply assumed that Westover was at the meeting at their request." Witherspoon believed in giving credit where credit was due.

"It just happened to come up," Barnes shrugged modestly. Nonetheless, he was pleased.

"Nevertheless, it was clever of you to suss out the truth. Now, which clerk told you, and what, precisely, did he say?"

"He's the senior clerk, sir. He sits in one of the back offices. His name is Miles Wittmer, and he's been with the firm for over forty years. He was hired by Mr. Donovan's grandfather. The old gent started the company in 1848. But that's neither here nor there." Barnes paused for breath. "I'd asked Mr. Wittmer about Westover's last day, and he told me much of what everyone else has said. He'd not noticed anything unusual about Westover, certainly nothing which would indicate the man was thinking of suicide. Wittmer told me a little about Westover's engine and how it was going to change the firm's fortunes for the better. When he was showin' me some of Westover's papers, he dropped a page, and it slipped under my chair. When I bent down to get it, he said not to bother, that it was just the cost sheet and the estimates had been set weeks before the first engine was built. And then he said, and this is the interestin' bit, that it was the cost of parts that had poor Mr. Westover insistin' on being at the board meeting."

"He was certain that it was Westover who wanted to be at the meeting?"

"I didn't press him on the point, sir," Barnes admitted. "I'd no idea it might be important. But he sounded fairly sure of himself as he was talkin'. Wittmer told me that according to office gossip, Westover wanted to go to the meeting so he could complain about James Horrocks buying cheaper struts than his specifications required."

"Cheaper struts?" Witherspoon wasn't sure what a strut was, he made a mental note to try and find out. "That's interesting. Did you find out anything else from Mr. Wittmer or the other clerks? I mean, anything beyond what was in their statements."

Barnes shifted uncomfortably. "Truth is, sir, I don't really know. I've not gone over the statements that carefully." He had, but he couldn't quite remember all the details of what he'd read. He didn't particularly want to share that with the inspector yet. It frightened him. He loved being a copper, and he especially loved working with the now-legendary Gerald Witherspoon. If his memory started to go, he'd have no choice but to resign. He didn't even want to think about that possibility. "Sorry about that, sir. I know I should 'ave been a bit more prepared . . . especially as I was the one who wanted to interview everyone again."

"Nonsense, Constable," Witherspoon interrupted just as the hansom pulled up to the curb. "You're always 'at the ready,' so to speak. I've not gone over the statements all that carefully myself. I simply wondered if there'd been something you read in them that made you want to have another word with the office staff. You're so very good at catching little things people say that might be of significance." The inspector opened the door, got out of the hansom, and waited in the blustery cold while Barnes paid the driver.

"Let's see what we can learn from Mrs. Donovan," he said as the cab pulled away.

The Donovan house was in the middle of a row of Georgian town houses. It stood four stories tall, was made of red brick, and was topped with a dark gray slate roof. The front steps were freshly painted, and the brass side sconces polished to a high sheen. The front door was painted jet black and boasted a bronze cast door knocker, which was a good ten inches in size.

"Yee gods," Barnes muttered, "that thing looks big enough to go clean through the door."

"Let's hope it doesn't," Witherspoon picked up the handle and let it drop against the strike plate. He winced at the loud noise the ruddy thing made and wondered what it must sound like from the inside.

The moments ticked by, and the door remained firmly closed. Witherspoon listened hard for the sound of footsteps on the other side but heard nothing. He was reaching for the knocker again when the door flew open and a tall, gray-haired woman garbed in black stared at them. "Yes?"

"We'd like to speak with Mrs. Donovan," the inspector said. "We're the police."

"I can see that," she flicked a quick look at Barnes's uniform. "Is Mrs. Donovan expecting you?"

As most people weren't expecting the police to drop by, the inspector thought it a silly question. But he understood the rather peculiar habits of the upper class. "I don't think so, but it is important we speak with her."

The housekeeper stepped back and motioned them inside. "I'll see if Mrs. Donovan is at home."

"This isn't a social call," the inspector said, but he was talking to the woman's retreating back. They stood in a large, open foyer with a beautiful persian carpet on the dark wood floor, thin blue and cream striped walls and a huge bushy fern on a round table next to the staircase. Along the wall opposite the staircase were paintings of pastoral scenes, seascapes, and two spectacularly huge bowls of fruit.

The housekeeper appeared at the end of the hall and waved them forward. "Mrs. Donovan will see you now."

They were led into a cozy, but well-appointed room. The two windows opposite the door were draped with blue and silver paisley patterned curtains, and a cheerful fire burned in the hearth. Silver candlesticks and framed daguerrotypes were scattered along the mantle piece.

"If you'd like to have a seat, gentlemen," the voice came

from a small door at the far end of the room. They turned and saw a tiny woman watching them. She was very, very small, not more than five feet and quite thin. Witherspoon didn't think she could weigh more than seven stone soaking wet. By the look of her face, she wasn't young. Witherspoon guessed she was closer to fifty than forty. Her hair was more brown than gray, and she wore it up in a topknot with fringe scattered across her forehead. "I'll be quite happy to speak with you." The faint rustle of her maroon-colored day dress sounded loud in the quiet room as she came toward them.

"Good day, madam. I'm Inspector Gerald Witherspoon, and this is Constable Barnes. We're here to ask you some very simple questions. We won't take much of your time."

She smiled and gestured toward the dark blue settee and matching chairs in front of the fireplace. "Take as much of it as you like, Inspector, I've nothing else to do today." Her voice was surprisingly deep.

The two policemen waited politely until she sat down and then they each took one of the blue armchairs flanking the settee. Witherspoon said, "That's most cooperative of you, madam. Now, uh, I'm sure you're curious as to why we're here."

"You're here, Inspector, because you think someone murdered Harlan Westover." She smiled faintly. "My husband and the other partners in the firm are most upset about the whole matter. They'd quite reconciled themselves to a suicide. Murder, of course, is quite a different matter."

"Uh, yes, you're right." Witherspoon's mind went completely blank. He wasn't accustomed to such unbridled cooperation. Generally, women of her class thought speaking to a policeman rather disreputable. Consequently, getting any information out of them was difficult.

"We understand you were at your husband's office on the day that Mr. Westover died?" Barnes asked.

"That's correct. There was a board meeting that day, and my husband promised to take me to Maitland's for luncheon. It's a lovely restaurant, do you know it?"

"I've seen it, ma'am, but I've never eaten there."

Witherspoon replied. "Did you happen to see Mr. Westover while you were at the office?"

"Yes, I was a bit early, or the meeting ran a bit late, I don't remember which," she laughed. "But I was sitting in a chair in the outer office waiting, when Mr. Westover came storming out. I said 'good day' to him but he didn't return my greeting. He just stalked past me and left the office."

"Did you think his behavior odd?" Witherspoon pressed. Totally ignoring the chairman of the board's wife seemed fairly odd to the inspector. He'd never ignore Chief Inspector Barrows's wife if she spoke to him, no matter how preoccupied he might happen to be.

"Very. I'd never known Mr. Westover to be rude. But I thought perhaps something had happened at the meeting, something which might have upset him. I couldn't imagine what could be wrong. My husband was thrilled with Mr. Westover's work. The new engine he'd designed and built represented a huge windfall for the firm. They'd already sold the prototype and were in the process of building more. Oh no, they'd not want to lose someone of Mr. Westover's talents."

"Was Mr. Westover thinking of leaving the firm?" Barnes interjected.

"Not as far as I knew," she replied. "But I know how worried my husband was that another firm was going to steal Westover away."

"Had any other firms tried?" the constable pressed.

She hesitated. "Not directly. But I know that the board was concerned about losing him. Of course, since he'd finished the prototype for the engine, they weren't quite as concerned as they had been."

"I take it the firm owns all rights to Westover's design." Witherspoon stated.

"That's correct," she replied.

"Do you know if Mr. Westover had any enemies?" he asked.

"Not that I'm aware of," she replied. "But I hardly knew the man. You really ought to ask my husband. He's known Mr. Westover for years."

"He knew him before he went to work for your husband's firm?" Barnes asked.

"That's right. Their fathers were at school together. My husband lured Mr. Westover away from Rupert and Lincoln, they're a big company in Birmingham."

"Did his old firm try to get him to stay on?" the constable asked.

"Of course," she laughed. "My husband and the other partners were terrified Westover would change his mind if they left him in Birmingham too long. They got him here as quickly as possible. They even found him a place to live once he'd agreed to come. You know how difficult it is to find decent accommodation these days. Luckily, my husband knew of some rather nice rooms that were available to let." She smiled brightly, "they were in a house he used to own as a matter of fact."

Witherspoon nodded. "Can you tell me if you noticed anything else about Mr. Westover after the board meeting?"

She thought for a moment and then shook her head. "Only what I've already said."

"Did you ask your husband what had happened at the meeting?" Barnes asked. "I mean, did he have any idea why Mr. Westover had been so rude?"

"I asked him, of course. But he said nothing had happened at the meeting and that Mr. Westover probably hadn't even noticed me sitting there," she snorted derisively. "My husband has very little faith in my powers of observation."

"Perhaps, ma'am, he should have listened to you a bit more carefully," Witherspoon said. "What time did you and Mr. Donovan finish lunch?"

"I'm not certain. It was probably about half past one."

"Did you come straight home from the restaurant?" the constable asked.

"I was in no hurry to get home, Constable. I went shopping and then to my dressmakers. I ordered three new gowns," she smiled slyly. "My husband will be furious when he gets the bill."

• • •

Smythe stood just outside the back door and watched Betsy step through the gate in the far corner of the communal garden. The gate was so well hidden by shrubs, you had to know just where to look to spot the ruddy thing. But as they all used that shortcut, especially when they were on a case, he knew if he waited out here he could talk to her without the others hearing.

He kept his gaze upon her as she stepped onto the footpath and started across the garden. Cor blimey, but he loved her. But Blimpey, damn the man, had made him think, made him start having doubts. He was older than Betsy. It hadn't bothered him until now, until he'd started thinking of some of the things Blimpey had wittered on about back in the pub.

She smiled in delight as she spotted him. "Are you waiting for me?"

"Always," he went toward her, holding out his bare hands.

"Why aren't you wearing gloves," she chided, as their fingers met. "It's cold."

"Don't fret, lass," he said softly. "I'm fine."

Betsy stepped back and looked at him. She could tell something was on his mind. "What's wrong?"

"Nothing, but I do want to talk to you before we go into the meetin'." He took her arm and led her back out into the garden, toward the huge oak near the center. "I've got something to ask you, and I want you to be honest with me."

"You're starting to worry me, Smythe," Betsy frowned. "What on earth is wrong?"

"Do you think I'm too old for ya?" he blurted. Blast, he'd not meant to say it like that.

"Too old?" she repeated. "Now why would you be thinking that you were too old for me?"

"There's more than fifteen years between us," he continued. "I'm goin' to be thirty-six in April . . ." his voiced trailed off as she stopped and stared at him.

"Smythe," she finally said, "if I'd thought you were too old for me, I wouldn't have said 'yes' when you asked me to marry you. Now who's been putting these silly ideas into your head?"

He could hardly admit that he was getting them from his

paid informant, so he just shrugged. "No one. It just occurred to me I might 'ave pressed you a bit. You know, before you 'ad a chance to really think about whether you wanted to marry me. That's all."

She cocked her head to one side and gave him a long, speculative look. "Are you sure you're not the one who's feeling a bit pressed?"

It took a moment for him to understand. "Now don't go thinkin' that, lass," he said defensively. "I'm the one that wants to get married. You're the one that's always puttin' it off."

"Me! You agreed that once we married, things would change and that neither of us was ready to give up our murders." She was incensed by the unfairness of the charge. Mind you, she'd been the one to realize that once they wed, there would most definitely be many changes in their lives. For starters, Smythe would want to give her everything, including her own home. Once that happened, no matter how hard they tried, life would be different. Neither of them was ready to face those kinds of changes. But blast it all, he'd agreed with her.

"You're right," he soothed, not wanting to ruffle her feathers any further. "I did agree. But just because neither of us wants a change just yet, I'll not 'ave you thinkin' I don't want to marry you. I want that more than anything."

"Then what's all this nonsense about?" she complained. "Oh, come on, let's get home. It's cold, and I learned ever so much today. I don't want to miss the meeting. You and I can sort this out later."

"There's nothing to sort out," he fell into step beside her. Betsy knew her own mind, if she didn't think he was too old, then well, he wasn't. But still, that conversation with Blimpey had left him feeling uneasy. "I just wanted to make sure you didn't mind the difference in our ages."

"Don't be daft," she took his arm. "It's not all that much, and it means nothing. I'd never even given it much thought until you brought it up."

Blast, he thought, maybe he should have kept his mouth shut.

The others were already seated around the table by the time they got to the kitchen. Wiggins was bent over, giving Fred a good petting. He straightened up as they entered the room. "I told Mrs. Jeffries you two would be along soon, told 'er I'd spotted you doin' a bit of courtin' in the garden."

"We weren't courtin'," Smythe said. "We were talkin'."

"Why don't you both have a seat and we'll get started," Mrs. Jeffries could tell the coachman was annoyed about something. She hoped he and Betsy weren't quarreling. But then again, it was quite natural for an engaged couple to occasionally have a difference of opinion. "I've quite a bit to report." She and Mrs. Goodge had already agreed that they wouldn't tell the others about Dr. Bosworth's news until the very end of the meeting. She didn't want to dampen their enthusiasm by telling them they might not have a murder at all.

"I wish I could say that," Wiggins gave the dog one last stroke and went to his chair. "Cor blimey, them tarts look good. I'm starved."

"You're not to make a pig of yourself," Mrs. Goodge chided. "Don't ruin your appetite. I've got a nice roast in the oven for supper."

"I think we'd best get right to it." Mrs. Jeffries poured the tea and began handing the cups around.

"Can I go first?" Betsy asked. At the housekeeper's nod, she told them everything she'd found out from the clerk Gilbert Pratting. She always made sure she repeated every little detail that she'd learned, no matter how inconsequential it might seem on the surface. They'd had too many cases solved correctly because of some tiny little fact that had been mentioned right at this very table.

"What's a strut?" Mrs. Goodge asked when Betsy had finished.

"It's a small part that helps fasten other parts," Smythe replied. "You know, it's one of them little bits that don't look important, but if they go missing, the whole contraption can fall apart."

"You mean like the time the pin thing broke off of my sausage maker and the handle fell off? That was a right mess, wasn't it! We had mountains of pork butt all over the kitchen and nothing to grind it with. Just goes to show how important the little bits in life are, doesn't it."

"That's right," Mrs. Jeffries added. She had her own questions to ask the maid. "So Pratting said that the clerk to the chief accountant said they'd not have jobs if Westover's engine hadn't sold?"

"That's what he said," Betsy replied, "and he wasn't unsure of himself when he was talking. He said it like it was the gospel."

"That means the firm is in trouble," Smythe muttered.

"Very probably," the housekeeper agreed. She took a sip of her tea.

"Maybe the firm's in trouble, but some of the partners aren't short of money," Mrs. Goodge added. "Oliver Arkwright has plenty, well, leastways his wife does."

"Did you hear that from one of your sources?" Wiggins asked cheerfully.

"That's where I hear everything," she replied.

"I wish we knew more about the argument that Westover had with James Horrocks," Betsy frowned slightly. "Too bad that lad got off the omnibus when he did. That might have been important."

"If 'e knew about it, I'm sure others in the firm do too," Smythe said kindly. "We'll find out what we need to know, we always do."

"You're right," the maid replied. "I expect I can find out about it tomorrow if I put my mind to it. Anyway, I've said my piece."

"What time is Lady Cannonberry supposed to be 'ere?" Wiggins asked.

Mrs. Jeffries started guiltily. Perhaps they should have waited for Ruth. But she still wasn't sure about the wisdom of discussing everything about the case with her. Ruth and the inspector were getting closer all the time. The housekeeper didn't want to be in the position of having encouraged the woman to keep secrets from Gerald Witherspoon. That wouldn't do their relationship any good at all. Yet telling Ruth she couldn't help out hadn't been a reasonable alternative either. She already knew what they were up to, and she was eager to do her bit. Besides, with Luty and Hatchet away, Lady Cannonberry's social connections might be very useful. They'd given her an easy assignment—to find out what she could about the partners in the firm. "She ought to be here any minute, we'll catch her up when she arrives."

"Don't worry, boy," Mrs. Goodge said. "We'll not leave her out of things. Now, as I was sayin', some of the partners aren't short of money. With or without the firm, the Arkwright's should be fine."

"Does he have money too?" Betsy asked.

The cook shook her head. "He had the aristocratic connections. She had the money. Her family is in trade and property. The gossip I heard is she only married him to get a step up socially."

Fred suddenly leapt up and bounded down the hallway. A second later, there was a knock on the back door. Wiggins was out of his chair like a shot and escorting Ruth into the kitchen a few moments later. She discarded her cloak and hat as she walked. "I'm so terribly sorry to be late, but honestly, it couldn't be helped. I was working on the case, and I simply couldn't leave without getting as much information as possible."

Mrs. Jeffries's heart sank. She hoped Ruth had been discreet. Getting information was important, but keeping their activities a secret was even more important. Not that all of them were always discreet. "Please don't worry about your tardiness, we only just started. Sit down and have some tea. We'll catch you up on what we've learned later. Mrs. Goodge was just telling us about the financial situation of some of the firm's partners."

"Tea sounds heavenly," she sank into the empty chair Wiggins held out for her. Betsy handed her a steaming cup of tea.

Mrs. Jeffries looked at the cook. "What else did you hear?"

"Not much more, only what Betsy's already mentioned, that James Horrocks has a reputation for being tight with money. But I've got my sources on the hunt, so to speak, and I ought to know more in a day or two."

"Excellent," the housekeeper said. She turned to Ruth, "would you like to share what you've learned with us?"

Ruth giggled, then her hand flew to her mouth. "Oh dear, I sound just like a schoolgirl. Honestly, I can't tell you how very excited I am to be a part of all this."

"We're delighted to 'ave you with us," Wiggins said quickly.

"Oh dear, I mustn't ramble." Ruth glanced at the carriage clock on the top of the pine sideboard. "I know we're a bit pressed for time, so I'll get right to it. I had a little chat with one of my husband's old friends, and he gave me some information on the background of Westover's firm." She stopped and looked at Mrs. Jeffries, "Don't worry, I was very discreet."

"I'm sure you were. Do go on."

"The firm was founded by Harry Donovan's grandfather. It was a family firm until ten years ago when Donovan needed to raise capital to expand. He wanted to start doing his own manufacturing and apparently that requires a great deal of money."

"Is that when the other partners bought in?" Smythe asked.

"That's when James Horrocks and Oliver Arkwright bought into the firm, Lawrence Melcher didn't buy in until two years later. It was when Melcher came along that the firm's name changed, it used to be called Donovan and Son. It was actually quite successful when the grandfather and the father were running it."

"I wonder why Arkwright's name isn't part of the company name?" Wiggins mused.

"I asked Jonathan that very question," Ruth said. "Apparently, Arkwright didn't put in enough money to get his name included."

Betsy shook her head. "There's something I don't understand, if the company isn't worth much, then why'd the other partners buy into it?"

"I don't know," Ruth admitted uncertainly. "But if you'd like, I could try to find out."

"That's a very good idea," Mrs. Jeffries said quickly. Company business was all very interesting, but it probably had nothing to do with Westover's murder. In her experience, people were generally killed for personal reasons. "Did you learn anything else?"

"Not really, only that Lawrence Melcher was persuaded to put his money into the company by Donovan. Since the company's fortunes have taken a turn for the worse, there's supposedly quite a bit of rancor between the two men. They had a dreadful argument at the bank a fortnight or so ago. It was so bad the manager asked them to leave."

Betsy shot a quick look at the housekeeper, who nodded almost imperceptibly. The message was clear, the maid was to find out what had happened at the bank. A fortnight ago was roughly the time that Westover would have been murdered.

Mrs. Jeffries smiled warmly at Ruth. "You've done wonderfully. We're very grateful for the information."

"Oh, I want to keep on helping," Ruth said quickly. "It's ever so exciting, and I do believe we're all meant to serve the cause of justice. Unfortunately, tomorrow I'm going to a committee meeting. We're trying to get women the vote, but perhaps I can beg off . . ."

"Oh you mustn't do that," Mrs. Jeffries interrupted. "Your work for the rights of women is important too."

Ruth looked doubtful. "Are you sure? Catching murderers is useful as well. One doesn't like to think killers are dashing about free to do it again."

"Maybe you can do both," Wiggins suggested helpfully. He was totally unaware of the surreptious frowns the others shot him. "You can go along to your meetin' and then come along back 'ere for our meetin'. Besides if you're busy in the afternoon, you can go out lookin' for clues in the mornin', can't she Mrs. Jeffries?"

"Of course she can," the housekeeper replied. She told herself that Wiggins was simply being kind and helpful. However, she decided that she and Wiggins might need to have a little chat tonight after supper. "Now, we really do need to move along. Smythe, have you anything to report."

"Not yet, but I've got some lines of inquiry I'm workin' on. I'll 'ave somethin' by tomorrow."

"Wiggins?"

"Nothin' from me," the lad admitted cheerfully, "but I'll keep at it. I've got a few irons in the fire."

Mrs. Jeffries sighed silently. She couldn't put off the news any longer. "I do have something to report. Dr. Bosworth stopped by today. He had some information for us. Now, before I give you the details, I want you to know that he was very uncertain as to what it actually meant."

Constable Barnes and Inspector Witherspoon waited in the drawing room of the Horrocks house. The fireplace was cold, the lamps unlighted and dark blue curtains wide open to the gloom of approaching evening. The room was getting darker by the moment. Surely, Constable Barnes thought, in a household this large, someone would come along and at least light the ruddy lamps. But so far, they'd seen no one but the maid who'd answered the door. He saw the inspector pull his overcoat tighter and noticed he'd not removed his gloves.

Maybe the interview with Edna Horrocks wouldn't take long, Barnes thought. He was tired, cold, and his feet hurt. But he refused to give in to the discomfort. He might be getting older, but he wasn't going to become lax in his duty or his demeanor. Occasionally, he might forget something, but he was still a good copper. They wouldn't even be here if he hadn't re-interviewed the staff at the office and found out about Edna Horrocks. He was startled by the sudden sound of footsteps in the hall.

"I hope that's Mrs. Horrocks," the inspector said softly. "I'd like to get this over and done with. I'm very tired."

Edna Horrocks swept into the room. She was an attractive woman in her mid-fifties. She wore a black and green striped dress with a dark green overskirt. Her wheat-colored hair was done up in a tight topknot. She didn't look pleased. She stared at them coldly out of a pair of deep set hazel eyes. "What do you want?" she asked.

Witherspoon was so taken aback by her rudeness, he blurted out the truth, "To find out why you were hanging about outside your husband's office on the day Harlan West-over was murdered." He clamped his mouth shut, mortified that he'd not been more polite. He'd never spoken so rudely to a woman in his entire life.

"I was spying on my husband," she shot back. The inspector's uncharacteristic bluntness had surprised her into speaking before she could guard her words. "Oh dear, I oughtn't to have said that." She closed her eyes, sighed, and then sank down on a chair near the door. "I'm sorry, Inspector. I've been terribly rude. Please sit down and let's start over."

"Of course, madam," Witherspoon replied. He nodded at the constable, and the two of them moved to the settee. "I do appreciate your honesty, though. Would you mind telling me why you want to spy on Mr. Horrocks."

"Why do you think, Inspector," she said wearily.

"I've no idea," Witherspoon replied.

She stared at him incredulously. "The usual reason, sir."

"Usual reason?" he repeated.

"I think Mrs. Horrocks is afraid Mr. Horrocks is seeing another woman."

"Thank goodness one of you understands," she said. "I knew there was a board meeting that day, you see, and that meant that James would be leaving the office right afterwards. I decided to follow him."

"You'd actually want to know your spouse was being unfaithful?" he murmured. Gracious, this was becoming a most odd police interview.

"Of course," she replied. "The only way I can get a divorce is if I've evidence of adultery."

It was completely dark by the time the inspector came through his front door. He desperately wanted to discuss this case with his housekeeper. "Good evening, Mrs. Jeffries. It's very cold outside, and I'm dreadfully tired."

She reached for his hat. "Good evening, sir. Not to worry, Mrs. Goodge has a lovely meal in the oven for your dinner. That'll warm you up nicely."

He took off his heavy overcoat. "I'd like a glass of sherry first."

"I thought you might, sir." She hung up his garments and

ushered him toward the drawing room. "It's already poured."

"Excellent."

A few moments later, he was settled into his favorite chair and Mrs. Jeffries was sitting across from him. "Inspector, have you thought anymore about what we discussed yesterday?" She did hate to be a nag, but this was one task he'd been avoiding.

Witherspoon winced. "Well, I've been awfully busy, what with the investigation . . ."

"Of course you have, sir. But as I said earlier, you really must take care of your social obligations."

"Can't I just invite the chief inspector and his wife to a restaurant?"

"It's not just the chief, sir. There's also a good number of others who you ought to entertain. There's your neighbor, Mrs. Cross, Lady Cannonberry, and that nice sergeant and his wife. You really must consider it, sir. It would be very good for your career."

An expression of panic crossed the inspector's face. "But I'm no good at that sort of social thingamabobby. I'd be the host, I'd have to make sure that things went along nicely, that people talked to each other . . ."

"You could ask Lady Cannonberry to act as your hostess," Mrs. Jeffries suggested.

Witherspoon immediately brightened. "Do you think she'd do it?"

"I suspect she'd love to, now do think about it, sir. As I said, a nice dinner party would do wonders for your career. Now, sir. Do tell me about your day. Is the investigation going well? Did you find out much today?"

"Quite a bit, actually," Witherspoon said quickly. He was relieved to be off the subject of the dinner party. He could face down a crazed killer waving a pistol and it wouldn't terrify him as much as the thought of playing host at a dinner party. But he knew his housekeeper was right, he did have social obligations to repay. He brushed the dinner party worries aside and began to give her the details of his day. As it had been quite a long day, he went to great pains to remember everything. He'd found talking over his cases did wonders for putting him on the right path, so to speak.

Mrs. Jefries listened carefully, occasionally asking a question or making a comment. By the time he'd finished telling her about his interview with Edna Horrocks, she'd managed to work several of her own ideas into their conversation. By the time he was on his way to the dining room for his dinner, he was utterly convinced that his own brilliant mind had produced a whole new perspective on this case.

CHAPTER 6

The morning dawned bright and cold. Smythe caught Betsy on the landing before they went down for breakfast. "Did ya sleep well, love?"

"Wonderfully," she said. She looked around and then stood on tiptoe and kissed him on the mouth. "Now come along, then," she said as she drew back, "let's not be late. I'm fairly sure Mrs. Jeffries got quite a bit of information out of the inspector last night."

"There's no 'urry, love," he murmured, as he reached for her. He wanted a few more moments alone with her, a few more moments where he didn't have to share her with the others or with one of the inspector's cases.

She deftly stepped to one side just as Wiggins came bounding down the staircase. "Mornin' all," he said cheerfully. "Brrr . . . it's cold. Even with the fire in the grate, I didn't think our room would ever get warm. Let's get on down to the kitchen, it's sure to be nice and toasty."

Betsy fell into step with the footman, and Smythe gave up. He trailed after them. He wasn't going to have a chance to talk to her alone again, not this morning. Blast a Spaniard, why had he ever brought up the subject of age? She'd never thought anything about it till he'd rubbed her nose in it. What if she started thinkin' about it, started thinkin' there was too great a difference between them? What then? Bloomin' Ada, but he'd been a fool. He'd tossed and turned all night, worrying about it.

They went into the kitchen and took their places. Over breakfast, Mrs. Jeffries gave them a full report on what she'd learned from the inspector.

"Cor blimey," Wiggins exclaimed, "you mean this Mrs. Horrocks was actually waitin' about, tryin' to spy on her husband?"

"Yes, and it obviously wasn't the first time," Mrs. Jeffries replied. "Mrs. Horrocks told the inspector she's sure her husband had spotted her. That's why he went to that pub for lunch. It was the sort of place she didn't dare go into unescorted. She waited and waited for him to come out, and when he didn't she realized he must have slipped out the back door. Apparently, it's not a happy marriage."

"Most marriages aren't," the cook interjected, "but most people don't go about wanting to get divorced. I've never heard of such a thing."

"Divorces do 'appen," Smythe said thoughtfully. "But even so, I don't see 'ow Mrs. Horrocks wantin' a divorce can 'ave anythin' to do with Westover's murder."

"Neither do I," Mrs. Jeffries agreed. "Not unless there was a connection between Mrs. Horrocks and Harlan Westover that we don't know about."

"I'll try and find out," Smythe reached for another slice of bread. "Maybe there was somethin' between the two of 'em, and maybe Mr. Horrocks found out about it."

"Does Horrocks have an alibi?" Mrs. Goodge asked. "I mean, other than the lunch at the pub. Oh bother, what's wrong with me! After his lunch, he's supposed to have gone to look at property on the Goldhawk Road."

"He did 'ave lunch at the pub," Smythe said. "I checked. But he was finished by one o'clock and Mrs. Horrocks was right, he did slip out the back door."

"It's a very weak alibi." The housekeeper frowned. "But then, everyone's alibi is fairly weak." She sighed. "I'm not even sure we're investigating the right group of people. For all we know, Westover might have been killed by someone who had nothing to do with his work. Someone from his past. Someone he'd wronged before he started working here in London."

"Not to worry, Mrs. Jeffries, if that turns out to be what 'appened," Wiggins said cheerfully, "then we'll suss it out sooner or later. We always do. Anyways, now that I've found out about Mrs. Horrocks and her wantin' a divorce, I think I'll 'ave a snoop around there. No tellin' what I might find out."

Despite her misgivings, Mrs. Jeffries smiled. It was impossible to be downcast in the face of such optimism. "That's a good idea, Wiggins, but before you do, why don't you have another go at Westover's neighborhood?"

Wiggins's eyebrows shot up in surprise. "All right, if you say so . . . uh . . . but what am I lookin' for?"

She wasn't sure herself. But she knew they were sorely lacking in hard facts. "The killer had to have gotten to the Lynch house by some means. He or she had to have entered the house, through either the front door or the back. Someone might have seen something . . ." her voice trailed off. "Good gracious, we've been quite foolish."

"How do you mean?" Mrs. Goodge asked.

"We really must speak with Mrs. Lynch," she replied. Her mind worked furiously. "We've got to ask her about the front door."

"Front door?" Betsy repeated. "Didn't the inspector say that Mr. Horrocks had said it was unlocked?"

"Yes, but just because he said it, doesn't mean it's true." She turned her gaze to Smythe, "For many people keeping their doors locked is as natural to them as breathing. I'm betting that an elderly woman, living with two lodgers had them both trained to lock the front door the moment they crossed the threshold." She knew she was on to something, but she wasn't certain what it was.

"But we know that Westover was upset," Betsy pointed out, "maybe he forgot to lock up when he came in."

"When something is a habit, we do it without thinking,"

Mrs. Jeffries replied. "I don't know that Mrs. Lynch insisted the doors be locked, but we must find out."

"You want me to talk to Mrs. Lynch?" Wiggins wasn't sure he was the best person for that task.

"No, I'll take care of it," she replied. "But do go back to the neighborhood this morning. There is still so much we need to find out."

"And as the police didn't even know they had them a murder, they wouldn't have done much in the way of questioning the neighbors," Betsy added. "You might find out all sorts of things."

The housekeeper poured herself more tea. "With Wiggins working that area, we'll at least be sure we haven't missed something obvious. Oh, by the way, Ruth will be here for our afternoon meeting. She might have some information for us as well."

"Is that it then?" Smythe picked up his mug and drained it. At Mrs. Jeffries's nod, he rose to his feet. "I'll be off then, there's a couple more hansom cab drivers I want to talk to today, and if it's all the same to you, I'll have a go at seein' if anyone saw Horrocks on the Goldhawk Road."

Betsy got up too. "Come along Wiggins, let's get cracking. I might as well go with you as far as Holland Park."

"I'm goin' to take the omnibus," he announced, as he stuffed the last bit of toast into his mouth. "It's too cold to walk very far."

Smythe shot Betsy a fast glance, but before he could say a word, she said, "Don't worry, I'll take the omnibus as well." She knew him so well, she was beginning to read his mind.

"The lad is right. It is too cold to be larkin' about the streets." He knew he sounded like a mother hen, but he couldn't help himself.

"Don't worry about me, I'll be fine. Most of my work today will be indoors. I'm going to do my best to find the bank the partners had that row in a few weeks ago," she laughed. "Let's keep our fingers crossed that Melcher and Donovan made a big enough fuss that people still remember all the details."

"I'd try the banks near the office." Mrs. Jeffries suggested.

Betsy headed for the coat tree. "There can't be that many banks in the neighborhood."

Mrs. Jeffries smiled encouragingly as the kitchen emptied out. But one part of her feared they were all wasting their time. She'd spent half the night awake, worrying about what Dr. Bosworth had told them. The truth was, they might be rushing about chasing their tails. Harlan Westover could very well have taken his own life. She'd given the matter a good, hard think and come to the conclusion that unless they got their hands on some very compelling evidence, they simply couldn't be sure if this was murder or suicide. Drat, but sometimes life was so very complicated.

Wiggins pulled up the collar on his thick, heavy coat to fight off the chill. He'd been up and down the street in front of Harlan Westover's house half a dozen times, and no one had so much as poked a nose out. It was too ruddy cold for anyone to be out and about.

He leaned against a lamppost at the end of the block and stared morosely at the quiet street. Nothing stirred. There were no housewives with shopping baskets, no maids armed with brooms or footmen with brass polish. There wasn't even anyone cutting across the green. What was he going to do? He refused to go home with nothing.

Discouraged, he started to turn away when a young lad came racing around the corner and almost crashed into him. The boy leapt to one side. "Sorry, gov, I didn't see you standin' there."

" 'Ow's that then, I'm not invisible," Wiggins replied with a laugh. "What's your rush, boy?"

"It's bloomin' cold," the boy said. But he stopped and stared at Wiggins out of a pair of curious green eyes. His cheeks were flushed a bright pink, and an unruly mop of curly brown hair was visible beneath a knitted green woolen cap. His short gray jacket was clean, but well worn, and the bright blue wool scarf wound twice around his neck was far too long to actually belong to him. "My mam tossed me out this mornin'. She said I was fit to drive her to drink and to go run off some of my fidgetin'."

"How old are ya?" Wiggins asked. He didn't hold out much hope the lad could tell him anything useful, but it was someone to talk to for a few minutes.

"Twelve," the boy grinned. "My name's Derek Wilkins. I live down the street. My mam's the housekeeper."

"Well, Derek," Wiggins said amiably. "I don't suppose you'd like to walk with me a bit. I'm waitin' for my friend, she's applyin' for a post as a maid at a big 'ouse around the corner. It's borin' as bits out 'ere on my own." It was a weak story, but it would do for a young one.

The lad shrugged. "Mam says not to talk to strangers, but you look 'armless enough. I reckon if you try anythin' I could outrun you. I'm a powerful good runner."

"I'll bet you are," Wiggins said. He started off down the street. The boy fell into step beside him. "Anyway, what kind of neighborhood is this? I don't want my fiancée workin' somewhere that isn't nice."

"Fiancée," Derek repeated. "I thought you said it was your friend."

"We ain't officially engaged, not yet. But bein' as you live 'ere, you'd be in a position to know if it's safe or not for Flossie."

"Nothin' much happens around here," Derek said.

"Are you sure?" Wiggins pressed. This wasn't going the way he wanted. "No robberies or missing persons or murders?"

"Well," the boy rubbed his nose. "Mrs. Markham's cat was stolen. That's what she claims, but Mam says the silly old thing probably run off. And Mr. Walters, he lives down at number 17, he lost his topcoat and gloves. Someone took 'em right off the coat peg when he left his door open . . ."

"That's it, then?" Wiggins tried to keep the impatience out of his voice.

"Oh, that poor Mr. Westover who lives across the street from us, he killed himself . . ."

"Killed himself?" Wiggins clucked his tongue. "When did this 'appen?"

" 'Bout a fortnight ago," Derek replied. He pointed toward the opposite side of the road. "He had rooms at Mrs. Lynch's, right up there."

"How'd he do it?"

"Blew his brains out," Derek said eagerly. "And what's more, I heard the gun goin' off. I tried to tell me mam, but she said I were makin' it up."

"Did you tell the police?"

"The police," Derek snorted. "They wasn't interested. When they come around the second time 'cause Mrs. Lynch was raisin' a fuss and callin' 'em fools, Mam said I wasn't to say anythin'. Said not to cause trouble. But I don't see how tellin' what I heard could cause trouble."

Wiggins was elated. If the lad was telling the truth, they would have an exact time of death. "I don't see 'ow it could either. Cor blimey, you must be a clever one to remember about the gun."

Derek tried to shrug as if it didn't matter, but he couldn't quite hide his proud grin. "Weren't nuthin'. I was outside, ya see. Mam wanted me to pick up a loaf down at the baker's. She'd forgot it that mornin'. I'd just started off when all of a sudden there was this 'orrible loud noise, like thunder, only sharper and quicker like."

"What did ya do?" Wiggins pressed.

"Do?" Derek seemed puzzled by the question. "There weren't nuthin' to do. I looked about tryin' to suss out the cause, but I didn't see anything so I went on to the baker's to get Mam's loaf. She'd be right snarky if I didn't get her the loaf, she needed it for the afternoon tea."

"Did anyone else come out because of the noise?"

The boy's brow wrinkled. "Nah, I don't think so. I don't remember seein' anyone. It was a cold day, and there was plenty of traffic on the road. I expect I'm the only one that 'eard anything, but then, I was practically standing outside Mrs. Lynch's when it 'appened."

"I don't suppose you know what time it 'appened?" Wiggins asked casually. From the corner of his eye, he watched the lad's expresssion.

"Course I know," Derek bragged.

"You 'ave a watch?"

"Don't be daft, course I don't 'ave a watch. I know because when I got to the baker's, it was almost ten past two."

"How long did it take to get to the baker's?" Wiggins asked patiently.

"About five or six minutes," Derek replied. "It's just across from Shepherds Bush Station. Mam don't like the one 'round the corner from us. That means the poor bloke musta done it a few minutes past two o'clock."

Betsy refused to be defeated. She pulled open the heavy door of the London and Leicester Bank and stepped inside. This was the third bank she'd tried this morning, and so far, she'd had no luck whatsoever. She stopped just inside the door and studied the territory for a moment. On the far side of the huge room, clerks dressed in stiff white shirts and narrow ties labored behind a long, high, wooden counter. Each clerk was separated from the one next to him by wooden partitions.

Betsy hesitated. She had a good story at the ready, but it hadn't worked at the last bank. That clerk had been in such a hurry his only concern had been to get rid of her as quickly as possible. She scanned the young men serving behind the counter. The one in the middle was tall, confident, and handsome as sin, the one next to him appeared to be involved in a very intense discussion with a middle-aged matron. Betsy's gaze stopped on the third clerk. He was perfect. Chinless, pale eyes, and already balding even though he was young, she was sure she could get him to talk. She started for her quarry and took her place in his line. It was the longest of the lines.

She waited patiently as the patrons ahead of her did their business. The customer in front of her finished his business and moved off. No one had gotten into line behind her, so if she got the fellow talking, she might learn something useful. Betsy put on her most dazzling smile and stepped up to the counter.

The clerk looked up as he shut the cash drawer. A blush crept up his pale cheeks as he took in her expression. Apparently, he wasn't used to pretty blonds beaming at him. "Uh . . . can I help you, miss?"

"I certainly hope so," she sighed dramatically. "I've got a most unusual problem, you see, and I'm not even sure I'm in the right bank."

"Oh . . . oh . . . do tell me how I can help," he sputtered.

She leaned closer and locked her gaze on his. "You see, about a fortnight ago, my grandmother happened to be in a bank in this area. She only popped in to keep warm. By that, I mean, it wasn't her bank. While she was there, two gentlemen got into such a terrible row. It was such a terrible argument, that the bank manager asked them to leave . . ."

"Oh yes," he said brightly, "I remember it quite well . . . it was Mr. Melcher and Mr. Donovan. It was quite awful. They started shouting at each other so loudly that Mr. Haggerty asked them to leave . . ." his voice trailed off as the clerk on his left shot him a frown.

But Betsy wasn't going to let some sour-faced bank clerk stop the flow of information. She brightened her smile even further and leaned so far over the counter it's a wonder she didn't bang her head into the fellow's chest. "Yes, yes, that's what my grandmother told me."

The clerk cleared his throat. "Uh, now uh, how can I help?"

"Do you happen to know where either of the gentlemen that were having the row actually live?" she asked boldly.

"You want to know where they live?" he repeated incredulously.

Betsy nodded eagerly, as though it were the most ordinary of requests. "Of course. That's why I'm here. You see one of them dropped his pocket watch. It's quite a nice watch. He dropped it just outside the door. Grandmother left right behind them. She said the man took his watch out, looked at it, and then was so upset that when he went to put it away, he missed his pocket completely, and the watch fell onto the pavement. He was lucky it didn't break."

"Goodness, it must be a jolly good watch," he said thoughtfully.

"Grandmother shouted at him," Betsy continued, "but he was in such a state that he didn't hear her."

He gaped at her. "I'm afraid I still don't understand."

Yee Gods, she thought to herself, the fellow was a bit of a dolt. "Grandmother picked the watch up," she explained patiently. "She tried to catch up with him, but she's an elderly woman and he was walking very fast. He disappeared before she could give the wretched thing back to him. So she took it home and has been fretting over how to get the silly thing back to the proper owner for two weeks now. That's why I've come."

"Why didn't she bring it back here?" the clerk asked. He sounded curious, not suspicious.

"Because she couldn't recall which bank it was," Betsy replied. "She only stepped inside for a moment to get out of the cold." She threw caution to the winds. "Look, can you meet me after you get off work or perhaps at your meal break? I really don't want to take up anymore of your time here, and I don't want to get you into any sort of trouble. But this is very important. Grandmother will have another stroke if I don't give that wretched watch to the proper owner . . ."

"I take my meal at half past eleven," he said quickly. "I could meet you then."

"Excellent, meet me at the tea shop on the corner. I'll be waiting." With that, she tossed him another dazzling smile, turned on her heel, and left. She didn't want to give him time to change his mind.

Smythe knocked softly on the back door of the Dirty Duck pub. It was outside of hours but he didn't want to wait for opening time to see Blimpey. There was too much to do today. He shivered as a blast of cold wind blew off the dark water of the Thames. From inside, he heard the faint sound of steps and then the door opened. A bearded fellow wearing a stained apron stuck his head out. "We're closed, mate. Come back later."

"I've got business with Blimpey. Tell 'im that Smythe is 'ere."

"I'm not his keeper, you know." The publican wiped his hands on his dirty apron.

"Let 'im in," Blimpey's voice came from inside. "He's a right persistent bloke."

The barman stepped to one side, and Smythe stepped through the door. Blimpey was standing at the far end of the corridor, leaning against the doorway of the public bar. "You're out and about early," he said amiably. "Come in and have a sit down. I was just havin' a bite of breakfast."

Smythe followed him into the bar. Blimpey went back to his spot in front of the fireplace. There was a cheerful fire burning in the grate and a plate of cheese and bread was on the table. Blimpey gestured at the food. "Once I'm married, I'll have a proper cooked breakfast. The only hot thing Sam can do is a pot of tea."

"Have you asked her yet?"

Blimpey dropped his gaze and shrugged. "Not yet. I want to do it properly. Wait till just the right moment."

"Haven't worked up the courage, eh?"

"Cor blimey, big fellah. How the hell did you manage?" Blimpey picked up his mug and took a long, slurpy sip of tea. "Scares me to death, it does. I've faced off coppers, thieves, and river pirates, but nothin's got me shakin' in my boots as much as the idea of askin' her to marry me. What if she says 'no'?"

Smythe gazed at him sympathetically. He knew how painful Blimpey's problem could be. He'd been there himself. But right now, he needed information. "That's just a risk you'll have to take. You might ask one of her friends how she feels about you."

Blimpey brightened immediately. "Cor blimey, that's a right good idea. I could ask Cora Werthers to have a word. At least that way I'd know if it was safe to bring up the subject. I don't want to lose her, you know. I'd rather have her as a friend as not."

"I understand." He'd felt the same way about Betsy.

Blimpey sighed and gave himself a shake. "Right then, on to business. You're 'ere a bit early."

"Knowin' you, I was fairly certain you'd 'ave somethin' for me."

"I've got a bit. It seems your Mr. Westover was quite the fellow. His old employers up in Birmingham were more than a little sorry to see him go. They offered him a barrel of money to stay on, but by that time, Donovan had already snared him and lured him to London. Rupert and Lincoln was in a right old snit about it. There was quite a bit of bad blood between the firms. Still is. Old man Lincoln vowed to put Donovan and the others out of business."

"That's a bit harsh."

"Not really," Blimpey said. "Westover wasn't just a bloomin' good designer, he was a brilliant engineer. I can't make 'ead nor tails out of all that mechanical nonsense, but apparently, havin' someone who's got the gift for it in your firm is good. I don't know the ins and outs of it, but when Rupert and Lincoln lost Westover, they started having one problem after another. They make steam engines, you see, for the railways. Westover was their chief engineer, and once he was gone, they couldn't seem to fix anythin' right. It might be worth havin' a look at Lincoln. He was in London a couple of weeks ago."

Smythe thought about it for a moment and then he shook his head. "I'll have a look. But if he was that angry, why kill Westover. Why not kill Donovan?"

"Maybe he considered Westover a traitor," Blimpey suggested.

"But he wouldn't wait three years," Smythe replied. "Or maybe he would. Do you have anything else for me?"

"Not much," Blimpey said from around a mouthful of bread. "I did find out that Harry Donovan's wife was the widow of John Welch."

"Who's he?" Smythe was beginning to get a bit confused.

"A fellow who made a lot of money importing tea. Died a few years back and left every cent to his good wife, who married Harry Donovan just in time to buy the building the firm is housed in, thus eliminating a very ugly eviction process. They've been at that address for a long time. Course now that Mrs. Donovan bought the leasehold, they'll not have to worry about having to move for awhile."

"Cor blimey, you mean the company was in so much trouble they couldn't pay the rent?"

"Couldn't pay the rent, nor the rates, nor their clerks' wages. If Donovan hadn't married the widow Welch when he did, his company would have been doing business from the front parlor of his house."

"How convenient for Mr. Donovan. A rich widow just larkin' about desperate to marry him."

"She wanted to marry him all right, but she's no fool. She bought the building as an investment. Mind you, she did give him a nice lease and put a bit of cash in the business."

Smythe nodded. "If Donovan was so broke, how did he have the money to lure Westover away from Rupert and Lincoln?"

"Different time, Smythe," Blimpey said. "He married the missus about seven years back. She put in enough to keep the concern going for a couple of years and then when that run out, he brought in Arkwright and Horrocks. After that, Melcher come along with his cash and Donovan was set for a bit." Blimpey smiled brightly. "Course, no matter 'ow much you have, it'll never be enough if you keep pissin' it away. From what I've learned, none of the partners in that company knows their arse from their elbows, let alone how to run a business. Sad too, Donovan's father and grandfather are probably spinnin' in their graves. Now those gents knew what they was about, they didn't have to bring in partners to keep the business goin'."

"Will you be able to find out more by tomorrow?" Smythe asked. He didn't know what to make of any of this. But he was sure that once he told the others, they'd all put it together. They were a clever bunch, even if he did think so himself.

"I've got my sources workin' on it." He sighed. "I just wish that women was as easy as work."

"So do I, mate," Smythe agreed. "So do I."

Inspector Witherspoon wasn't sure what to do next. He'd interviewed the partners and their spouses, and Constable

Barnes had spoken to everyone at the office. Twice. "I still don't have any idea where we are with this case," he said to Barnes. They were in a Lyons Tea Room trying to get warm. Witherspoon took another sip of tea. He was taking his time. He wasn't in any hurry to go back out into the cold. Besides, he hadn't a clue where to go next.

"I think we ought to interview Mrs. Arkwright again, sir," Barnes suggested. "She's a bit flighty, but she seems observant, nonetheless."

Witherspoon perked right up. "I say, do you have some questions you'd like to ask her?" This might not be such a dreadful afternoon after all.

"Well, it seems to me she might know a bit more about everyone's movements on the day of the murder."

"Really?"

"Yes, she admitted she was at the firm on the day of the board meeting, the day Westover died."

"She met her husband for luncheon," the inspector added. "She told us that."

"Don't you think it a bit odd, sir," Barnes mused. "She never mentioned that she'd seen Mrs. Donovan there that day. She was waiting for her husband too."

"We don't know that the two women actually saw one another," the inspector pointed out. "Mrs. Donovan waited in the office proper, while I got the impression that Mrs. Arkwright had waited outside." He frowned, "Of course, I don't recall Mrs. Arkwright actually mentioning where she was waiting."

"She said she saw Westover when she and her husband were getting into a hansom," Barnes grinned. "But that doesn't mean she wasn't in the office and didn't see or hear something else that might end up being useful. Besides, I think she's a bit of a chatterbox, sir. If there's something goin' on at Donovan, Melcher, and Horrocks, I warrant we might have a chance of gettin' it out of her."

"I do believe you've got a point," Witherspoon replied. He was suddenly quite eager to get on with it. He reached into his pocket, pulled out some coins, and laid them on the table. "Let's stop at the restaurant Mr. and Mrs. Arkwright had lunch at as well. I want to have another go at the waiters."

"Right, sir. Best that we cover everything." He was biding his time, it wasn't quite the moment to steer the inspector back to the police reports. "For that matter, sir, I think it's odd that all the board members left the office that day. According to what the clerks said, that was very odd. There was generally always one of the partners on the premises. It was sort of an unwritten rule."

"Yes, but that meeting must have been quite upsetting. Someone committed a murder afterwards."

"Acrimony seems to have been the order of the day at that firm," Barnes said.

Mrs. Jeffries was doing a bit of dusting in the front parlor when Betsy arrived back at Upper Edmonton Gardens. The housekeeper stuck her head out into the hall when she heard the maid coming up the back stairs. "Hello, Betsy. I hope you've had a successful day."

"Hello, Mrs. Jeffries. It's been fine, so far," Betsy giggled. "I can't wait till we have our meeting."

"I think Mrs. Goodge has got someone in the kitchen, so I expect we'd best leave her be for a bit longer."

"I'll just finish tidying up the linen closet after I've changed my shoes." She took off her cloak. "You do think she'll be ready for our meeting, don't you?"

Mrs. Jeffries waved her feather duster airily. "Oh, I'm sure she'll be finished by then. Mrs. Goodge is very good at moving people along once she's got what she needs from them. I take it from the happy expression on your face that you had a run of good luck today."

Betsy grinned. "I found out ever so much. I just hope it's useful. How about you?"

"I popped over to Mrs. Lynch's," Mrs. Jeffries replied. "I found out what I needed to know."

"You spoke to Mrs. Lynch?"

"No, but I managed a word with Mr. Baker."

"Who's he?" Betsy asked.

"Her other tenant. He confirmed what I thought . . ." she

broke off at the sound of more footsteps coming up the back stairs. "That sounds like Wiggins."

A moment later, the footman appeared at the top of the stairs. He waved in greeting. "Hello, Mrs. Jeffries, Betsy. Cor blimey, it's cold outside. I saw that Mrs. Goodge had someone with her in the kitchen. Do you think she'll be finished by our meetin' time? I think Lady Cannonberry is on her way across the garden."

"I'd best get downstairs then," Mrs. Jeffries tucked her duster under her arm and headed for the back stairs. "You two come on down when you're ready." She trotted down the stairs and was relieved to find the kitchen empty and Mrs. Goodge putting the kettle on.

"Not to worry," the cook assured her, "I kept my eye on the clock." She pulled the big brown china teapot off of the drying rack.

"I wasn't in the least anxious." Mrs. Jeffries headed for a covered plate at the far end of the long table. "Is that for us?"

The cook nodded. "It's lemon tarts, I thought we deserved something really nice today."

The housekeeper knew that meant Mrs. Goodge must have struck gold. She was always generous with treats when she'd learned a lot.

Within a few minutes, everyone had arrived and taken their places. It was obvious all of them had something to report. Ruth Cannonberry was practically bouncing up and down in her chair, Betsy's eyes sparkled, Mrs. Goodge hummed as she poured out the tea, Smythe looked extraordinarily pleased with himself, and Wiggins was grinning from ear to ear. Gracious, this was a fine how do you do. What on earth was she going to do? She almost wished Dr. Bosworth had kept his information to himself. Then she caught herself, what was she thinking? Of course Dr. Bosworth had been right to tell them what he knew.

"Mrs. Jeffries," Mrs. Goodge raised her voice. "Are you all right?"

"Oh dear, silly me," she smile apologetically. "I was thinking about our case. Do forgive me. Now, who would like to go first?"

They all spoke at once. Mrs. Jeffries raised her hand for silence. "Gracious, it seems we're all very eager to speak. Why don't we take it one at a time. Ruth, you're our guest, you go first."

"I don't want to step out of turn," Ruth began, "but if you insist. As you all know, I didn't think I'd have time to do much investigating, not with my women's meeting and everything, but you'll never guess, I heard ever so much at the meeting."

"Just goes to show you never know where you're goin' to find somethin' interestin'," Wiggins said eagerly.

"I don't know if it's useful or not, but I found out that Oliver Arkwright wouldn't have a farthing if it weren't for his wife."

Mrs. Jeffries hid her disappointment. They already knew that.

"I understand she's from a wealthy family," Mrs. Goodge said tactfully.

"Oh yes, I know you already know that, but I'll warrant that what you don't know is that Mrs. Arkwright wants her money back. She had a frightful row with her husband about money she loaned his firm. Mrs. Merkle heard all about it from her maid who got it directly from Mrs. Arkwright's maid."

"How can she get her money back?" Smythe asked. "He's her husband. What's hers is his and what's his is hers."

Ruth shook her head. "Not anymore. Not since the Married Woman's Property Act. Surely you must have heard of it? It was passed in Parliament several years ago. It gives married women control over any money they bring into their marriage and any money that they inherit while married. Mrs. Arkwright not only brought quite a bit into the marriage, she's about to inherit quite a bit more."

"I thought she already had inherited," Mrs. Goodge said. "Didn't her uncle die recently?"

"He didn't die, he just went into a coma. But he's not expected to live much longer."

"Why'd she loan her husband money if she didn't want him to keep it for awhile?" Wiggins asked.

"She did it so that he could buy in to the firm. He'd convinced her that it was a good investment. Frankly, Mrs. Merkle is of the opinion that Penelope Arkwright loaned her husband the money to buy in as a partner to get him out of the house," Ruth replied. "Apparently, before that, he spent most of his time at home."

"No wonder she loaned him the cash," Mrs. Goodge muttered darkly. "Imagine having to put up with a man under your feet all day."

"They aren't very happily married," Ruth continued. "Mrs. Merkle's maid says that he's always reminding her that her family is in trade while his is related to the Queen."

"That's not very nice," Betsy said.

"She's getting her own back," Ruth grinned. "Mrs. Arkwright has threatened to take her husband to court to get her money back. That'll embarrass him and his family."

"You can do that?" Wiggins asked incredulously.

Ruth nodded. "It was a proper loan. She has a note and made him put up his house as collateral."

"So if she takes him to court and he can't repay the loan, does that mean she gets his house?" Wiggins asked.

"I think so," Ruth replied.

"Cor blimey, that don't say much for the institution of marriage," Smythe muttered.

CHAPTER 7

Betsy got the floor next. "I had a bit of luck finding out about that row between Melcher and Donovan."

"You didn't have any trouble finding the bank, then," Mrs. Goodge commented.

"It was the third one I tried," Betsy replied. "And I was lucky enough to find someone who'd witnessed the whole thing." She paused and shot a quick glance at Smythe. His expression was interested, but not overly so. She felt just the tiniest bit guilty about how she'd flirted with that poor bank clerk to get the information she'd needed, and she was sure that guilt was written all over her face. Her beloved was getting very good at reading her expressions, and even though he wasn't generally a jealous man, she'd just as soon not have him asking her any pointed questions about her sources. "The clerk who witnessed the argument is a real chatterbox. Told me all about it while we were waiting for the omnibus." This time, she didn't look at Smythe. "The row was very noisy. Everyone heard them. Lawrence Melcher got absolutely furious with Harry Donovan and accused him of running the business into the ground."

"That does seem to be the general assessment of the management of that firm," Mrs. Jeffries murmured. An idea popped into the back of her mind and just as quickly popped out again.

"What else did they say?" Mrs. Goodge pressed.

"The clerk hadn't heard the first part of the argument," Betsy explained.

"You said 'e'd 'eard the whole thing," Wiggins reminded her.

"Only from when the shouting started," Betsy said. "But from the exchange he heard, it was obvious the two men had been arguing well before they began screaming at each other. The jist of it was that Donovan wanted Melcher to guarantee another loan at the bank and Melcher didn't want to do it. Melcher, apparently, has plenty of money of his own. He shouted at Donovan that there wasn't any use in getting a loan, Donovan would only fritter it away."

"What did Donovan say?" Smythe asked eagerly.

"Donovan yelled that Melcher was being unfair, that it wasn't his fault that the firm had had a run of bad luck, and that the loan would only be temporary. Once the orders for the new engine began rolling in, they'd have more than enough to pay off all the loans." She paused for a breath. "Melcher shouted back that if Donovan wanted more money, he'd better try getting it from his wife, because Melcher wasn't giving him another penny. Furthermore, there weren't going to be any orders, not if Westover had anything to do with it."

She stopped and waited for the others to understand the implications of that last bit of information.

"Was the clerk absolutely sure about that?" Mrs. Jeffries asked.

"Absolutely," Betsy nodded her head in emphasis. "I knew that bit was important, so I made him repeat the conversation almost word for word. He was sure of what he'd heard."

"What happened then?" Mrs. Goodge asked.

"At that point, they'd gotten so loud, the manager asked them to please leave. From what the clerk said, they were still shouting at each other as they walked down the street." Betsy shrugged apologetically. "But he couldn't hear what they were saying. But it was loud enough that people on the street were staring at them. The clerk saw that clearly enough. That's about it, then. I didn't find out anything else."

"Well done, Betsy," Mrs. Jeffries said. "That is very useful information. But then, I'm sure the rest of you have interesting things to report as well." She didn't want anyone to think what they had to say wouldn't be important. "Though I must say I'd really like to know whether this row was before or after Westover's death."

"It was before," Betsy said quickly. "I'm sorry, I ought to have mentioned that. Donovan and Melcher had the row on the twelfth, which was the day before the board meeting. The clerk remembered because the row happened just a few minutes before the bank had its monthly board of governors meeting, and the manager was so upset he didn't even notice the govs had arrived, let alone greet them properly. Several of them were most put out. My source said the clerks got a good laugh at that. The manager isn't very well liked."

Mrs. Jeffries nodded thoughtfully. "Now that is interesting. It means the partners knew before the meeting that Westover was unhappy about something."

"Probably those cheap struts," Mrs. Goodge suggested.

"Sounds like they knew he meant to do something about it as well," Smythe added. "Anyway, if it's all the same to everyone, I'll have a go next." He told him everything he'd learned from Blimpey, making sure he didn't leave out any details. "So it seems that no matter how much money people invest in the company, within a few years, it's gone."

"Sounds like it would 'ave been gone even sooner if it 'adn't been for Mrs. Donovan," Wiggins commented.

"And Mrs. Arkwright," Mrs. Goodge pointed out. "Arkwright couldn't have bought into the firm without his wife's money."

"Some people just aren't very good at business," Smythe said. "But that doesn't seem to stop 'em."

"Does anyone want to 'ear what I found out?" Wiggins asked. "It's gettin' on."

"Go on lad," Smythe said kindly. "I've said my bit."

Wiggins told them about his meeting with Derek Wilkins

and the lad's certainty about hearing the gunshot. "So at least we know what time the murder took place. That's important, isn't it?"

"Very," Mrs. Jeffries said, and she meant it. "The boy was sure of the time?"

"He was. He was sure it was a few minutes past two."

"And after two that afternoon, none of the partners had an alibi," Mrs. Jeffries said thoughtfully.

Mrs. Jeffries sat in her chair by the window, staring out at the faint flickering gaslight across the street. She was thinking, or rather, she was letting her mind drift from one snippet of information to another. This was a technique she'd perfected over the last few years, one she used when a case seemed unduly difficult, or even worse, unduly muddled.

She took a deep breath and let the thoughts come and go as they would. They knew when the murder took place now, but that didn't help all that much. With so many people not having a true alibi, where did one start?

The firm's partners were apparently appallingly bad businessmen, but that probably had nothing to do with Westover's death. Half of the city was filled with inept businessmen. There were always articles in the newspapers about one bankruptcy or another, but there didn't appear to be a corresponding number of murders. And why would any of the partners want to kill Westover? He was the one goose the company had that just might lay a golden egg. Admittedly, they appeared to know that Westover was upset about those cheap struts, but there were many ways to mollify an angry employee. All they would have had to do was to guarantee to replace the things. Surely that would have been easier than one of them murdering the poor fellow.

What if it wasn't murder at all? She frowned as Dr. Bosworth's words came back to haunt her. Could that growth have affected Westover's behavior? Could it have caused him to do something completely out of character like take his own life? If only they knew for certain one way or another. She suddenly realized that there might be a way to find out. Inspector Witherspoon had told her that Mrs. Lynch claimed Westover didn't own a gun. Which meant that he would have had to have gone out and acquired a weapon. One didn't buy a pistol at the corner shop. She decided to put a flea in Constable Barnes's ear. He had much better sources than she did when it came to finding out how one acquired a weapon on short notice. If Westover had purchased a gun, either legally or through some backstreet sources, that would be very strong evidence for the suicide theory.

She shifted in her chair as her eyes focused on the dim flickering gaslight. The one thought that bothered her the most, the one thing they didn't have a clue about was the most important. Why would anyone want to murder Harlan Westover? No one appeared to benefit directly from his death. His estate was too small to kill for, and he had no known enemies. The partners knew he was angry about what they'd done to his engine, but that was hardly a motive for murder. Besides, the engine didn't belong to Westover. It belonged to the company, so even if he was angry, he was no threat to the firm. So who wanted him dead? More importantly, why?

As soon as the inspector had left the house the next morning, they gathered around the kitchen table. With one eye on the clock, Mrs. Jeffries told them everything she'd learned from the inspector after supper the night before. It didn't add much to their store of knowledge, but they were all of the opinion that every little bit helped. "Today the inspector is going to go back to the Ladbrook Grove Police Station. He wants to go over the police reports again. Then he's going to speak to Westover's solicitor."

"He's not done that yet?" Betsy was a bit surprised. "Usually that's one of the first things he does."

"True, but this investigation is a bit unusual," Mrs. Jeffries said defensively. "I think he's having a difficult time. It's really not his fault. After all, the original police reports classified the death as a suicide. Oh, you know what I mean, we all know how seriously he takes his duty. He's not incompetent, he has simply gone about this investigation a little differently. The truth is, he's a bit stuck on this case."

Mrs. Goodge snorted. "He's not the only one. We're movin' at a snail's pace ourselves."

"We're doin' fine, Mrs. Goodge," Wiggins said firmly. "We'll find out who the killer is; we always do. I think we've learned ever so much."

"I agree," Mrs. Jeffries said firmly. She got to her feet. "As a matter of fact, I suggest we all get started. Does everyone have something in mind for themselves to do?"

"I do," Wiggins declared. "I'm goin' to have a snoop about the Horrocks house. I didn't get a chance to get over there yesterday."

"There's a couple of hansom drivers I'm still tryin' to track down," Smythe said.

"I think I'll have a go at the Arkwright neighborhood," Betsy announced. "No one's really taken a good look at them."

"Ruth has a friend she's going to talk to this morning," Mrs. Jeffries told them. She headed toward the coat tree. "And I think I'm going to go out and see if I can catch up with Constable Barnes."

"Constable Barnes?" Wiggins repeated. "Why'd you need to talk to 'im?"

"He might be able to clear up a little matter for me," she replied. "And even better, I want to give him a few hints about some of the things we've learned." This was as close as she'd ever come to telling the others that she suspected Barnes knew and approved of what they did for their inspector. "He's a very astute man."

Everyone stood up. Mrs. Goodge began clearing off the table. When Betsy started to reach for the empty bread plate, the cook shooed her off. "You go on, now. I'll clear this lot up. Mrs. Jeffries and Wiggins are right. We will find this killer, but we've got to get crackin'."

"Are you sure?" Betsy didn't want the cook overdoing it. She was getting up there in years.

"Get on with you, girl," Mrs. Goodge laughed. "I might be old, but I've been cleaning up since you were a twinkle in God's left eye. You get your hat on and get out there findin' us some clues."

Smythe looked at the darkening sky and frowned. It was well past nine in the morning and there'd not been a hint of the sun. From the way the clouds were rolling in, he didn't think he was likely to see much of anything but buckets of rain. He hoped Betsy had remembered to take her umbrella before she left the house. Cor blimey, he was turning into an old woman. Betsy was no fool, and she could take care of herself. But he loved taking care of her. He shivered as a cold, damp wind cut through him all the way to his bones. Blast a Spaniard, but it was going to be a nasty day, and his beloved was out in the thick of it.

A hansom cab turned the corner and dropped off a fare. Smythe whistled, then held up his hand to catch the driver's attention. He'd already asked about and found out that this particular driver tended to work this neighborhood regularly.

"Can you give us a minute?" he said as he approached the cab. "I'd like to talk to ya. I'll make it worth your time." He reached in his pocket, pulled out a shilling, and held it up."

The driver grinned as he caught sight of the coin. One of his front teeth was missing. "You can have more than a minute if that's what you're payin'." He climbed down from his seat.

"I need some information." Smythe handed him the coin. "I hear you work this neighborhood pretty often."

"That's right. This is my patch. Most of my fares is from hereabouts."

"Do you ever bring fares to that house?" he jerked his thumb toward the Horrocks house on the far side of the road. "Maybe a gentleman?"

"The Horrocks place?" The driver shook his head. "I've taken a few fares there, but I don't remember just takin' a gentleman on his own. Leastways, not recently."

Smythe was very disappointed. He'd been hoping this case would turn out to be something simple like an enraged husband killing his wife's lover. He tried another tactic. Maybe Mrs. Horrocks went to Westover's house. "Do you remember taking Mrs. Horrocks over to a house on Brook Green?"

The driver frowned. "Why are you so interested in the Horrocks? You're not the law, are ya?"

"No, I'm not the law, and I'm not wantin' to do 'em any 'arm. I'm just investigating uh . . . uh . . . an insurance claim, that's all."

"Insurance claim?" The driver looked at him suspiciously. "What kind of claim? Look 'ere, mate, I'm not wantin' any trouble. Not with the likes of the folks that live around 'ere. They'd 'ave my 'ead on a pikestaff if they knew I was goin' on about their business."

Smythe decided to try a different approach. "You took my money," he protested. "What do you think I was payin' for, your company?"

"You paid me a shillin', mate, and that's not enough for the kind of details you're lookin' to buy."

Smythe didn't like being held over a barrel, but he did want more information. He had a feeling there might be a bit more coming his way if he swallowed his pride and opened his pockets. He dug out a handful of coins. "Here's five more shillings if you'll answer my questions."

"Now that's worth talking for, mate," the driver pocketed the money. "Now, what was your question again?"

Smythe held on to his temper. "Have you ever taken Mrs. Horrocks to a house over on Brook Green?" The whole matter no longer seemed important, but blast it, he'd paid the fellow, and he was determined to get what he could for it. They hadn't any evidence that there was anything between Mrs. Horrocks and Westover.

"Nah, never took Mrs. Horrocks to Brook Green."

Smythe felt like he'd just had his leg pulled, but he wasn't going to let the bloke make him any angrier. "You sure?"

"Sorry, guv, nothing like that. Like I said, I've brought lots of fares to the Horrocks," he replied, "and I've taken Mr. and Mrs. Horrocks here and there, but I don't recall ever taking Mrs. Horrocks to Brook Green. I took her to Hammersmith once, but that was over a year ago."

"Alright then," Smythe muttered.

The driver turned back toward the hansom. "Course now

I did take Mr. Horrocks to a house on Brook Green."

"Mr. Horrocks? When? How long ago was this?" Smythe asked eagerly.

"A couple of weeks back. I don't recall the exact date, but it was bloomin' cold. I remember it very well. Mr. Horrocks was so upset about somethin', he overpaid me, and frankly, as he's a bit of a tightwad, I took note of it."

"Do you remember exactly where you took him?"

"Course I do, it were only two weeks ago."

"Can you take me there? I'll make it worth your while," Smythe said. He no longer cared if the driver was taking advantage of him or not, as long as the fellow was telling the truth. He'd know when they got to Brook Green.

"Climb in, mate," the driver was already climbing back up to his seat. "And I'll have you there in two shakes of a lamb's tail."

Mrs. Jeffries walked up to the police constable behind the tall counter of the Ladbrook Grove Police Station and said, "Are Constable Barnes and Inspector Witherspoon on the premises?"

The constable, a chubby, older man with salt and pepper hair and bushy eyebrows, stared at her in surprise. "Yes ma'am, they're here. Do you want to speak to them?"

"Only with Constable Barnes," she replied. She held up a pair of spectacles. "I'm Inspector Witherspoon's housekeeper, he's forgotten his spectacles again. I don't wish to interrupt him while he's busy, so if you could just ask the constable to step out here a moment, I'd be most appreciative."

"Yes, ma'am," he stepped away from the counter and disappeared through a doorway.

Mrs. Jeffries didn't feel in the least guilty for having pinched the inspector's eyeglasses out of his coat before he'd left this morning. She had only done what was necessary. The door opened and Constable Barnes stepped into the room. "Why Mrs. Jeffries, how nice to see you."

"And you, Constable." She held up the spectacles. "He forgot these again. Could you give them to him?"

Barnes grinned and came out from behind the counter. "Certainly."

"Uh, Constable, could you step outside with me for a moment?" she asked. "I'd like to have a quick word with you about something else."

His grin broadened. "I was hopin' you'd say something like that."

A few minutes later, Constable Barnes stepped back into the empty office he and the inspector were using. "Mrs. Jeffries brought these by," he handed the spectacles to Witherspoon.

"Gracious, I could have sworn I left them in my coat pocket," he said. "Oh well, I'm very lucky to have such a devoted staff."

"You certainly are, sir," Barnes replied.

Inspector Witherspoon put on his spectacles and looked out the narrow windows of the station. "It looks like rain is coming, and we've still a number of people to see today. I still want to have a word with Mrs. Arkwright again. It's too bad she wasn't at home yesterday afternoon."

Barnes went back to the empty desk he'd been sitting at and picked up the file he'd been reading. Witherspoon was studying the report written by the first officer on the scene—it was less than one page long. Constable Barnes was reading the final report, which included the cornoner's verdict—it was all of seven pages long.

"Mrs. Arkwright's housekeeper said she'd be available this afternoon," Barnes replied. One part of him was thinking about what Mrs. Jeffries had told him. He hoped he'd have time to get on it before the day ended.

Witherspoon frowned. "I don't see anything here that I didn't see the first time we went through this lot. Perhaps this wasn't such a good idea."

"As you've said before, sir, it never hurts to be thorough. Perhaps if there had been a bit more attention paid when Mr. Westover's body was found, we'd already have our killer." Barnes shook his head in disgust. "I can't believe this, sir, they really did a shoddy job. They didn't ask any questions of anyone, including James Horrocks. You should always question the person that finds the body, sir. Any copper knows that."

Witherspoon agreed, but he didn't want to be unduly critical of his own. "I'm sure the officers did the best they could. But you're correct. They didn't follow proper procedure. I wonder why?"

Barnes glanced at the report again. "I did some checking, sir, and the first lad on the spot was PC John Howard. He's only been on the force a few months."

"Inexperienced. That explains it then."

"Inexperienced and upset by a dead body," Barnes snorted. Then he quickly tried to cover it with a cough. Witherspoon was notoriously squeamish around corpses. But the inspector had never let his discomfort keep him from doing his duty.

"We really ought to interview PC Howard," Witherspoon murmured.

"He's on duty at Shepherds Bush today. I checked the roster with the desk sergeant."

The inspector nodded. He'd been avoiding this part of the investigation. It was never pleasant questioning a fellow officer, especially when there was evidence that they'd mucked up a case quite badly. But it couldn't be helped. "After we speak with PC Howard, we'll have to talk to all the officers on the case. That includes the inspector who signed it closed." He reached for his tea and took a sip. "I don't recall the inspector's name."

"That's because the signature is almost illegible," Barnes ducked his head to hide his grin. He knew he ought to feel guilty about this, but he didn't. "But I can make it out now. It's Nigel Nivens, sir. Inspector Nivens had a murder right under his nose, and he signed it off as a suicide."

"Oh dear, this will be awkward. How on earth did this happen? Inspector Nivens doesn't work out of this station."

Barnes shrugged. "You know how it is, sir, he might have been working out of here on a burglary case and uh . . . volunteered to take a look at it when he heard there was a dead body." The constable was deliberately being diplomatic. More likely, Nivens heard there was a body and thought it meant murder. Solving murders is what made a policeman's career, and Nivens wanted that more than anything. The stupid sod probably used his Whitehall political connections to intimidate his way onto the case, and then signed it off without so much as a second thought when it looked like a suicide. Typical Nivens, Barnes thought, barge in, muck it up, and then drop the case when it couldn't further his career.

Witherspoon shook his head in agreement. "I'm sure you're right. Well, awkward as it might be, we will have to question Inspector Nivens. But I'm sure he'll not mind."

He'll pitch a fit and raise a fuss, Barnes thought. "Of course sir. He's at the Yard today. I think he's got a meeting with Chief Inspector Barrows this afternoon."

"Gracious, Constable, you are efficient these days. How on earth do you know Inspector Nivens's schedule?" Witherspoon asked.

Barnes could hardly admit that he'd known all along that Nivens was the original senior officer on this case and that he'd kept his feelers out for Nivens's whereabouts. He felt a bit guilty for keeping that information from the inspector, but he'd had to do it for Witherspoon's own good. Someone had to look out for his inspector. When he'd seen Nivens's signature on that final report, he'd realized that a confrontation was inevitable. Despite Witherspoon's success in solving murders, the fellow was blissfully ignorant of the political realities that affected every government bureaucracy, including the police. Nigel Nivens wasn't in the least ignorant of these realities. He had a huge network of political allies that stretched from the local precinct houses all the way to the home office. "Constable Booker, he's the deskman out front, he mentioned it to me when I arrived this morning. For some reason, he thought it was a meeting involving all of us." Barnes knew that a confrontation with Nivens would go much better in front of Chief Inspector Barrows. The chief inspector had his own political allies and wasn't in the least intimidated by Nivens. Usually.

"I see. Right then, we'd best get moving." He drained his tea and then looked toward the window. "Oh dear, it has started to rain."

It was pouring, but Barnes didn't care. He'd brave a deluge if it meant he got to watch Nivens squirm. "Are we going to the Yard, sir?"

"We do have to talk to Westover's solicitor, and we also need to follow up with Mrs. Arkwright."

"We've time to fit them both in before we go to the Yard," Barnes pointed out. "Nivens isn't meeting the chief until four this afternoon."

"I don't want to interrupt the chief inspector's meeting . . ."

"But sir, he won't mind," Barnes interrupted. "He wants us to keep him informed, and if we pop in this afternoon, we could give him a report at the same time. Kill two birds with one stone, so to speak." He held his breath, desperately hoping his inspector would agree. Nigel Nivens had been trying to ruin Witherspoon for years, and it was time to put the fellow in his place. "By the time we're finished, PC Howard ought to be on duty so we can swing back around this way and have a word with him and PC Smith. They're both on evening duty this week."

"PC Smith?"

"He's the other constable who was on the original case."

Witherspoon hesitated for a long moment. "That does seem to make sense. I don't suppose Nivens will mind speaking to us in front of the chief. He's a reasonable sort of person."

He'd be furious enough to spit nails, Barnes thought. And every copper who'd ever worked under Nivens would give a week's pay to see him squirm.

Lady Ruth Cannonberry smiled kindly at the maid who handed her a cup of tea. "Thank you, dear," she said, taking the delicate Wedgewood cup and placing it on the table next to her.

"It's been such a long time since we've seen you," her hostess, Miss Emmaline Parker said. She was genuinely pleased to see her guest. Lady Cannonberry was compassionate, kind, and more importantly, intelligent. Miss Emmaline Parker was a very rich woman with very few friends. Her outspoken views on politics had seen to that. She was a radical, an atheist, and thought most people in society useless parasites. But she liked Ruth Cannonberry, even if the woman had been married to a lord and was currently having some sort of relationship with a policeman of all things. Emmaline Parker, who didn't care all that much for the male of the species, didn't understand it but thought it brave of Ruth nonetheless. "I understand you've been out of town taking care of your late husband's relatives. Honestly, Ruth, hasn't anyone ever told you that once you're widowed, you're not responsible for his relatives anymore? It's not like they can't hire a nurse. The whole bunch is rich as sin."

Ruth laughed. "Don't be so harsh, Emmaline. I'm all they've got. No one likes to be on their own when they're ill."

"Malingerers, all of them," Emmaline grinned, and for a moment, her long, bony face was pretty. Even seated, one could tell she was a tall woman. Her hair was dark brown and pulled straight back into a bun at the nape of her neck. She was in her late thirties, but made no effort to appear younger. She dressed for comfort rather than fashion. That day she wore a heavy gray wool day dress, plain enough to please a Quaker. "So now that you're back in town, I do hope we can see one another a bit more often."

"Absolutely." Ruth liked Emmaline, she was intelligent, interesting, and funny. "Now, I do have an ulterior motive for coming along this morning. Not that seeing you isn't a worthwhile endeavor in itself, of course."

Emmaline laughed. "This is getting more interesting by the minute. Do go on, you mustn't keep me in suspense."

Ruth took a deep breath. She was mindful that she had to be discreet, but she was also aware that this was one of the people in London who might have the information she needed. "I know you're very well informed on what's going on in the business community, and I needed your advice."

"My advice? Are you certain? Most people think my views are far too radical to be of consequence," Emmaline replied. She was very flattered. "Are you certain you don't want to speak with your late husband's bankers?"

"I'm sure. From what I've observed, you never lose money on your investments . . ."

"Maybe I keep quiet about it when I do," Emmaline interrupted.

"Nonsense, you're not capable of keeping quiet about anything," Ruth shot back. She clamped her hand over her mouth when she realized what she'd said. But Emmaline hadn't taken offense.

She laughed. "Oh, that's good. It's also true. All right, go ahead, ask away. But mind you, my methods are very unorthodox. Did you have any particular company in mind?"

This was the tricky part. Ruth didn't want to give any hint that she was really investigating a murder, and later, once an arrest was made, Emmaline would remember this conversation. So she'd prepared herself by getting the names of several firms to ask about. She'd asked her butler. She hoped he knew what he'd been talking about. "I've been approached to invest in several firms. I'm hoping you'll know which one ought to be the best." She smiled and took a deep breath. "I've heard rumors that Carstairs might be a good firm to invest in, my next door neighbor has it on good authority that they're looking to raise capital."

Emmaline looked thoughtful. "They're quite reputable, but I'd be careful with them. Jonathan Carstairs isn't well, and his brother is supposedly going to take over the day-to-day running of the firm. The brother's a bit dim."

"Oh. Well, what about Riley and Wotmans?"

"They're quite good. Conservative and reliable. You'll not make a fortune but you'll get a steady return on your investment, more importantly, you'll not lose anything."

"And Donovan, Melcher, and Horrocks?"

"Stay away from them. Don't give them a farthing," Emmaline exclaimed. "Now that their engineer is dead, they'll be out of business within the year, you mark my words."

"That does sound strange."

Emmaline leaned closer. "Now I'm not one to gossip, but wait until I tell you about this lot. You mustn't give them any money, Ruth. You must promise me."

"You make them sound postively dangerous."

"They are dangerous," Emmaline insisted. "At least to rich women. That's how they raise their capital, you know. Every time they're in real financial trouble, they bring in another managing partner with a rich wife." She broke off and frowned at Ruth. "Is someone encouraging you to buy into this firm? A man?"

It took a moment before she understood the implication behind her friend's words. She laughed. "Do you mean am I being courted for my money? Absolutely not."

Emmaline smiled in relief. "I thought you'd be too sensible for something like that, but in matters of the heart, people can be awfully foolish, and as I said, this firm has a reputation for running on other people's money, especially women."

"Really?"

"Oh yes, they've been in trouble ever since the second Mr. Donovan died. Harry Donovan, that's the son who took over about fifteen years ago, is a fool. He's virtually run the company into the ground. His own father didn't want him taking it over, he used to berate him publicly about what an idiot he was, but because of circumstances, Harry ended up with the firm."

"How long has this company been in business?" Ruth asked.

"The company was started by Harry's grandfather. He did quite well out of it, bought the family a big house in Mayfair and made sure his children married well. The next Donovan did even better with the firm than the grandfather. He had two sons, Albert and Harry. Albert was the eldest and was going to take over the firm when his father passed on, but Albert died of typhoid fever. Harry wasn't the man his brother was, he drank, gambled, and generally wasn't considered very bright, but when his father died, there was no one else to take the business. As I said, it's been in trouble ever since. Harry Donovan just seems to have a habit of making one bad decision after another."

"That's so very odd. Now, what did you mean about the engineer being dead? That's a very strange reason for a company going out of business."

"Not this company. Let me pour us another cup of tea, and I'll tell you the whole story. You're not in a hurry, are you?"

Westover's solicitor was a middle-aged man named Alastair Greeley. His office was on the second floor of a building on the Marylebone High Street. Greeley was a tall, dark-haired man, with a broad forehead and deep-set hazel eyes. "I've been expecting you, Inspector," he said politely as he gestured for the two policemen to sit down. "I understand the investigation has been reopened."

"That's correct," Witherspoon replied. "We've had new evidence come to light."

"Good," Greeley broke into a wide smile. "I never did agree with the suicide verdict. I tried to tell the other inspector that it was impossible for my client to have taken his own life, but the fellow wouldn't listen to me."

Witherspoon waited until Barnes had gotten out his little brown notebook before he spoke. "That's most unfortunate. But we're here now and anything you could tell us will be most helpful."

Greeley raised his eyebrows. "Let's hope so, Inspector. But it has been over a fortnight since the murder was committed."

"First of all, can you tell us why you think Mr. Westover didn't take his own life."

"Several reasons. To begin with, he was quite a devout Roman Catholic. He went to mass every week. Secondly, he'd bought tickets to go on holiday in Italy, and thirdly, the man simply didn't have the character to take his own life."

"I see," Witherspoon had hoped for something a bit more substantial than that. "We understand that Mr. Westover had no close family."

"That's correct. He's got some cousins in Bristol. I've been in contact with them."

"Are they his heirs?" Barnes asked.

"They'll inherit everything," Greeley replied. "But I shouldn't see them as suspects if I were you. The cousins are two elderly ladies, and I don't think they came to London with murder in their hearts and a gun in their hands. They were quite distraught when they heard the news."

"How big an estate is it?" Witherspoon asked. He was rather annoyed with himself for not getting this information sooner. But gracious, this case was most odd. Most odd, indeed.

Greeley shrugged. "It's a bit more substantial than one would think. There's a house in Birmingham and some stocks. But believe me, sir, Harlan Westover wasn't murdered for his money."

"Would you explain that, sir?" Witherspoon asked.

"I intend to, Inspector," Greeley replied. "Harlan Westover came to see me a few days before he died. He was very concerned about something going on at his firm and wanted to know if he had any legal recourse against them. Unfortunately, he was quite vague as to what the trouble might be. I told him that unless he could give me a few more details, I couldn't give him any advice."

"You have no idea what he thought the company had done?" Barnes asked.

"It had something to do with the factory, I think. He mentioned that he had to pop around there and have a word with the foreman. Then he'd know for sure and he'd get back to me." Greeley closed his eyes and sighed. "He apparently found out what he needed to know, because he made an appointment with my clerk to come see me again. The appointment was for the day after his death. That's another reason I know he didn't take his own life."

"Why didn't you bring this up at the inquest?" Witherspoon asked.

"I was out of town on another case, and the judge wouldn't grant a postponement. I sent a note to the other inspector, hoping the police would do something before the verdict was rendered, but your Inspector Nivens refused. He insisted Westover was a suicide. He was wrong, and furthermore, he's a very stupid man."

"Is there anything else you can tell us?" the inspector asked quickly.

"Only that I hope you catch whoever did this to Harlan. He was a good and decent man. He didn't deserve to lose his life like that."

"No one does, sir," Witherspoon replied.

CHAPTER 8

Wiggins stood on the corner and stared glumly down Argyll Road. Cor blimey, he hated these posh neighborhoods. This morning, he'd been so certain that he was being ever so clever. He'd told the others he was going to go to the Horrocks's neighborhood, but that had been just a ruse to throw them off the scent. After his triumph yesterday in being the one to find out Westover's time of death, he'd gotten greedy for glory, for being the one to bring in the best clue. He'd planned on going along to every neighborhood where a suspect lived, make contact with someone from the household, and then find out which of them actually owned a gun. That would have been really good. He'd even wondered why the police hadn't done it. But blast a Spaniard, he'd been to the Arkwrights and not seen hide nor hair of a servant to natter with, now he was here at the Melcher neighborhood, and it was just as empty. Dead as a bloomin' doornail. What a waste. There wasn't even much traffic around this way today. Wiggins shifted his weight and pulled his coat tighter against his chest. He didn't know what to do next. He decided it was time to head for his original destination, the Horrocks house, when all of a sudden, the side door of the Melcher house opened and a young woman came out. She was carrying a large basket.

Wiggins took off like a shot. He caught up with the girl just as she stepped onto the sidewalk. He scurried around so that he was abreast of her. "Can I carry that for you, miss?"

"Thanks all the same," she replied, staring at him suspiciously. "But I've got it."

"You can trust me," he said, determined not to give up. "I work for a policeman. My name's Wiggins, and I work for Inspector Gerald Witherspoon. That basket looks awfully heavy."

Just then she stumbled, and he grabbed her arm, steadying her so she wouldn't fall. "You all right, then?"

"Ta." She smiled gratefully. "This bloomin' thing weighs a ruddy ton." She glanced over her shoulder at the Melcher house, hesitated, and then shoved the basket toward Wiggins. "I suppose it's all right. I mean, if you work for a police inspector." She was a plump girl with light brown hair tucked under a housemaid's cap, blue eyes, and a moon-shaped face. Beneath her thin cloak she had on a gray dress covered with a white apron. "God knows I'll not be able to carry it all the way to the laundry."

Wiggins eagerly took the burden from her. "Most houses 'ave their laundry picked up," he said, giving her a friendly smile.

"We generally do too," she replied. "But Mrs. Miller, that's our housekeeper, found these things of Mr. Melcher's under his bloomin' bed, of all places. The stupid cow insisted I had to take them in right away. Can you believe it? The laundry boy is due by tomorrow mornin', and she couldn't even wait a day!"

They had come to the corner. "Which way?" Wiggins asked.

She pointed to her left. "We take it to Mrs. Clifton and she's right behind the butcher's."

"Right then," he started off in the direction she pointed. "What's in 'ere? Bricks?"

She shrugged. "Clothes and shoes. We don't have a proper footman, so we takes Mr. Melcher's shoes to Mrs. Clifton as well. She does the whole lot, and then her boy brings it back the next day. But honestly, I don't know why Mrs. Miller couldn't wait. It's cold out 'ere. I suppose she didn't want Mr. Melcher findin' out she'd not cleaned his room properly. I mean, that's the only thing it could be. She didn't want Mr. Melcher findin' out she hadn't cleaned under his bed for two weeks. Lazy cow! She'd have my head if I waited two weeks to clean under the settees and cupboards in the drawing room."

Wiggins caught his breath as the import of her words hit him full force. He suddenly realized he had to be very, very careful here. "Uh, sounds like you work at a very strange place."

She made a face. "It's not all that strange, our master is just on his own. You know what I mean. No wife to run the household, so he relies on Mrs. Clifton. If you ask me, she's getting too old to be takin' care of such a large place. Mind you, the way she tells it, if it hadn't been for her, these things," she jerked her head at the basket, "would have been lost for good. But I know she's lyin'."

Wiggins shifted the basket slightly and slowed his steps. His mind was working furiously. "Uh how do you know she's lyin'?"

"She said she found these clothes at the back of his wardrobe. But I saw her pulling them out from under the bed. She won't let me or Dulcie up to clean Mr. Melcher's room, so I reckon he tossed these ruddy things under the bed a couple of weeks back and forgot to mention them. She's been too lazy to clean under there properly, so she made up a story about where she found the clothes."

"Uh, how much further is it?" Wiggins asked carefully. He didn't want her to stop talking, but he needed some measure of how much time he had left.

"Just a few more doors up," she replied. "It's awfully nice of you to do this for me."

"It's my pleasure, miss." Wiggins didn't want to get his hopes up. The clothes in the basket probably had nothing to do with Westover's murder. He didn't think he'd be that lucky two days in a row. Still, you never knew, maybe they were a clue. From what she said, they'd been under a bed for the better part of two weeks. He had to find a way to get a look at them.

"It's just here," she turned down a walkway and led him around the back of a two-story brick building. A narrow, rickety staircase went up the rear wall. Wiggins was afraid if he didn't act fast, he'd lose his chance.

"Why don't you stay here," he suggested, "and I'll take 'em up to your laundry. Them stairs look awfully tiring."

She smiled broadly. "That's right nice of you. You are a good fellow, aren't you. I guess that'd be all right. Just tell Mrs. Clifton it's for Mr. Melcher's account and we need it back by tomorrow."

Wiggins nodded and started up the stairs. He glanced over his shoulder at the girl. Cor blimey, she was watching him like a cat tracking a mouse. He wanted to see what was in the bloomin' basket. He stumbled and dumped the basket on the stairs. The sheet covering fell off, and the clothes tumbled out onto the staircase. "Sorry," he called out to her as he bent to pick up the garments. He picked up a heavy, black shoe, gave it a cursory glance, saw nothing interesting and dropped it back into the basket. He picked up the other shoe, two dirty hankies, some undergarments, several soiled towels, and lastly, a man's dress shirt. He examined each piece as best he could. But everything looked normal. He popped the shirt onto the top of the pile and was reaching for the sheet, when a dark red spot on the sleeve of the shirt caught his eye. As he picked up the sheet, he took a long, hard look at the shirtsleeve. There were more dark spots splattered on the white fabric. Cor blimey, he was no expert, but he was sure them spots must be blood.

"Yo . . ." the girl shouted, "is everythin' all right?"

"Yeah, I just want to make sure everything's back in properly," he called. He turned his back to her, took a deep breath, and then shoved the soiled shirt into his coat. Then he hurried up the stairs. The door opened as he reached the top. The entire time he was giving Mrs. Clifton the laundry, he silently prayed that parts of the pinched shirt weren't sticking out anywhere where she could see.

• • •

The rain had stopped by the time that Inspector Witherspoon and Constable Barnes got to the Arkwright house. This time, they were shown into the drawing room. A tiny fire sputtered pathetically in the fireplace, and a lamp was lighted against the gloomy day. There were heavy blue damask curtains on the windows and a pale gray carpet on the oak floor. There were several likenesses of the Queen scattered about the room, the largest one being set in the place of honor in the center of the mantel. Witherspoon wondered if Arkwright had ever considered having a photograph of his wife done.

"Hello, Inspector, Constable," Mrs. Arkwright said as she swept into the room. She took a seat on the dark blue settee and gestured toward the matching overstuffed chairs. "How very nice to see you. Do sit down. Shall I ring for tea?"

"That's most kind of you, Mrs. Arkwright, but please don't bother," Witherspoon replied. "We've just had some." He and Barnes sat down. "Is your husband here as well?"

"He'll be right in," Mrs. Arkwright smiled brightly. "How is the investigation coming along? I do hope you catch whoever murdered poor Mr. Westover. I didn't know him well, but he was such a nice man."

"We'll not rest until his killer is caught," Witherspoon assured her. "Murderers eventually make a mistake and give themselves away."

"It's so terribly upsetting," she continued. "Just when Mr. Donovan was so very certain everything was going to be all right, this has to happen. Of course, the firm has had the worst luck. Some would say it was more than just bad luck . . . I mean, sometimes I think that some people really aren't adept at running a business . . ." She broke off as her husband stepped into the room.

Oliver Arkwright didn't look pleased. "I don't see why you're bothering us again," he snapped. "We've already told you everything we know."

Witherspoon rather wished he could have had a few more minutes alone with Mrs. Arkwright. "I know that you think you have, sir. But I've a few more questions. We've been to see Harlan Westover's solicitor, and he's given us some very interesting information."

Arkwright's eyebrows shot up. "I don't know what he could have possibly told you . . ."

"He said that Mr. Westover was thinking about taking legal action against your firm."

"I don't know what you're talking about," Arkwright sputtered. "Legal action, that's absurd. There's no reason he'd want to take legal action against us. We did nothing wrong."

"He was going to talk with the foreman at your factory and then go to the board with his complaint." The inspector added.

"He only gave us a progress report," Arkwright said defensively. "I don't know what you're talking about, and this solicitor, whoever he is, doesn't know what he's talking about either. Does he have any proof . . ."

"Exactly where again did you go after the board meeting?" Barnes interrupted. He could see that Arkwright was getting rattled and often, a change in the direction of the questions helped that process along.

"I've already told you, I took my wife to luncheon at Wentworths," Arkwright replied, but some of the bluster had left his voice.

"And what time did you finish your luncheon?" Witherspoon pressed. They had checked with the restaurant, and the waiters had confirmed that the Arkwrights were present that day. But no one recalled precisely when they'd left.

"Again, I've already told you. We finished luncheon about two o'clock."

"Oh no dear," Mrs. Arkwright interjected. "It was actually closer to one thirty. I remember precisely. The clock on the bank tower had just struck the half hour as I was getting into the hansom to come home."

Arkwright glared at his wife. "Penelope, I'll thank you to let me answer my own questions."

"Then I suggest you answer them correctly," she replied cooly. "You know perfectly well when we finished luncheon and left the restaurant, you looked at your watch."

"Am I to understand that the two of you went your separate ways after leaving the restaurant?" the inspector pressed. He was annoyed with himself for not finding this out earlier. Gracious, this was very remiss of him. "I was under the impression you'd come home and spent the afternoon here together."

"I've no idea how you got such an idea, I never said that we were together," Arkwright retorted.

"But you certainly implied that the two of you came home that day," Witherspoon insisted. "But as you didn't, I'd appreciate it if you could each tell me exactly where you were that afternoon." He made a mental note to double check anything either of them said. Goodness, how could he have been so negligent in this investigation? A wave of shame swept through him. His actions thus far bordered on incompetence.

"I came right home," Mrs. Arkwright volunteered. "You can check with the maids. They were both here when I arrived. Then I went right up to my room and had a rest."

"Do you remember what time you got in?" Barnes asked. He was angry at himself. As a good copper, he should have verified all this sort of detail right after the first interview. Blast, but he must be getting old.

She frowned as she thought back. "I think I heard the clock chiming two as I came in the front door. But as I said, you can check with the maids. Bessie was cleaning the front stairs, and she saw me." She shot her husband a malicious smile.

Witherspoon watched the interplay between the Arkwrights carefully. He was no expert on married life, but he suspected these two didn't much care for one another. "Thank you, Mrs. Arkwright." He turned to the husband. "And you, sir? Where did you go after you put your wife in the cab?"

"I put myself in the hansom," Mrs. Arkwright said. "My husband had already stomped off in a temper. We'd had words, you see, and he was quite angry at me."

"Penelope, please be a bit more discreet." Arkwright's voice was pleading now. "The police aren't interested in our private business."

"But I think they are," she retorted. "Especially as our

argument related very much to your company." She looked at Witherspoon. "My husband was furious with me because I wouldn't give him anymore of my money to pour into the company. As a matter of fact, I told him if the company didn't repay what I'd already loaned them, I'd take them to court."

"Penelope, please be quiet. Our argument has nothing to do with Westover's death," Arkwright said.

The inspector stared at Arkwright. "Why did you need money to put into the firm if this new engine of Mr. Westover's was going to be so successful?"

"That's not really pertinent to your investigation," Arkwright argued.

"It's for us to decide what's pertinent and what's not," Barnes said.

Arkwright's eyes narrowed angrily. "I don't think I have to answer any more questions. As a matter of fact, I believe I'll contact my solicitor."

"He wanted the money to get his name on the company," Mrs. Arkwright said. She glared right back at her husband. "The other partners all have their names on the company. Oliver wanted that as well. But Harry Donovan wouldn't change the name of the firm until he came up with more cash. Now that they had their golden engine, Oliver didn't want to be left out in the cold."

"You know nothing about it," Arkwright hissed at his wife.

"I know something happened at that board meeting that you didn't plan for," she yelled. "I know that because you were beside yourself with anger that afternoon. You could barely eat."

"I was worried, not angry. For God's sake, shut up before you put my head in a noose." Arkwright shook his head in disbelief as he stared at his wife's stony face. "God, I knew you were unhappy, but I didn't think you hated me this much."

She said nothing.

Arkwright's shoulders slumped, and he tore his gaze from

his wife and turned to the two policemen. "I think you'd better leave, Inspector."

"Not until you tell us where you went that afternoon," Witherspoon said softly. He felt rather bad for the poor fellow. It was obvious Penelope Arkwright truly loathed her husband and equally obvious that he hadn't had a clue as to her true feelings. Until now.

He sighed and closed his eyes. "If you must know. I went for a long walk."

"That's true, Inspector," Mrs. Arkwright added. "I know because one of my neighbors, Mrs. Gilley, saw my husband over on Brook Green later that afternoon." She smiled sweetly at her spouse and then looked back at the two policemen. "What a coincidence, Oliver. You must have been so close to poor Mr. Westover just as he was dying. What a pity you didn't go around to see him. You might have saved his life."

Wiggins stepped into the back hallway of Upper Edmonton Gardens and carefully closed the door behind him. It wouldn't do to barge in on Mrs. Goodge when she was with one of her sources, made her right testy it did. He cocked his head toward the kitchen but he didn't hear anything. Deciding it was safe, he walked up the hallway and stepped inside the kitchen.

Mrs. Goodge was sitting at the table, staring morosely at the carriage clock on the top of the pine sideboard. Fred spotted him and shot to his feet, wagging his tail and looking just a bit embarrassed that his beloved Wiggins could slip into the house without Fred hearing him!

Alerted by the dog, Mrs. Goodge looked at Wiggins. "You're back early," she said.

"Good boy," he patted the dog. "It looks like it's goin' to rain again, and I decided to come home."

"Sounds like your day has been as miserable as mine," she shook her head. "I've not found out a ruddy thing. This miserable rain has kept everyone away. The grocer's boy just dropped our order and left without so much as a by-your-leave, the chimney sweep from down the road went home early, and I got a note from my old friend Melba that she hurt her ankle and can't come to see me. I was countin' on learning something from Melba. She used to be the cook at a house on Surrmat Road, and that's just around the corner from where the Donovans live."

Wiggins could see that Mrs. Goodge was very upset. She got like that when she felt she wasn't contributing enough to the case. He hated seeing her get all sad and miserable. "I came home early because I need your advice," he said.

"My advice?" she repeated. "What about?"

Wiggins dropped into the chair next to her. Nothing cheered her up more than giving advice. He had been going to wait until they had their meeting before he told the others, but maybe he could cheer the cook up first. "I've found something and I don't know what I ought to do."

"Something to do with the case?" Mrs. Goodge asked earnestly.

He nodded. "Evidence. I've got evidence and the truth of the matter is, I stole it."

Mrs. Goodge gaped at him. "What on earth have you done, lad? You've not broken in to someone's house . . ." she broke off as she realized what she was saying. The truth was, in the course of their investigations, they'd broken into houses before.

"No, it's nothin' like that," he replied, glad to see that she was getting indignant. That was better than her being sad. "I just happened to get my hands on this," he pulled the shirt out of his coat and laid it in front of the cook, "and I think there's blood on the sleeve. I think it's Mr. Westover's blood but I don't know for sure."

Mrs. Goodge didn't bother with silly questions. "Whose shirt is this?"

"It belongs to Mr. Melcher. I stole it from the laundry basket."

"Maybe we should wait until the others get here before you say anymore," Mrs. Goodge said softly.

"I don't think so," Wiggins replied. "Uh, I came home early hopin' you could tell me if I done this wrong or not. I mean, maybe I ought to nip back to the Melcher house and

hide this shirt in case we need the inspector to find it. Oh
cor blimey, I'm not sayin' this right."

Mrs. Goodge held up her hand and got to her feet. "Wiggins, Mrs. Jeffries and the others are out. We've got plenty
of time. I'll make us a cup of tea and you tell me exactly
what happened. Then we'll decide what needs doin' and
what doesn't."

Inspector Nigel Nivens was already sitting in front of the
chief inspector's desk when Witherspoon and Barnes arrived
in Barrow's office. Nivens, a plump middle-aged man with
dark blond hair and pale blue eyes, wasn't pleased when the
other two men stepped inside the office.

Chief Inspector Barrows waved them forward. "I got your
message, Witherspoon. Come on in, then, we've a lot of
ground to cover." He indicated the inspector was to take the
chair next to Nivens.

Barnes stood respectfully by the door. The constable struggled to keep his face expressionless, but it was difficult, he
knew that Nivens was probably beside himself by now. Let
the man worry, he was the one who'd mucked up the case.

"I thought this was going to be a private meeting," Nivens
said.

"Why would you think that?" Barrows looked up from the
papers he'd been reading. He turned his attention to Witherspoon. "I understand you need to ask Inspector Nivens
some questions about his handling of the Westover murder."

"It wasn't a murder," Nivens said defensively, "it was a
suicide."

"You're wrong." Barrows smiled nastily. "That's one of
the reasons you're here in my office. Harlan Westover was
murdered and because you didn't investigate properly, the
man's death was ruled a suicide. These," he tapped the police
reports in front of him, "aren't worth the ink used to write
them. I'm appalled that one of my officers would do such a
shoddy investigation, and I'm appalled at myself for not realizing it when these reports first crossed my desk."

"I think you're being a bit unfair, sir," Nivens blustered.
"My report was based on an assessment of the evidence that

I had at the time of the investigation." He tossed a quick glare at Witherspoon. "It's only been since he stuck his oar in, that the case was called a murder."

"I asked him to stick his oar in," Barrows shot back. "And I wouldn't have had to do that if you'd done your job properly."

"I did do my job properly," Nivens insisted. "The evidence pointed to suicide."

"Then can you please tell me how on earth a man could get into a locked room to commit suicide, when the only known key was thirty feet on the other side of the door?"

Nivens opened his mouth to speak and then clamped it shut again. Finally, he said, "All right, I'll admit that I did overlook the significance of that evidence . . ."

"You overlooked everything," Barrows picked up the reports and waved them in the air. "You didn't interview the neighbors, you didn't investigate anything about the victim's life, you simply assumed that because he was lying there with a hole in his head and gun under his hand that he'd killed himself. That's precisely what the killer wanted you to think."

"Now look here, chief inspector," Nivens began, "you've no call to berate me like this. I made an honest mistake . . ."

Witherspoon didn't dare look at Nivens, he felt terrible for the poor man. "He's right, sir," he put in softly. "I think it was just an honest mistake."

"We don't have any room for these kinds of mistakes," Barrows roared. "It hasn't been that long since the Ripper, gentlemen, and in case you have forgotten, we never solved those cases either. The public still doesn't have a lot of faith in our abilities. When the press gets wind of the fact that we mucked up another case, it'll not do us any good at all."

"Perhaps the press won't find out," Witherspoon ventured. This meeting wasn't going at all as he'd hoped.

Barrows and Nivens both stared at the inspector. Even Barnes closed his eyes in disbelief.

"Don't be naive," the chief inspector said. He sank back in his chair and turned to stare out at the darkening sky. "Of course they'll find out and when they do, we'll look like incompetent fools."

Witherspoon cast a surreptious glance at Nivens, who was staring straight ahead, his eyes focused on a spot over Barrows's head. Drat, this had been a most unpleasant encounter, most unpleasant indeed. He wasn't fond of Inspector Nivens, but he hadn't wanted to see him raked over the coals quite so badly.

Barnes was struggling to keep his expression blank. This had been better than he'd hoped. He couldn't wait to tell the lads. Nivens was hated by just about everyone who'd ever worked under him. He was notorious for blaming the uniformed blokes when things went wrong and taking the credit when things went right. He cast a quick look at Nivens. The man was staring into space, his expression thoughtful and his eyes calculating. Barnes was suddenly uneasy. By rights, Nivens ought to be blazing angry, spitting fire, and threatening Barrows with his Whitehall connections. He was too calm. What was he up to now?

Barrows sighed loudly. "It's getting late, and the most useful thing we can do is get this case solved as quickly as possible. Witherspoon, go ahead and ask Nivens your questions."

The inspector relaxed a bit, relieved that they could move onto a discussion of the facts of the case itself. He saw that Barnes had taken out his notebook.

Nivens's mouth curved into a slight smile. "You're quite right, sir. It is time to answer some questions."

Witherspoon cleared his throat. "I don't have all that many, Inspector Nivens. But I would like to know a few more details about the crime scene, so to speak."

Nivens said nothing for a moment. Then he said, "I'm afraid you don't understand, Witherspoon. This was my case, and I'm the one that should be asking the questions."

Smythe hoped the blooming rain had finally stopped for the day, it was damp enough down here by the river without it pouring onto his head as well. He pulled open the door of the Dirty Duck and stepped inside. The pub had only opened fifteen minutes earlier, but it was already crowded. He spotted Blimpey sitting at a table next to the fireplace.

Blimpey waved him over, and Smythe pushed his way through the crowded room. He slid onto a stool across from his informant. "What'll you 'ave?" he asked.

"What'll you have?" Blimpey repeated with a wide smile. "It's on me today."

"Cor blimey, you must be in a tearin' good mood. I'll have a beer." Smythe studied his companion for a moment and then he grinned. "She musta said 'yes'."

"That she did, my boy. That she did." Blimpey caught the barman's eye, held up two fingers and mouthed the word "beer". He turned back to Smythe. "I took your advice before I said my piece and had one of her friends ask a few pertinent questions of the lady. Once I knew she was amenable, well, then Bob's-your-Uncle." He broke off and grinned at the barmaid who brought their drinks. "Put it on my tab, luv," he told her. As soon as she was gone, he picked up his glass and raised it toward Smythe.

Smythe did the same. "All the best, Blimpey, and I mean it."

"Same to you, friend, same to you." He took a quick sip from his glass. "Mind you, we've already set a date, not like you and your lady. We're doin' it in June. Nell's got a sister comin' over from Canada for a visit. We thought we'd wait till then so she could be here for the nuptials."

Smythe shifted uncomfortably at the reminder that he and Betsy hadn't set a date. "That's a nice time for a wedding. Maybe Betsy and I will beat you to it, though. Anyway, what 'ave you got for me."

Blimpey put his glass down and leaned forward. "I decided that as you'd been so helpful to me with my . . . delicate situation, that I'd do a bit of snoopin' about on the 'ouse, so to speak."

"You didn't have to do that, Blimpey," Smythe replied. "All I did was give ya a bit of advice." Nevertheless, he was touched.

"You're a good friend, Smythe. There's lots that would have had a bit of fun at my expense if they'd known what was troublin' me. But you were a real gent about it. Anyways, I put my feelers out over in Stepney. Found out a bit, I did."

"Isn't that where the Donovan factory is?"

"That's right. Struck gold, too." He laughed and took another quick swig. "Seems your Mr. Westover was in a right old state before he died. My sources told me that a day or two before he supposedly blew his brains out, he went along and had a word with the foreman of the factory."

"And what did he find out?" Smythe couldn't believe his luck.

"Seems that your Mr. Westover had designed an engine that was supposedly goin' to put the company firmly in the black, if you know what I mean."

Smythe patiently sipped his beer. He knew all this, but he didn't want to put a damper on Blimpey's day. "That's right, I remember."

"Well, as I mentioned yesterday, the company wasn't doin' all that well financially. They kept havin' to raise capital to keep operating. But this engine was different from their usual goods, it was actually quality. Some would even say it was ahead of it's time. Very powerful."

"I know all that, Blimpey," Smythe said. "What's it got to do with Westover's death."

"It's got everything to do with it," Blimpey smiled smugly. "Seems that the factory foreman told Westover that the struts used on an important part of the engine weren't the ones Westover had specified on his plans. They'd bought cheaper struts to save a bit of the ready. Westover had a fit right there on the factory floor. He was shoutin' so loud the whole place heard him."

Smythe knew about the struts, but he didn't know about the shouting. "What was he sayin'?"

"He started screamin' that the engine wouldn't be safe unless it had the proper struts. That it was too powerful and that it'd blow up and kill someone."

"Why didn't he just make 'em change the struts to the ones he'd specified?" Smythe asked.

"They couldn't. That's why he got so angry. He'd come

to see the foreman to insist he change the struts, seems Westover had known about them bein' cheap for a few days. But the engine had already been shipped out. That's the reason he got so het up."

"Bloomin' Ada, no wonder he got so angry."

"And the factory had orders for more engines. Apparently, word about the engine had already got out, and everyone and his brother wanted one. But that's neither here nor there, what is important was that Westover told the foreman that he had to cable the company that was buyin' the thing, that he had to warn them it wasn't safe. The foreman told him he couldn't do somethin' like that, that Westover would have to take it up with the partners. Westover said he would, that he'd go along to their board meeting and make them do what was right. He'd not have it on his conscience that his engine had killed people."

"So that's why he was at the meeting," Smythe murmured.

"And that's probably why he was killed," Blimpey added. "The firm was in trouble, and that engine was goin' to save all their arses. They'd not want any engineer coming in and tellin' them the thing was about to blow up and kill a bunch of people. More importantly, they'd not want their engineer tellin' anyone else the ruddy thing was dangerous. Not when they had orders comin' in left and right."

Mrs. Jeffries decided to postpone their meeting until after the inspector came home. Neither Smythe nor Betsy were home in time for their usual afternoon meeting, so she sent Wiggins over to Lady Cannonberry's with a note telling her to come around about eight o'clock that evening.

As soon as Wiggins left, she turned to the cook. "He was acting a bit strange. He couldn't seem to meet my eyes."

"Young people always act strange," the cook muttered. "I expect he's just a bit preoccupied with this case. We all are. Oh look," she pointed toward the window at the far end of the kitchen, the one that faced the street. "A hansom's pulling up. That's probably the inspector. Should I get a tray ready?"

"Give me half an hour," the housekeeper replied. She hurried toward the back stairs. "I want to find out if he's learned anything useful today."

She made it to the front door just as the inspector stepped inside. "Good evening, sir," she said as she helped him take off his hat and coat. "Did you have a productive day?"

"I've had a very productive day, Mrs. Jeffries. But it was also rather difficult. I didn't get near as much accomplished as I'd hoped. Constable Barnes and I were going to interview the original police constables on the case, but we simply ran out of time. That's the way this entire case seems to have gone, two steps forward and one step back. Then again, one doesn't achieve something without effort."

"Would a glass of sherry help, sir?"

"Most certainly," he headed for the drawing room. She was right on his heels.

She went to the cupboard and poured out the sherry as he settled himself into this favorite chair. "It's been a most upsetting day, Mrs. Jeffries, but I do believe we're making progress. Mind you, things got a bit dodgy today."

"In what way, sir?"

"I almost lost the case to Inspector Nivens."

"Inspector Nivens," she yelped. She almost dropped the sherry but recovered quickly and only spilled a few drops. "What's he got to do with it?"

Witherspoon smiled as he took the drink from her. "At present, nothing. But he was the first inspector on the case originally."

"You never mentioned that," she said softly. She was alarmed that he'd left out such information in their earlier discussions. What else had he left out?

"I didn't know until today," he admitted. "The signature on the original report was illegible, and I didn't give the matter much thought. Today I realized that we had to speak to the original investigators, and, luckily, Constable Barnes had been able to decipher Nivens's handwriting. Oh, by the way, thank you for bringing my spectacles to the station."

"It was nothing, sir. Do go on."

"Apparently, even though Nivens had mucked it up, so to speak, he felt that being the original officer on the case entitled him to get it back. Luckily, the chief inspector didn't share that view. Of course, it might still get a bit messy. I believe Inspector Nivens has some very influential friends in high places."

"But the case is still yours?"

"Oh yes," he replied. "But the chief did warn me to get cracking."

"In other words, he wants it solved right away."

CHAPTER 9

They were all assembled at the kitchen table at precisely eight o'clock. Wiggins had gone across the garden and escorted Ruth so she wouldn't have to make her way over in the dark.

"I think we've quite a bit of information to get through," Mrs. Jeffries said firmly, "so why don't we go around the table. Let's start with you, Ruth. Did you have any success today?"

"Oh yes," Ruth nodded eagerly. "Well, I don't know if the information is useful, but I did hear a bit more about the principals in the case. It's mainly just a verification of what we already know, that the firm is in financial trouble." She paused for breath and then told them everything she'd learned from Emmaline. She was careful to make sure she repeated everything. "And there seems to be an unfortunate tendency of the company to bring in a new partner with a rich wife when the firm is running out of cash," she finished.

"That's the truth," Smythe muttered. "Despite Harry Donovan bein' such a proud one, it sure didn't stop 'im from using other people's money."

"And it's usually ladies' money," Wiggins added. "That don't seem right."

"That might be changing," Ruth continued. "Harry Donovan has spent the last few weeks bragging to anyone who'd stand still for thirty seconds that his firm was going to be doing brilliantly. He's even started hinting that he was thinking of buying his partners out and returning complete ownership to himself."

Smythe frowned. "Why would he do that? It's not like he's got any heirs to inherit from him."

"Perhaps his pride has taken such a beating over the years that he's desperate to prove he's as good as his father and grandfather," Ruth suggested with a shrug.

"Pride goeth before a fall," Mrs. Goodge quoted.

"And it's a silly reason to buy out yer partners," Wiggins added, "especially when it's already been proved that he's not very good at runnin' the business on 'is own."

"Doesn't seem like the bloke was particularly good at runnin' it even with the partners," Smythe put in.

"I wonder if the other partners know of Donovan's plans?" Mrs. Jeffries murmured, her expression thoughtful.

"My source didn't say," Ruth replied, "and I wanted to take care in how much I asked. I don't want to draw undue attention to my curiosity."

"Yes, we quite understand," Mrs. Jeffries replied. But knowing if the other partners knew of those particular plans might be important. She made a mental note to pursue this line of inquiry. It could well be pertinent to motive. If one of the other partners suspected they were being pushed out, they might have been tempted to ruin Donovan by murdering Westover and making sure that goose didn't lay another golden egg. But she'd think about that later, when she was alone. She turned her attention to Betsy. "Any luck today?"

"Not really," Betsy replied. "I tried hanging about the Arkwright house, but that didn't work. No one so much as stuck a nose out of any of the houses around there. Then I happened to spot the inspector and Constable Barnes coming down the street, so I scurried off as fast as I could. So all I've got to show for my trouble is sore feet. But I'm sure I'll do better tomorrow. You can't get lucky every day."

"Of course you will, Betsy," Mrs. Jeffries encouraged.

"Perhaps tomorrow you might try and find out some more about the partners' various maritial problems." She had no idea what, if anything, those kinds of difficulties might have to do with Westover's murder, but one never knew where one would find a solution.

"And they've got plenty of 'em," Smythe added. "At last count two of 'em had wives threatenin' legal action, and the other one's wife wants a divorce."

"Puts you right off the whole idea of marriage, don't it?" Wiggins commented.

"Don't be silly," Betsy glared at the footman. "There's lots of people that are happily married."

"And lots that ain't," Wiggins replied. "But not to worry, you and Smythe'll do all right. You're not like most married people. You like each other."

"Thank you, I think," she said.

"I do rather like the lass," Smythe gave her a cheeky grin. "and we'll do better than all right."

"Have you got any idea who killed him yet?" Mrs. Goodge leaned back in her chair and looked at the housekeeper.

"Not yet," Mrs. Jeffries admitted, "but I'm sure we'll come across something that'll point the way very soon." She refused to let the others see how concerned she was about this case. She had no idea who killed Harlan Westover, and there weren't even any nagging little patterns playing about at the back of her mind. Furthermore, after what she'd learned from Inspector Witherspoon today, she'd realized they'd overlooked some obvious sources of information. She was quite annoyed with herself.

"I 'ad a pretty good run of luck today," Smythe said. "I think maybe I stumbled across somethin' important."

"Good," Mrs. Goodge said firmly.

"Mind you," he warned, "it might be nothing." But he knew it was important. He just didn't want to make the others feel bad. He told them everything he'd learned from Blimpey. He didn't mention Blimpey by name, of course. His pride wouldn't let him admit to the others that he got most of his information by paying for it.

No one said anything for a few moments after he'd finished. Finally, Mrs. Jeffries said, "Gracious, Smythe, I think you've found our motive. Thank goodness you had the intelligence to trot along to that factory and ask a few questions. I'd been giving myself a good scolding because we'd neglected to direct any of our inquiries there."

He could feel a flush climbing his cheeks. "Like I said, I just got a bit lucky. I was a bit at loose ends after leavin' Brook Green so I took a chance on findin' somethin' out from the factory workers. That reminds me, I found out somethin' else today." He told them about the hansom driver taking Horrocks to Brook Green. "I'm not saying Horrocks is the murderer. The driver wasn't sure about the exact date," he stressed. " 'E just knew it 'ad been close to a fortnight ago that he took 'em there."

"Cor blimey," Wiggins yelped. "That's no good. I'm sure the killer must be Melcher . . ."

"Not so fast, Wiggins," Mrs. Goodge warned. She was slightly put out that Smythe had stolen their thunder, so to speak.

"What are you talking about?" Mrs. Jeffries watched Wiggins carefully. The lad generally didn't get this excited without good reason. "Why Melcher as the killer?"

"Because I stole his shirt," Wiggins exclaimed, "and it's got blood on the sleeve. Westover's blood. Tell 'em, Mrs. Goodge. Tell 'em what I found out today. Melcher is bound to be our killer."

Everyone started talking at once.

" 'Ow did you get your 'ands on 'is shirt?" Smythe demanded.

"Wiggins, what have you been up to?" Betsy cried.

"Goodness, Wiggins, that was certainly resourceful of you," Ruth said.

"I'm afraid I don't understand this at all," Mrs. Jeffries frowned. "Have I missed something?"

"Everyone, be quiet," Mrs. Goodge shouted.

Startled, everyone immediately fell silent and stared at her.

"Sorry, I didn't mean to shout," she smiled sheepishly. "But it's important you hear the whole of this. I'll explain how Wiggins happened to get his hands on Lawrence Melcher's shirt." She took a deep breath and then told them what had happened. "So you see, Wiggins was in a bit of a state. He had to steal the shirt because it might be evidence, but by stealin' it, he put himself in a bit of a precarious position, you might say."

"You might say that," Mrs. Jeffries agreed.

"Did I do somethin' wrong, Mrs. Jeffries?" Wiggins asked worriedly. "Should I 'ave left it in the laundry basket?"

"Not at all," she said. "Your actions were perfectly correct. Could you go and get the shirt, please?"

He leapt to his feet. "It's in the dry larder." Fred jumped up and dashed after Wiggins. The dog didn't like to let the lad out of his sight.

Mrs. Goodge waited until Wiggins had disappeared. "I didn't know what to tell the lad when he brung it in and told me how he'd got his hands on it," she said softly. "He was in a bit of a state."

"What's wrong?" Ruth asked quietly. "It's evidence, isn't it?"

"Yes, but it can be traced directly to him," Mrs. Goodge answered. "The girl can easily identify him."

"I see," Ruth nodded. "And if we give it to the inspector and he starts asking questions, it'll lead right back to Wiggins."

"I'm afraid so," Mrs. Jeffries replied. "We've found evidence before, but generally, it doesn't point a finger directly at one of us. Or if it did, we would find a way to muddy the waters a bit. But Wiggins didn't really have much choice in the matter. If he hadn't acted, we'd have lost the evidence."

"Down, Fred," Wiggins's footsteps could be heard, and a moment later, he and the dog hurried into the room. " 'Ere it is," he waved the shirt in the air.

"Thank you, Wiggins," Mrs. Jeffries said calmly. "Put it on the table, and we'll all have a good look."

Wiggins did as instructed, laying the garment neatly in the center of the table. He arranged it so the bloodstained sleeve was draped across the front of the shirt. "I know we can't really give this to the inspector," he said cheerfully. "That'd be too risky. The maid could point me out in a quick minute if the police started asking questions. On the other 'and, I didn't want this shirt goin' into the wash, just in case it was important. I thought we ought to see it."

Mrs. Jeffries cocked her head to one side and studied the shirt. "You're absolutely right, Wiggins, it is important that we see. Now, we've got to think how we can get this evidence and all the other things we've learned tonight to the inspector. But before we discuss precisely how we're going to manage that feat, let me tell you what I found out from the inspector this evening. Before we go putting a noose around James Horrocks's neck, you might be interested to know that Oliver Arkwright was seen on Brook Green the day of the murder."

"Arkwright? So both he and Horrocks might have been there that day." Mrs. Goodge pursed her lips. "Things are certainly getting muddled. Oh, sorry, Mrs. Jeffries, go on with what you were sayin'."

"Thank you, I heard a bit more than that." She gave them a complete report. When she got to the point where Nigel Nivens name came up, there was a storm of protest.

"The nerve of the man," Mrs. Goodge snapped.

"First he mucks it up, then he wants it back?" Betsy yelped.

"Stupid git," Smythe muttered. "It's a wonder someone 'asn't put their fist in that man's face before now."

"The inspector isn't goin' to be taken off the case, is 'e?" Wiggins wailed.

"I'm a bit confused." Ruth glanced around the table. "Gerald's never mentioned this person before. Who's Nigel Nivens, and why do you all dislike him so much?"

Smythe and Betsy were the last to leave the kitchen. The moment Betsy put the last teacup away, he grabbed her about the waist, swung her around to face him, and gave her a quick kiss.

She stared at him and didn't like what she saw. Despite the playful kiss, there was a wary look in his eyes and tightness about his jaw. Something was wrong. "Mrs. Goodge will be shocked if she comes in to get a drink."

He shrugged. "She knows we're 'ere, she'll not be back."
He knew the others in the household did their best to give
him and Betsy a bit of privacy. "I want to talk to you."

"I don't want to hear any nonsense about our age difference," she warned.

"That's not it," he replied. He took a deep breath. He knew
he was getting ready to step on thin ice, but he needed an
answer. "I think we ought to set a date."

"For the wedding?"

"No, for callin' on the queen. Of course for the wedding."

Betsy had known this was coming. She'd put him off once,
and he'd understood. She didn't think she could manage it
a second time. "What's the hurry? I thought we'd agreed that
neither of us was prepared to give up our investigating."

"We don't know that we'd 'ave to give up anything," he
said softly.

"But we agreed to wait a couple of years."

"I know, but what's the 'arm in settin' a date?"

"The harm is once we set a date, we'll have to stick to
it."

"What's wrong with that?" he cried. "Don't you want to
marry me?"

"Of course I do," she shot back. "But you know as well
as I do that once we marry, everything will change. There
won't be anymore investigating, there won't be anymore
meetings and following suspects and sussing out clues. Once
we're gone, it'll be over."

"Luty and Hatchet manage to help out," he pointed out,
"and they don't live here."

"And they miss a lot of things, too," she reminded him.
"If you're not on the spot, you're going to miss out. We both
know that, and neither of us is ready to give this up."

"There's no reason we couldn't stay on here for a bit after
we was married."

She stared at him closely. "Do you really mean that?
You'd not want to move us into our own home right off?"
Though, in truth, she'd been thinking about how wonderful
it would be to have a real home of her own. Smythe could

give her anything she wanted, and one part of her really did want a place all her own.

"I'm thinkin' we could find a way," he replied. "We're intelligent people, Betsy. I know that once we marry, things will change. But that doesn't mean we'll have to give up our investigatin'. Besides, all I want to do now is think about settin' the date."

She hesitated. There were so many reasons to keep things just as they were. She knew this man, once they married, he'd not be content with her being a maid in some else's home. He'd want to give her the world, and he could. He was a rich man. But much as she loved him, loved the idea of having her own home and her own family, she couldn't give up their cases. Not yet. Helping to catch murderers made her feel special, as if she was doing something so noble it was almost a religious calling. But she also loved him and she could tell this was important to him. "All right, then," she sighed. "I guess we can set the date."

He stepped back, stared at her for a moment, and then folded his arms over his chest. "You don't have to sound so miserable about it. It's a weddin' I'm wanting, not your execution."

"That's not it, and you know it," she retorted. "And no offense intended, but you're not standing there with a big happy grin on your face either. You look right annoyed about something, and you have ever since the others went upstairs." That was a bald-faced lie, but she said it anyway because she felt so guilty.

He nodded. "You know me so well, lass."

"Huh?" She caught herself. "I knew it. What's got your back up?"

"Nothin'. Well, it's somethin', but it sounds downright petty to say it out loud."

"Go on, then. Be petty, it'll make you feel better." She punched him playfully on the arm. "And don't try telling me it's because I didn't want to set a date."

"That's part of it," he smiled sheepishly. "I guess I was a bit put out at Wiggins producing that ruddy bloodstained shirt and stealin' all my glory. I was so sure my information was going to point the way to the killer."

She gaped at him for a moment, then she laughed. "You're jealous of him for getting ahead of you."

"I told you it was petty," he said.

"Your information was important," she said. "We've finally got a motive."

"But do we have the right one?" He took her arm and headed for the back stairs. "That's the question."

"I think so. Westover probably went to that board meeting and threatened them. That's probably why he was killed. He knew who'd bought his engine and where it was being shipped. He was probably murdered to keep him from sending a cable telling the buyers to send it back before it blew up and killed people."

Smythe shook his head. "I don't know, lass. Would someone actually kill a man to keep him from sending a cable? Especially when we know that the only thing wrong with the engine was just some cheap struts. And those could be easily replaced." He took her hand, and they started up the darkened staircase.

"But they already had a terrible reputation as a company," Betsy said. "Maybe whoever killed Westover didn't want any bad news about the engine getting out. Not with all those orders pouring in."

"Let's think about it after we've had a good night's sleep." Smythe stifled a yawn. "We do need to start thinking about a date, though."

"Of course we do," she agreed. "But let's wait till the case is solved. I don't want to have to think about something as beautiful as our wedding while we're trying to catch a ruthless killer."

Mrs. Jeffries was up well before the rest of the household. She left the others a note on the kitchen table instructing them to make sure the inspector ate a good breakfast and that she'd see them all for tea later in the afternoon. She tucked the parcel containing Melcher's bloodstained shirt under her arm and stepped out the back door. It wasn't yet daylight, and it took a moment for her eyes to adjust to the dim light of dawn. She pulled her cloak tight about her and started across the garden to the gate on the far side.

After their meeting, she'd done a good deal of thinking. She still had no idea who their killer might be, but the beginning of a pattern was starting to form in her head. All the partners had a motive and it appeared as both Oliver Arkwright and James Horrocks might have been to see Westover on the afternoon he died.

She reached the gate, pulled it open, and stepped out into the empty street. Turning, she made her way the short distance to Holland Park Road and reached the omnibus stop just as an omnibus pulled up. She got on board, paid her fare, and then settled back in her seat. If she were very lucky, she'd reach her destination just as her quarry emerged from his house.

She took the omnibus to the Hammersmith Bridge, got off, and started across. Traffic into the city was already getting heavy. She stopped and leaned over the stone balustrade, looking at the dark, gray waters of the Thames. Would they ever solve this case? She simply didn't know. She hoped Wiggins was right and that they'd find something soon to point the way to the killer.

She tore her gaze away from the water, crossed the road, and walked the rest of the way to her destination. She rounded the corner just as the front door of the second house down opened and Constable Barnes stepped out.

Mrs. Jeffries stopped. She wanted to make sure that the constable was alone. She didn't want Mrs. Barnes poking her head out with any last-minute words for her husband. But the door stayed closed.

Barnes adjusted the strap of his helmet and started up the street. He stopped in midstride as he saw her. "Mrs. Jeffries? Is everything all right?"

"Good morning, Constable. Everything is fine. I simply wanted to have a chance to speak with you privately."

He cast a quick, nervous glance back at his house. "Let's get around the corner. I don't want Mrs. Barnes asking any awkward questions."

"Oh dear, I am sorry," Mrs. Jeffries said. "I wasn't thinking."

Barnes relaxed a bit when he was no longer in sight of his house. "Don't fret, Mrs. Jeffries. My wife's not a jealous woman. She's just a bit nosy. If she saw you meeting me, she'd pester me silly until I told her everything."

"And what is everything?" Mrs. Jeffries asked softly.

He looked at her, his expression thoughtful. "I believe you already know that, don't you. You and the rest of the inspector's staff help him a bit on his cases, don't you?"

She wasn't going to insult his intelligence by denying it. "Yes, we do. How long have you known?"

"I started suspecting quite a long time ago. But I didn't know for sure until recently."

"Are you going to a . . ."

"Going to what?" Barnes chuckled. "Run telling tales to the inspector about his staff picking up a bit of gossip or passing on some street talk that they hear? Now that wouldn't be right, Mrs. Jeffries, not right at all. Why worry the man with silly talk like that? He's got a lot on his mind."

It took a moment for her to fully understand him. "Of course," she agreed. "One wouldn't want you to go telling tales out of school. Speaking of the . . . uh . . . well, silly gossip that one picks up, I happened to have heard a few things of interest and even stumbled across a bit of what might be evidence." She handed him the parcel, took a deep breath, and then plunged straight in to her tale. She told him everything. By the time they reached the omnibus stop for the trip back to Holland Park Road, she'd passed on every scrap of information they had.

"That's quite a bit of silly gossip," he commented as the omnibus pulled up. He took her arm and helped her board.

Neither of them spoke until they'd made their way to the back and taken their seats. "I'm not sure what this proves," he tapped the paper-wrapped parcel, "and I shall have to think of a way to get this and the rest of your information to our inspector. But never fear, I'll manage it."

"He already knows some of it," she replied. "I dropped a few hints in his ear last night. But I'll leave it to you to direct him as you see fit." Mrs. Jeffries had complete faith in Barnes's intelligence and his discretion. "I'm getting off at Hammersmith Station. So we've not much time. Did you find out anything about Westover getting a gun?"

"So far, there doesn't seem to be any evidence of him buying one through any of the local gunsmiths. But he could have written off and bought one through the post." He grimaced. "And my inquiries on the less legitimate ways of obtaining a weapon haven't turned up anything. But just because I can't find any evidence of a purchase, doesn't mean he couldn't lay hands on a gun."

"But I don't think he did," she mused.

"I don't either," he agreed. "After everything we've learned, I'm sure he was murdered."

"So am I," she replied. "But then I think of Dr. Bosworth's evidence about the growth on the poor man's brain and how that might have had an effect on his behavior . . ."

"But it might not," Barnes argued, "and the evidence of foul play just keeps gettin' stronger."

"How much of a danger to our inspector is Nivens?" she asked.

"Chief Inspector Barrows clipped his wings a bit yesterday," Barnes replied. "But that'll not stop him for long. You and your lot best be careful. Nivens suspects the inspector is gettin' help."

"We'll take extra precautions to make sure he doesn't spot us. I'm sure his pride is wounded."

"That it is," Barnes warned, "and he'll be wantin' to take his fury out on our inspector. But for all his political connections and bluster, he's a bit of a coward. I think we'll be all right. Especially if the inspector hurries up and solves this case."

The omnibus pulled up in front of the busy Hammersmith Station, and the constable swung out of his seat to let her out. "Let me know if you find out anything worthwhile today," he said. "And I'll make sure our inspector learns everything your lot has found out."

• • •

"The inspector kept asking me where Mrs. Jeffries had gone," Betsy said as she came into the kitchen. She carried a tray with the inspector's dirty breakfast dishes.

"He was down here askin' me the same thing," Mrs. Goodge replied. "I told him she'd gone to see the fishmonger and the butcher."

"I know." Betsy frowned as she put the tray down on the far end of the kitchen table. "He told me. But then he kept wondering if Mrs. Jeffries had gone because she wanted to order something special from the butcher's and the fishmonger. I hadn't any idea what to say."

"He's worried," Mrs. Goodge snorted. "He's afraid Mrs. Jeffries has already gone ahead and started planning that dinner party she's pressing him to have."

"Men," Betsy laughed and began picking the dirty dishes off the tray. "They're brave enough to face ruffians with pistols, but the idea of social obligation scares them to death."

"Don't bother with that," Mrs. Goodge jerked her head at the mess. "I'll take care of it."

Betsy looked doubtful. "Are you sure? It'll only take a few minutes to get this lot cleaned up. I'm only going over to the Arkwright neighborhood."

"This case isn't goin' to solve itself," the cook retorted. "Now go on with you, and let me get crackin'. I've got some sources dropping by in a bit, and I want this kitchen cleared."

Betsy did as she was told and was out the door a few minutes later. Once the maid was gone, Mrs. Goodge was alone. Smythe had left just after breakfast to do some snooping near the Donovan house and Wiggins had taken it into his head to go back to the Lynch neighborhood. Mrs. Goodge hoped the lad kept a sharp eye out. She suspected the inspector and Constable Barnes might be over in that area today.

It didn't take the cook long to finish the chores. She had just put the last plate on the rack, when there was a knock on the back door. She hurried down the hall, opened up, and blinked in surprise. "Melba? This is a surprise. I didn't expect to see you today." Melba Robinson was a small, thin woman with frizzy gray hair and bright blue eyes. She wore a heavy black coat, buttoned from the tip of her sharp chin down to the tip of her toes.

"I hope you don't think it's a liberty, bein' as I was supposed to come by yesterday."

"Oh no," Mrs. Goodge ushered her inside and down the hall towards the kitchen. "You're very welcome. Let me take your coat."

Melba was already in the process of unbuttoning the garment. "I'm ever so sorry about yesterday. But the most dreadful thing happened. I locked myself outside."

"How awful," Mrs. Goodge replied.

"Not to worry, I got inside," Melba got enough buttons open to slip off the coat and nimbly stepped out of it. She hung it on the coatrack.

"You have a spare key hidden outside?" Mrs. Goodge asked. She ushered the other woman towards the table. "Let's have tea. I've some nice apple tarts baked."

"There's no spare," Melba shrugged. "Tea would be lovely, thank you."

"Do sit down," Mrs. Goodge pointed at a chair and then hurried to put the kettle on. "If there's no spare key, how'd you get inside? Surely you didn't climb through a window." She really didn't care, but she'd found that it didn't matter what her sources started talking about, it only mattered to get them talking. Melba Robinson lived very close to the Donovan house, and if there were any gossip to be had about them, she'd have it. Melba's house wasn't one of those posh Mayfair mansions, it was a simple modest row house that she'd bought with money both inherited from relations and saved out of her salary over the years.

"Of course not," Melba giggled. "Mind you, I'm still pretty spry for someone my age. I could probably have gotten in that way if I'd had to, but it wasn't necessary. I went to my neighbor, Mr. Courtland, and he let me in."

"He climb in a window?" Mrs. Goodge said absently. She racked her brain for a way to bring up the Donovans. She put a plate of apple tarts in front of her guest. "Tea'll be ready in a minute."

"Don't be daft," Melba snickered. "Mr. Courtland can barely walk. He used to own my house, you see. I bought it off him five years ago this spring. When I told him what I'd done, he mucked about in this old wooden box of his, and lo and behold if he didn't find an old key to my front door. Mind you, it was covered in rust and barely worked, but it got us inside. He'd had it all along and forgotten it was there."

The kettle whistled and Mrs. Goodge finished making their tea. "That's handy," she said. "Him havin' a key and all. Uh, isn't it awful about that neighbor of yours?"

"What neighbor?" Melba demanded. "I've heard nothing about any of my neighbors." She picked up a tart and put it on her plate.

"The Donovans . . ."

"Oh them," Melba interrupted. "Well, it's only to be expected, now isn't it? Mind you, none of us that live 'round there is surprised about it. Well, it was bound to happen, wasn't it?"

For a moment, Mrs. Goodge wasn't sure what to do. Her pride didn't want to let on that she didn't know what Melba was talking about, yet she was greedy for information. In less than a heartbeat, greed won. "I'm not sure I know what you're talking about, Melba."

"What were you talking about, then?" Melba demanded.

"Mr. Donovan's business," Mrs. Goodge replied. "I wondered if you'd heard about the death of his chief engineer. It were ruled a suicide . . ."

"It was murder," Melba interrupted again. "The police have been around to speak to the Donovans and to some of the neighbors."

"Did they talk to you?"

"No, my home is too far away from those posh houses where the likes of the Donovans live. But they spoke to Minnie Carroll, and she told me they're askin' about Mr. Donovan." She paused and took a big bite of apple tart. "Said they wanted to know if she'd seen Mr. Donovan come home on the day the poor engineer fellow died and if she did, what time was it. But Minnie hadn't noticed anything."

"Oh," Mrs. Goodge was very disappointed.

"Mind you, it seems to me they ought to be keepin' an eye on Mr. Donovan. Seems to me if what I heard was right, poor Mrs. Donovan had better take care."

Mrs. Goodge snapped to attention. "What? What's this about Mrs. Donovan?"

Betsy spotted the housemaid as she came out from the side of the Arkwright house. She knew the girl was a servant because she'd come out the servant's entrance and not the front door. But where was the girl going? It was too early in the day for it to be her afternoon out. Even the nicest of households didn't let girls out until after the noon meal, and it had just gone ten. Puzzled, she watched as the girl turned and headed up the street. Perhaps she was on an errand for her mistress? But then why wasn't she wearing her maid's cap?

Betsy decided to follow her. The girl moved quickly, as though she were late for an appointment. Betsy stayed at a reasonable distance, not wanting the girl to see her. But being discreet was very difficult. The girl kept stopping and looking over her shoulder, as though she knew she was being followed. The first time it happened, Betsy pretended to be looking in a shop window, but the second time, she had to dodge behind a post box.

Finally, the girl turned into a tea shop on the Kensington High Street. Betsy held back, wondering if she ought to go in as well. If the girl had spotted her, she'd be done for. But if she hadn't, she might learn something. She took a deep breath and stepped inside the shop.

The place was very crowded. There were people standing at the short counter, and most of the tables were filled as well. It took her a moment to spot her quarry. She was sitting at a table in the center of the room talking earnestly to a middle-aged man.

Betsy hesitated. There was an empty table next to them, but she knew the practice in these sorts of places was to get the tea first and then find a place to sit. Obviously, the man had gotten both their beverages, as there was a steaming cup of tea in front of the girl. But Betsy didn't want to risk someone at the counter grabbing that table. Blast. She made up her mind and hurried toward it. If anyone asked, she'd just pretend she was waiting for someone.

From the corner of her eye, she watched the girl as she pulled out a chair and sat down. The girl didn't appear to notice her. Betsy sat down and unobtrusively twisted herself so that her ear was towards the girl and the man.

"I'm sorry, sir," the girl said to him, "but that's all I was able to hear."

Betsy heard the man sigh. Then he said, "It's all right. Did she say what time he was coming?"

"No, sir, only that she would be seeing him this afternoon." The girl took a quick sip of tea. "I'm sorry, Mr. Arkwright. I wish I had more to tell you. But frankly, sir, she's a bit careful on what she says around us. She doesn't tell me any details."

Betsy held her breath. So, the maid was secretly meeting with her employer, Oliver Arkwright. The secrecy was apparently so that Arkwright's wife wouldn't find out, and it was equally apparent Arkwright wasn't meeting with the girl for the usual reason.

"But you're sure he's coming today?" Arkwright pressed. "It's very important that you be certain."

"Absolutely, sir. I heard her tell cook to have some nice cakes ready for this afternoon. She said Mr. Wellbanks, her solictor, was coming and they'd be wantin' some tea."

CHAPTER 10

Inspector Witherspoon and Constable Barnes turned into the courtyard of the Ladbrooke Grove Police Station. As they crossed the cobblestones, Barnes said, "Perhaps another chat with some of the partners' servants might be in order, sir."

"Really? Do you have any specific sorts of ideas about what we might ask?" Witherspoon pulled open the heavy double oak doors, and they stepped inside.

Barnes nodded at the police constables milling about behind the counter. "I think so, sir. It uh . . . suddenly occurred to me that as Westover was killed with a gun, the killer might have gotten blood on himself."

"But surely, if that were the case, he'd have gotten rid of the damaging evidence." Witherspoon headed toward the counter.

"Not if he didn't know it was there," Barnes replied. "It's quite easy to get a drop or two on a lapel or a shirt sleeve and not even realize it's there." He winced inwardly at how pathetic his argument sounded, but it was the best he could come up with.

"You're right, Constable. I'm no expert on firearms, but surely it's rather difficult to shoot someone at what must have been very close range, without getting a bit of blood on oneself. Blood does tend to splatter." He smiled politely at the officer behind the counter. "Good day, sergeant. We're here to have a word with PC Howard and PC Smith."

"We're all ready for you, sir," the sergeant replied. "We've set you up in the same interview room as before. Go on in, and I'll have someone go get the lads."

They crossed behind the counter, through a door, and into a dim, narrow hallway. The interview room was the last door at the end. In the center of the room was a table with two chairs on each side of it. A tall wooden file drawer with a gaslamp sitting on top of it stood by the window.

"Did you want to interview them together, sir?" Barnes asked.

Witherspoon frowned. "Is there any reason we shouldn't?"

"They did muck up the original investigation, sir," the constable replied. "And they might be worried about being reprimanded. We'd probably get more out of them speaking one on one."

The door opened, and an older PC stuck his head inside. "PC Howard is here, sir. Are you ready for him?"

"Where's PC Smith?" Barnes asked.

"He's at the Marylebone Magistrates Court. He's giving evidence on another case. He ought to be here soon, though."

Barnes and Witherspoon looked at each other. "We're ready for PC Howard," the inspector said. The constable nodded and ducked back out into the hall. They could hear him say, "Come along, lad, they're ready for you."

"Looks like we'll be interviewin' them separately after all," Barnes muttered as he took a seat behind the table. Witherspoon sank down in the other one.

PC Howard was a tall, lanky young man with a bony face, deep-set brown eyes, and russet-colored wavy hair. "Good day, Inspector, Constable." His back was ramrod straight, but his expression was wary.

Witherspoon smiled reassuringly at the young man. "Good day PC Howard. Do have a seat," he gestured at one of the empty chairs.

Howard licked his lips nervously and sat down.

Barnes opened his little brown notebook. "You were the first police officer to arrive on the scene when Mr. Harlan Westover died, is that correct?"

"That's right, sir, I was patrolling over on Brook Green when all of a sudden, this fellow comes running across the grass shouting that he needed help."

"What time was this?" Witherspoon asked.

"It was about half past twelve." He paused. "I think."

"What happened then?" Barnes pressed.

"I went with the gentleman around the corner to Charter Street. He told me that a man was dead and that it looked like he'd been shot. That's when I blew my whistle, sir." He paused again and took a breath. "That's proper procedure, sir. If you know there's been a weapon used, you're supposed to call for help immediately."

"Of course it is," Witherspoon reassured him. "I suppose you got an answering whistle from PC Smith."

"That's right, sir. It come right away so I knew PC Smith was close by. I went on into the house with this gentleman who I later found out was Mr. James Horrocks. By then, there were plenty of people larking about, so I knew someone would show PC Smith where we'd gone."

"Was Mr. Horrocks saying anything?" Barnes asked.

PC Howard shook his head. "Not really. He'd gone quite pale, like he was in shock. We got upstairs, and Mr. Horrocks stayed on the landing. I went inside and saw the victim sprawled on the settee. I felt for a pulse and made sure he was dead. Just then, PC Smith come in, and he checked the fellow as well." He shrugged uncomfortably. "To be honest, sir, I was a bit taken aback. I'd never seen anything like that and neither had PC Smith. PC Smith went out and asked Mr. Horrocks some questions. He come back into the room, and I was goin' to nip back to the station and call out the police surgeon. PC Smith was goin' to search the victim's rooms, but all of a sudden, Inspector Nivens arrived. He took right over."

"Exactly what did he do?" Barnes asked softly.

"He spoke to Mr. Horrocks, found out who the victim was and that he'd worked for Mr. Horrocks's company. Then he stepped inside, had a quick look about, and announced it was a suicide. I said we'd not had a chance to search the premises or ask any questions . . . but he said not to waste our time." PC Howard shifted nervously. "I didn't like it much, but what could I do? He was an inspector. PC Smith tried arguing with him, he told him that we'd not asked nearly enough questions of Mr. Horrocks, but Inspector Nivens told him it wasn't necessary. That Mr. Horrocks was a well-known businessman and he'd take care of speaking to him later. PC Smith even pointed to the fact that there was a drop of blood on the settee. But Inspector Nivens told him not to be impertinent and to do what he was told."

"Where was the blood?" Barnes asked sharply.

"On the arm of the settee," Howard explained. "But it wasn't on the arm of the side where Westover's corpse was lyin', it was on the other side. PC Smith was sure the body had been moved. Which means it was murder, sir. People don't move themselves from one end of the settee to another, not once they're dead."

Mrs. Jeffries stepped through the heavy door of the West London Hospital. She stood in the foyer, surveying the area and planning her strategy. Straight ahead of her was a long narrow corridor with doors and hallways branching off at various intervals. The walls were painted an ugly shade of green that vaguely matched the gray green color of the linoleum.

The place smelled of sickness and antiseptic. Mrs. Jeffries started down the corridor. She passed a door that led into a large ward, but she didn't go in, instead she carried on to the end where a nurse sat behind a desk. The woman looked up at her approach. "May I help you, ma'am?"

"I'm not certain," Mrs. Jeffries gave the woman a timid smile. She had planned her strategy carefully and hoped it would work. "Actually, I've a rather odd problem. I'm not even sure I'm at the right place."

"You don't know where you ought to be?" the nurse said sternly. "I'm afraid I don't understand."

"Let me explain," Mrs. Jeffries replied. "My cousin died recently."

"Did he die here?" the nurse asked.

"No, but he was brought here for a postmortem."

"A postmortem?" the nurse frowned. "Then you'll have to go around to the back. We've nothing to do with postmortems here. We only have sick people on this ward. The operating theaters and the morgue are in the back."

"But I don't need to get him," she said quickly. "I'm looking for his clothes, you see. He's been dead and buried for over a fortnight, but no one seems to know what happened to his things. I've been around to the police, but they've no idea and they told me to come along here. He was fully clothed when his body was brought in. He was wearing a new coat and one of his good work shirts. My nephew Harold is the same size as cousin Harlan and he could use those clothes. Especially the coat." Mrs. Jeffries had decided on the practical approach. Nurses, porters, and orderlies were good solid working people. They knew the value of money, and a relative retrieving a dead man's clothes would not shock them.

The nurse thought for a moment. "You'd best see Mr. Glass, he's the porter. He'd be able to tell you if the clothes are still here."

Mrs. Jeffries didn't have to ask what that meant. In a city teeming with poverty, a perfectly good set of unclaimed clothing would soon end up at a street market or secondhand shop. "Where could I find him?"

The nurse gave her directions, and Mrs. Jeffries made her way to the other end of the building. Mr. Glass, the porter, was sitting behind a desk at the end of a hallway. He was reading a newspaper. Behind him was a closed door. She suspected the door lead to the morgue.

She stepped up to the desk and explained her situation.

Glass, a thin man with a dour expression and greasy brown hair, stared at her for a long moment. "How do I know you're Westover's cousin?" he finally said.

Her heart sank. The clothes were probably long gone. "How do you know I'm not?" she retorted.

"Anyone could walk in here and claim they was anyone, now, couldn't they?" he replied. "How am I to know you're telling the truth? We can't just go giving people's things to anyone who wants 'em."

"I suppose I could get Inspector Witherspoon to vouch for me," she began.

Glass's eyes widened. "Inspector, you mean like a police inspector?"

"Oh yes," she smiled brightly. "He was the one who suggested I come here. He was sure the clothes would still be here. They were, after all, evidence in a police inquiry. By rights, they should have been sent along to the police station as soon as the postmortem was finished."

"There's no need to be bringin' in any police inspectors," Glass got to his feet. "You look like a nice person. I'm sure someone of your sort wouldn't go about pretending to be someone they're not." He edged toward the door behind him. "You just wait here a minute, and I'll nip back and have a look."

"Thank you," she gave him a bright smile.

He disappeared through the door and slammed it behind him. Mrs. Jeffries was fairly certain that Harlan Westover's things were still here. She had no doubt that Glass had planned on selling the things, but had kept them for awhile in case a relative or a solicitor showed up to claim them.

The door opened, and Glass stepped back out. He carried a bundle wrapped in brown paper and tied with heavy string. He handed her the parcel. "Here you are, ma'am, all nice and tidy like."

Mrs. Jeffries gave him a shilling. "This is for your trouble, Mr. Glass. Thank you for taking care of my cousin's things."

Glass blinked in surprise as he took the coin. "That's all right, just doin' my job." But he was pleased nonetheless.

She tucked the bundle under her arm and hurried off. She still had much to do. When she got outside, the day had brightened, but it was still cold and overcast. Traffic on King Street was heavy, but she managed to get a hansom. "Upper Edmonton Gardens in Holland Park," she told the driver. She wanted to examine Westover's clothes before they had their afternoon meeting. She also wanted to have a good long think about the case. She was beginning to see a pattern and hoped that it was the one that would lead to the killer.

Wiggins danced from one foot to the other in an effort to keep his feet warm. He'd not had much luck today, but he wasn't giving up. He'd found a good spot to keep an eye on things, a nice doorway of an empty house that gave him an excellent view of the Donovan house. But so far, he'd seen nothing. Maybe he ought to give up. But then what would he do? He supposed he could go along to the Melcher neighborhood. As far as Wiggins was concerned, Melcher was even more of a suspect than Donovan. He pushed away from the doorframe, and just then, the front door of the Donovan house opened and Mrs. Donovan, followed by her butler, stepped outside. "Shall I get you a hansom, ma'am?" he asked.

She waved him off. "I'll walk." She started down the street. Wiggins let her get half a block ahead of him and then was after her. She walked for a good distance, finally slowing her steps when she reached the commercial area in Knightsbridge. Wiggins didn't worry about being spotted, she never once turned to look behind her.

She stopped at a low, two-story stone building, paused, and went inside. Wiggins dashed across the road and got close enough to read the lettering on the wooden sign above the door. It read, "PG Baines & Son. Solicitors."

He kept walking on past the building until he got to the corner. Turning, he stopped and watched the door, waiting for her to come out. He had quite a long wait, long enough that he realized he was drawing attention to himself by standing on the corner. Keeping his gaze on the office, Wiggins crossed the road to the commercial district. Shops lined both sides of the road at this end of the street so he could stroll back and forth amongst the throngs of shoppers unnoticed. But he kept a sharp eye on that door.

He reached the end of the street closest to the office when the door opened and she stepped outside. A balding, elegantly dressed gentleman wearing spectacles was with her.

Wiggins managed to stroll past them just as the man said, "Are you absolutely sure about this? The preparations are all in place. Once he's served, it'll be very difficult for you."

"That doesn't matter, I won't be there. I'm leaving to-morrow morning," Mrs. Donovan replied.

Wiggins unobtrusively slowed his steps.

"We'll take care of it immediately, then," the man said. "My clerk will go before the . . ."

Unfortunately, no matter how slow Wiggins went, he couldn't hear the rest of the sentence. He was out of earshot. He got to the corner, turned it, and then dived back to keep his eye on his quarry. Mrs. Donovan had finished her con-versation and had turned and started up the road toward the shops. Wiggins waited until the solicitor went back inside, and then he took off after her. But the crowd of shoppers had thickened, and he lost her. Blast a Spaniard, he thought, she's up and disappeared.

Mrs. Jeffries quietly eased open the back door and stepped inside. Holding her parcel, she tiptoed down the hall. She kept her head cocked toward the kitchen, listening to see if Mrs. Goodge was with one of her sources. But she heard nothing.

"Mrs. Goodge," she said as she came into the room, "are you alone."

"I'm 'ere as well," Smythe said.

"We've just sat down for a quick cuppa," Mrs. Goodge said. "My source just left and Smythe hasn't had any luck today. What's that you've got?"

"Harlan Westover's clothes," Mrs. Jeffries popped the par-cel on the table and began pulling off the string.

"Cor blimey, where'd you get those?" Smythe asked. His voice held a hint of admiration.

"From the West London Hospital where he was taken for the postmortem," she replied. "The police never bothered to pick them up, and neither did any of Westover's relations." She pushed aside the wrapping paper and pulled out a dark gray jacket. She held it up and all of them had a good look.

"Why don't you check the pockets," Mrs. Goodge suggested.

Mrs. Jeffries laid the coat on the table and began rummaging through the pockets. "Smythe, do the trousers."

Smythe pulled them out of the parcel, gave them a cursory examination, and shoved his hand in the front left pocket. "What's this, then?" He held up a key ring; on it were two keys.

"Those must be Westover's house keys," Mrs. Goodge yelped.

"Cor blimey, you'd a thought the first coppers on the scene would 'ave taken these. This is evidence, Mrs. Jeffries."

Mrs. Jeffries dropped the jacket onto the table, she'd not found anything in the pockets except a pencil stub. "It certainly is," she stared at the keys. "It proves that Westover probably let the killer in."

"How does it prove that?"

"We've already established that Mrs. Lynch had her lodgers well trained. They locked the door behind them the moment they stepped over the threshold."

"So if Westover came in and locked the doors behind him and then dropped the keys in his pocket, the killer either had to have a key to the front door or Westover had to have let him in," Mrs. Goodge concluded eagerly.

"What should we do with these?" Smythe held the keys in the air.

"We'd best prove that those are his house keys," she replied. "I don't want to get caught out making faulty assumptions. May I leave that up to you?" she asked the coachman.

"I'll handle it as soon as we're finished 'ere," he replied. "Don't worry, I'll take care not to alarm Mrs. Lynch. She'll not know I'm there."

"Is there anything else worth seein'?" Mrs. Goodge demanded.

"There's some undergarments," Mrs. Jeffries tossed them to one side, "a pair of socks and his shirt." She held the shirt up. "But his shoes are missing."

"They were probably pinched by someone at the hospital,"

Smythe suggested. "Good shoes are worth a bit on the street."

"That's got a great ruddy stain on it," the cook pointed to the collar.

"Looks like ink," Smythe murmured. "Wonder how long he walked around with that on his shirt."

"Most of the day, I expect." Mrs. Jeffries folded the garment and laid it back on the paper. She picked up the other pieces, began folding them, and stacked them neatly on top of the shirt. "As soon as Smythe confirms the keys, we need to get this parcel to Constable Barnes."

"Does he know about us, then?" Mrs. Goodge asked.

Mrs. Jeffries hesitated.

"Come on, Mrs. J., we all know that Barnes was close to sussin' us out," Smythe said.

"He suspects we help a bit, but I don't think he quite understands how deeply involved we are. Not to worry, though, he's devoted to our inspector. He can keep his own counsel."

"And workin' with our inspector 'asn't hurt 'is career." Smythe dropped the keys in his pocket and got up. "I might be a bit late to our meetin' this afternoon, I'll probably wait till it's gone a bit dark before I try these keys."

Constable Barnes closed the door of the interview office and followed Witherspoon down the hall.

"Are you all finished, sir?" the sergeant asked as they came into the main room of the station.

"For the moment," Witherspoon said politely. "We appreciate the help you've given us."

"I'll bet you're close to an arrest, aren't you, sir," the sergeant said enthusiastically. Like many of the rank and file of the Metropolitan Police, he was a great admirer of the legendary Gerald Witherspoon.

"Well, uh . . ." the inspector tried hard to think of something optimistic yet noncommittal. He hadn't a clue whom to arrest.

"We're workin' on it," Barnes said. "You lot will be the first to know when it happens."

The sergeant laughed. "That's right, good coppers always play it close to the chest."

"Where to now, sir?" Barnes asked Witherspoon. He hoped it was someplace that took them a long time to reach, because he had quite a lot of information he wanted to drop in the inspector's ear. Too bad he couldn't come out and just tell him everything he'd learned from Mrs. Jeffries, but that wasn't possible. He'd been feeding the man hints all day about this case. But he wasn't sure if Witherspoon had gotten any of them.

"I was thinking we ought to have another go at talking to the partners. We need to know a bit more about that engine they shipped off to South Africa. It seems to me that engine might be the key to this whole case. Also, I'd like to ask them some questions about the firm's financial situation."

Barnes silently heaved a sigh of relief. "That's a good idea, sir. We've plenty of time to go over there and have a word before they close for the day."

"We'll even have time for a bit of lunch," the inspector said cheerfully. "Come along, there's a nice café just up the road. I could do with a nice chop and a bit of mashed potato."

They had almost reached the front door, when it burst open and Nigel Nivens charged into the room. He skidded to a halt as he spotted them. "I've been looking for you two."

"And it seems you've found us," Witherspoon replied. "Is there news? Has the chief sent you to fetch us?"

"I'm not Barrows's ruddy errand boy," Nivens snapped.

"Then why are you here?" Barnes asked cooly. He looked Nivens squarely in the eye.

"You know good and well why I'm here." Nivens's hands balled into fists. "I made it perfectly clear yesterday that I wanted to be present when you interviewed PC Howard and PC Smith."

"I'm afraid that just wasn't possible," Witherspoon said. "Chief Inspector Barrows was quite resolute on the matter. He wanted us to interview them on our own."

"This is my case," Nivens's face contorted in fury, he raised his fist and stepped toward Witherspoon.

Barnes quickly stepped in front of his inspector. "It *was* your case, sir. It's our case now."

From the corner of his eye, Barnes saw the sergeant start out from behind the counter. The constable knew he wasn't a young man, but he'd been a street copper for thirty years. He was still fairly certain he could handle himself and protect his inspector if tempers got out of hand.

Nivens flicked a quick glance at Barnes, then backed away. "You're going to be sorry you did this," he swore. "I'll not have my career destroyed by the likes of you two."

"Gracious, Inspector Nivens," Witherspoon was deeply shocked. "No one is trying to destroy your career."

I am, thought Barnes. Fellow never should have been a copper in the first place.

"The hell you're not," Nivens snarled. "You've tried to ruin me ever since you stole those Kensington High Street murders out from under my nose. Well you're not getting away with it. You're not going to make me look like a fool again."

"No one's making you a fool," Witherspoon said. "Inspector Nivens, I really have no idea what you're talking about. I'm simply doing my job."

Nivens glanced over Witherspoon's shoulder. A sizeable crowd of constables had gathered around the sergeant. None of them were looking particularly friendly toward him. He began backing toward the door. "You'd best take care how you write your report, Witherspoon. If you make me look incompetent, I'll make you regret the day you joined the force, and don't think I can't do it, I've got plenty of friends in high places."

Witherspoon hated confrontation, especially with fellow officers, but he wasn't going to allow himself to be threatened. "I'll write up my report as I always do, Inspector, with diligence, care, and an allegiance to the truth. Not my career. You may have many friends in high places but that is certainly no concern of mine and most assuredly will not influence one word of my report."

"You really are a fool," Nivens said coldly, "and I'll make

you pay if it's the last thing I ever do." He turned and stormed out the door.

The inspector stared after him, his expression utterly stunned. He shook his head in disbelief. "I've no idea why that man hates me so much."

"He was the rising young star on the force until you came along," Barnes said quietly. "Mind you, he was a lousy copper. Bullied suspects into false confessions, bullied the lads every chance he got, and was a real boot licker when it suited his purpose. That's why this case never had a chance with Nivens on it. Harlan Westover was just an engineer, James Horrocks and the partners are rich and powerful men. He'd not want to look at them too closely. Why do you think he was so quick to call the case a suicide right after he questioned Horrocks?"

"I can't believe it." Witherspoon started for the door. "How did he get away with it all this time?"

"He never leaves any proof, sir," Barnes sighed as they stepped outside. "The lads know it's always their word against his. He's got plenty of rich and powerful friends to protect him, and, well, occasionally he does solve a burglary. Anyway, sir, not to worry, he's not the only one with allies. You're a good copper, sir, and after that Ripper fiasco, there's plenty at the home office that'll be watching out for you. They know you're a good copper."

They were all late for their afternoon meeting. It was almost ten past five before Mrs. Goodge got the table laid. She put out the teapot as Mrs. Jeffries came in. "I'm sorry to be so late," she began, but stopped when she saw the empty chairs. "Where is everyone?"

"Late," Mrs. Goodge replied tartly. "But I was late too, so I can't grouse about it. I sat down in my rocker to have a bit of a rest and nodded off."

Mrs. Jeffries laughed. "Not to worry, I did the same thing, only I was sitting at my desk. I do hope the others get here soon."

"Me too," Mrs. Goodge put the teapot down next to a plate

of jam sandwiches. "I have a feeling we're going to have a lot to talk about."

Everyone else, except Betsy, arrived within minutes, and they took their usual places around the table. Mrs. Goodge handed around the sandwiches and cakes, while Mrs. Jeffries poured the tea.

"Should we wait for Betsy?" the cook asked. Just then they heard the back door open and the sound of running footsteps. "That's her now."

Betsy came into view. The others gasped when they saw her. Her face was smeared with dirt, her cloak was covered with mud streaks, and there were leaves dangling from her disheveled hair.

Smythe was on his feet and across the room like a shot. "Bloomin' Ada, are you all right?" he grabbed Betsy and pulled her closer into the light. "What happened to you, lass? Are you all right? Are you 'urt? Should we call the doctor?"

"I'm fine, Smythe," Betsy soothed him with a weary smile. "I'm not hurt, just filthy, and it's my own fault."

"Betsy, come have a chair and tell us what happened," Mrs. Jeffries suggested.

"You 'ave a nice hot cuppa now," Smythe lead her to her chair, and still holding her hand, took his own seat. "Cor blimey, you better 'ave learned something good from bein' in this state."

Betsy giggled. "Oh I'm sorry, I didn't mean for anyone to make a fuss, but I know what I look like. There's a very simple explanation. I had to hide in the bushes when I was following Mr. and Mrs. Arkwright. They decided to go for a walk along the river after she'd seen her solictor." She took a sip of tea and then told them about following the maid to the café. "Well, naturally, once I knew Mrs. Arkwright was seeing her solicitor, I went back and hung about the house. The solicitor went inside and a few minutes later, Mr. Arkwright came home and went in as well. About half an hour after that, the solicitor left and right behind him, the Arkwrights come out together. So I followed them, I wanted to find out what they were talking about, you see. But I didn't manage to get close enough to hear them till they went down to the river. They popped down on a bench, and I had to dive into the bushes to get close enough to hear what they was saying." She sighed. "I'll not bore you with the details, but the jist of it was that Mrs. Arkwright isn't going to sue her husband to get her money back. He was ever so grateful. He told her he loved her and that he would pay her back. He said he was going to sell some property off the family's estate up in Northumberland. I think they've come to some sort of . . . well, I think they realized they still love each other."

"Well blast a Spaniard," Mrs. Goodge snapped. "That's no good. I was sure Arkwright might be our killer. He was seen on Brook Green the day Westover was killed."

"He could still be the killer," Wiggins said.

"I don't think so," Betsy said. "They talked about Westover, and Arkwright swore he hadn't gone into the Westover's rooms. He claimed he went to the door, tried to open it, and then lost his nerve and left. I believe him. Mrs. Arkwright does too." Betsy shrugged apologetically. "That's all I got today."

"Are you sure you're all right?" Mrs. Jeffries pressed. "You must be cold, it's quite damp down by the river. We can wait if you'd like to go up and change into something warm."

"Let's get on with the meeting, I'm fine." Betsy smiled at Smythe. "Really, I am, I'm just a bit dirty."

"Can I go next?" Wiggins asked. At the housekeeper's nod, he told them about Mrs. Donovan and how he'd followed her. "She went to her solicitor's too," he nodded eagerly at Betsy, "but she didn't tell him to stop doin' anything." He repeated what he'd heard the woman say to her lawyer. "And then she disappeared into the crowd and I thought I'd lost her for sure." He crammed a bite of sandwich into his mouth. "But I caught up with her again just as she was goin' into the railway bookin' office. I nipped in 'ot on 'er heels and got right in line behind her. She booked a first class ticket to Paris. She's leavin' from Victoria tomorrow at eleven o'clock."

"Are you sure about this?" Mrs. Jeffries pressed.

"Heard it as clear as I can 'ear you," Wiggins grinned. "What do you think it means?"

"I don't know. Possibly nothing more than a woman wanting to get away from her husband," Mrs. Jeffries replied.

"Apparently there's quite a number of women wanting to be rid of their spouses," Ruth interjected. "I'm sorry. It's not my turn yet."

"It's all right," Wiggins said quickly. "I was finished."

"Yes, do go on, Ruth," Mrs. Jeffries took a sip of tea. "Who is leaving their spouse? One of our suspects?"

"Edna Horrocks. She's moved out of the Horrocks's house and is going to file for divorce," Ruth replied. "She's moved back to her family's estate in Wiltshire."

"She must be really fed up," Mrs. Goodge pursed her lips. "People like that usually don't divorce, they live separately. Are you sure she's actually going to divorce him?"

"I'm positive," Ruth said. "And her family is actively encouraging the divorce. They hate him. He's quite a rich man, but he's such a miser he's made her live like a pauper for years."

"He's rich?" Mrs. Jeffries asked. "I thought all of his money was tied up in the firm?" She was annoyed with herself for not finding this out earlier.

"Oh no, not all of it," Ruth said. "He's far too cautious a person to put all his eggs in one basket. He's got a number of other investments and plenty of real estate that's free and clear."

"So even if the company goes bankrupt, he'd be all right," Smythe muttered.

"As would Arkwright and Melcher," Ruth added.

"So it's just Donovan who would be in dire straits if the company went under," Mrs. Jeffries knew this was important. Suddenly, a number of things began to make sense. But she needed to have a good, long think about this before she was sure.

"Can I go now?" Mrs. Goodge asked. "It's gettin' late, and the inspector'll be home soon."

"If Ruth's finished?"

"I'm done," she replied. "Go on, Mrs. Goodge, what did you find out today?"

Mrs. Goodge told them about Melba's visit. "Mind you, gettin' any sense out of the woman was like pullin' teeth, she kept witterin' on about gettin' locked out of her house and her neighbor, who used to own the house, havin' to let her in. But I finally got a few useful bits out of her." She looked at Wiggins. "Mrs. Donovan went to see her solicitor today because she's havin' him serve her husband tomorrow. The firm's gettin' a notice to quit the premises. Leastways that's what Melba thought it was called."

"But why now?" Smythe asked. "Seems to me the company might just have a chance to be a success."

"That's probably what Mrs. Donovan is afraid of," Mrs. Goodge replied. "According to Melba, she hates her husband and has been looking for a way to hurt him for years. What better way than to wait until he's almost a success and then snatch it away from him."

"Why does she hate him so much?" Betsy asked.

Mrs. Goodge shrugged. "Who knows? But it happens that way sometimes. Anyway, that's all I've got."

Mrs. Jeffries looked at Smythe. "Does the key fit?"

He nodded, pulled them out of his pocket and handed them to her. "They do. I waited until Mrs. Lynch was in the kitchen and then nipped up the front stairs. Both keys fit, so he must have let the killer in."

"Where'd you get keys?" Betsy demanded.

Mrs. Jeffries told her and the others how she'd obtained the parcel from the hospital. They discussed the case for another half hour before they had to stop and take care of the evening chores.

By the time the inspector came home, Mrs. Jeffries's head was buzzing with so many ideas she could barely keep them all straight.

Over their customary glass of sherry, she found out what he'd learned that day. It was enough to add even more fuel to her mental fires.

The inspector retired right after dinner, he claimed he was simply tired, but Mrs. Jeffries thought he seemed a bit upset about something. He didn't eat as much as usual.

She went up to her own room and closed the door behind
her. She didn't bother to undress, but instead, went to her
chair by the window. She sat down, relaxed her body, and
let her mind drift free. Somewhere in all this information
was the identity of the killer. She knew it. She could feel it
in her bones.

CHAPTER 11

It was still dark outside when Mrs. Jeffries came downstairs. She made herself a pot of tea and sat down at the table, trying to put her thoughts into some semblance of order. She'd spent a good part of the night awake, alternately thinking and letting her mind drift free. By morning, she'd decided what course of action was needed. She only hoped it was the correct one to lead them to the killer.

She heard footsteps on the back stairs, and a moment later, Smythe appeared. He was fully dressed. He grinned at her. "Couldn't sleep?"

"No, I spent most of the night thinking about our case." She got up and fetched another cup.

"So did I," he admitted, taking the seat next to her. "Come to any conclusions?"

"I'm not sure," she poured him tea and handed him the cup.

"But you've got an idea?"

"I think so, but I'm not absolutely certain." She knew she shouldn't be so hesitant, but the conclusion she'd reached in the wee hours of the morning was based on very little hard evidence. On the other hand, it simply made more sense than any other idea she'd come up with. "When you were at the Lynch house yesterday evening, did you happen to notice the locks?"

"It was gettin' dark, Mrs. Jeffries, the only thing I cared about was seein' if the keys fit. To be honest, I didn't pay any attention to the lock proper. Why? Is it important?"

"It might be. I'm sorry to have to ask you this again, but can you nip over to the Lynch house and have a good look?"

"What am I looking for?"

"Age. I want you to see if you can tell if the lock is the original one. I know that might be a bit difficult . . ."

"That shouldn't be too 'ard," Smythe interrupted. "Those houses over on Charter Street are over fifty years old, if it's an original lock it'll be one of them old-fashioned kind with the big strike plate, if it's been changed, it'll 'ave one of them small mortise locks on it."

She stared at him in amazement. "Gracious, how do you know all that?"

"I did a bit of carpentry and 'ousebuildin' when I was in Australia." He shrugged modestly. "Anything else you need done?"

"I need someone to get Westover's clothes to Constable Barnes this morning *before* he comes to pick up the inspector. But I'll have Wiggins take care of that. He can waylay him at the corner."

"Should I get the lad up?" He started to rise, but Mrs. Jeffries waved him back to his chair.

"Not yet, we've got several hours before the constable is due here." She took another sip of the hot tea. "And I need to know about that stain on Westover's shirt."

"The ink stain?"

"That's right, I want to find out if Westover had it on his shirt when he left the office after the board meeting. It's quite a big stain, so if it was there at that time, it would have been plainly visible. Betsy might be able to find that out quickly enough. She can waylay that clerk she spoke to a couple of days ago before he goes into the office."

"I heard my name being bandied about." Betsy came into the kitchen. "Do you want me to do something? What is it?"

Mrs. Jeffries repeated her instructions as she poured the maid a cup of tea. "And I'll need you both back here by half past eight. That's when Constable Barnes is due," she finished.

Betsy nodded eagerly and took a quick sip of tea. "What if my source didn't see Westover that day? Do you want me to find someone else to ask?"

"If you can," Mrs. Jeffries replied. "But I suspect we're going to be up against a very rigid time frame, so you must be back here at half past eight. Let me give you some money, you'll need to take a hansom, it'll save a lot of time."

Betsy stood up. "I'll just get my cloak, then. It's upstairs."

"You've got a few minutes," Smythe protested. "Finish your tea."

She headed for the back stairs. "It's too hot, I'll finish it when I've got my cloak and gloves."

"You can walk her up to Holland Park Road," Mrs. Jeffries pulled some coins out of her pocket. "It'll be light by the time you get there."

"And I can go on to the Lynch house as soon as I see her safely off."

Within a few minutes, the two of them were out the back door and Mrs. Jeffries was left alone once again. She hoped her theory was right, but there was only one way to prove it. And it all depended on the answers these two brought back.

She poured herself another cup of tea and sat back to wait for the others to get up. She'd know in a few hours if she was right or wrong.

Inspector Witherspoon woke with the beginnings of a headache. He hadn't slept well. The altercation with Inspector Nivens had disturbed him greatly. But he wasn't going to let his discomfort stop him from doing his duty. He washed, cleaned his teeth, dressed, and went downstairs. Mrs. Jeffries was waiting at the foot of the stairs. "Good morning, Mrs. Jeffries."

"Good morning, sir. You're up early. It's only half past

seven. I don't believe that Mrs. Goodge has your breakfast ready yet."

"That's all right," he shrugged. "I'll pop down to the kitchen for a spot of tea. As a matter of fact, I might as well have breakfast down there this morning. No point in everyone tromping up and down the stairs with my bacon and eggs."

"Are you sure, sir? You might be a bit more comfortable in the dining room." Drat, the others weren't back as yet. They could hardly give her a report with the inspector sitting there as big as life.

Witherspoon went past her, turned down the hall, and started for the back stairs.

"Excellent, sir," she trailed behind him. "While you're there, we can discuss the dinner party."

Witherspoon skidded to a halt. "Dinner party? Oh dear, I'm afraid I've not given that much thought lately. The case, you see. Uh . . . perhaps I will eat in the dining room. Yes, I believe I will. If you could ask Betsy to bring me a pot of tea, I'll read the paper while Mrs. Goodge cooks my breakfast. No point in upsetting the household routine, is there?"

"The tea will be right up, sir. Your paper's on the dining table."

Afraid she'd bring up the subject of that wretched dinner party, he flew down the hall to the dining room and disappeared inside.

Mrs. Jeffries went down to the kitchen. "The inspector is up early."

Mrs. Goodge, who was sitting at the table drinking her tea, rose to her feet and headed for the cooker. "The others aren't back yet. But at least you got Wiggins out to give that parcel to Barnes."

"The inspector wants a pot of tea while he's waiting for breakfast. I'll make it." She fixed the tea and took it upstairs. As she was coming back to the kitchen, she met Betsy coming down the hall.

The girl's cheeks were flushed and she was breathless. "I had the hansom put me out around the other side of the garden," she explained. "I didn't want the inspector seeing me getting out of a cab this time of the morning."

"Were you successful?" Mrs. Jeffries asked as they went into the room. She put the tray on the table.

"Very," Betsy unfastened her cloak. "Westover's shirt was white as snow when he left the office that day."

"You didn't have any trouble gettin' the information?" Mrs. Goodge pressed.

"Not at all." She glanced around the kitchen, saw that Smythe was still out and said. "All it took was a bit of flirting. Honestly, men are such sillies sometimes. I didn't even have to come up with a convincing . . ." she broke off as she heard the back door open.

Smythe came into the room and smiled when he saw she was safely home. "Good, you're back." He unbuttoned his coat. "Cor blimey, it's cold out there. The locks are original, Mrs. Jeffries. Doesn't look like they've been changed since they were put in place."

"Thank you, Smythe. Sit down and have a bite of breakfast now. You too, Betsy." Mrs. Jeffries frowned thoughtfully. She picked up the empty tray off the table and laid it on the counter next to the cooker.

"Well, are you goin' to tell us who the killer is?" Mrs. Goodge demanded. She cracked an egg on the side of the skillet and dropped it into the hot grease.

Mrs. Jeffries barely heard the cook, she was too busy thinking. "Uh . . . yes, yes, that's the way it must have happened. It's the only thing that makes sense." She turned sharply and said to Smythe. "Get up. You need to get to Constable Barnes before he gets here. Bring him to the back door, I've got to talk to him before he sees the inspector."

Smythe, who'd been in the process of pouring himself a cup of tea, leapt up and charged for the back door. "I'll try and 'ead 'im off at the corner."

"Look for Wiggins," Mrs. Jeffries called. "I sent him out with the parcel of clothes, and hurry, please. I've got to speak with Barnes."

"What do you want Barnes to do?" Mrs. Goodge asked as she lifted the fried eggs onto a hot plate.

"Stop our killer from getting away."

•   •   •

Inspector Witherspoon frowned at the contents of the parcel spread on the dining room table. He shook his head in dismay. "Thank goodness you had the presence of mind to retrieve these things, Constable. It's evidence."

"Look at this ink stain, sir," Barnes said. "Seems to me that means that Westover must have written something after he got home from the board meeting."

"Why afterwards?" Witherspoon asked. "Why not before he left the office?"

Barnes was ready for this question. "I think someone would have mentioned it," he said. "He was a very fastidious gentleman, and we did keep asking the staff if there was anything odd about him that day. Someone would have noticed a huge stain like that on his shirt, and they'd have mentioned it to us. You know how people are, sir. They'll tell you all the details if you ask enough." It was weak, but it was the best they'd been able to come up with on short notice. "So I think we'd best get over to the Lynch house and have us a quick search. The man wrote something when he got home that day, and it was probably something to do with the meeting. Something that might point directly to his killer."

Mrs. Jeffries, who was standing in the hall eavesdropping, sincerely hoped they were on the right track, so to speak. It had just gone half past eight, if she was correct, they had a very short window of time to find their evidence and make the arrest.

"Let's get over to the Lynch house, then," Witherspoon said. "I'll just tidy this parcel up."

"Let's leave it, sir," Barnes said quickly. "I'm sure Mrs. Jeffries or someone else on your staff will do it up nicely and send it along to the station."

"Of course we will," Mrs. Jeffries dashed into the room. "Sorry, I couldn't help but overhear your conversation. We'll take care of this, I'm sure you've much to do today." She and the constable exchanged meaningful looks.

"Thank you, Mrs. Jeffries, we are quite busy." He edged toward the door. "Aren't we, sir?"

"Yes, I suppose we are." Witherspoon smiled gratefully at Mrs. Jeffries and trailed out behind the constable.

Barnes kept up a steady stream of conversation about the case as they took a hansom the short distance to Brook Green. He wanted to make sure he planted a number of suggestions in his inspector's ear.

Mrs. Lynch wasn't surprised to see them. "Are you making any progress, then?" she asked as soon as they stepped inside. She led them up the stairs.

"We should be making an arrest shortly," Barnes said quickly. Witherspoon shot his constable a puzzled frown but said nothing.

"Good, whoever murdered poor Mr. Westover deserves to be hanged." She opened Westover's door. "No one's been in here except your lot. But it's a good thing you came along today. His solictor is sending someone in tomorrow to get all of Mr. Westover's belongings." She stood to one side to let them pass. "I'll let you get to it, then. Close the door behind you when you're done."

Witherspoon crossed the room and stood next to the desk. "I suppose if he wrote something, he'd have done it here."

"Stands to reason, sir," Barnes replied as he walked over to the small bookcase by the fireplace. "I'll have a look in these bookcases, sir."

For the next few moments the room was quiet, save for the opening and closing of drawers and the rustling of papers. Witherspoon said, "There's nothing here on the desk." He picked the huge dictionary and flipped open the cover. "Wait a minute . . . what's this?"

"What is it, sir?" Barnes asked.

Witherspoon dropped the book back onto the desk with a loud thud. He held the paper where he could read it. "Good gracious, it appears to be an account of the board meeting." He paused and finished reading the document.

"What does he say, sir?"

Witherspoon handed the paper to Barnes. "Have a look for yourself. Harlan Westover told the board of directors that his engine wasn't safe. That the struts Horrocks had ordered were too cheap and they wouldn't hold. He demanded the board cable the company in South Africa that had bought the engine and tell them to replace the struts."

"That doesn't seem unreasonable," Barnes replied, as he started to scan the pages. He'd been hoping for something a bit more dramatic than that.

"Apparently everyone agreed with him except for one person. Harry Donovan. Donovan claimed the firm's reputation couldn't stand anymore bad news. It would ruin them in the industry. As the major shareholder, Donovan refused to allow them to send the cable."

"It says here that Westover resigned and told Donovan he was going to send the cable himself." Barnes looked up at Witherspoon. "Perhaps we'd better go have a chat with Mr. Donovan."

Witherspoon nodded. "I think that's quite a good idea."

Barnes sighed in relief and surreptitiously pulled out his pocketwatch and checked the time. It was a quarter to ten. He'd promised Mrs. Jeffries he'd do his best to get Witherspoon to the Donovan house before Mrs. Donovan left for Victoria Station. If they took a hansom and didn't run into any traffic jams, they ought to make it in time. "There's a cab stand on the other side of the green."

Witherspoon tucked the note in his coat pocket. "Good. I think Mr. Donovan has some explaining to do."

"Will you be making an arrest, sir?" Barnes asked as they stepped out into the hall. He closed the door.

"I'm not sure," Witherspoon replied. They started down the stairs. "It's evidence, but I don't know if it's enough evidence."

Barnes nodded. He knew that the note was enough evidence, but only if taken together with the scenario that Mrs. Jeffries had hinted at during their brief meeting this morning. "Why don't we see what Donovan has to say for himself," he suggested.

They got into a cab and drove toward Mayfair. The traffic wasn't awful, but they weren't making particularly good time. Barnes pulled his watch out for the second time just as they rounded the corner to Wywick Place. Ten fifteen. Good, if they were lucky, she hadn't left yet.

"Are we running late, Constable?" Witherspoon asked as the hansom pulled up in front of number seven. "Do we have an appointment I've forgotten? That's twice you've check the time."

"No sir," Barnes forced a laugh as he swung out of the cab. "I think the watch might be running a bit slow, that's all."

Witherspoon stepped down and reached into his pocket for some coins. All of a sudden the door of the Donovan house burst open and a maid came running out.

"Help, help," she screamed. "He's killing her. He's killing her."

Barnes caught the woman as she careened toward them. "Get a hold of yourself," he demanded. "What's wrong?"

More screams came from inside the house.

Witherspoon leapt towards the front door. Barnes shoved the maid to one side and charged after the inspector. They ran up the short walkway and into the foyer.

"Leave me alone, you bastard!" a woman's voice came from the drawing room.

Several servants were heading for the drawing room, but the inspector waved them back. "Let us handle this," he yelled. "Go to the corner and get the constable on patrol."

"Hold on, sir," Barnes called. "Wait for me."

"I'll kill you, you stupid bitch!" Harry Donovan's enraged voice filled the house. "You'll pay for this."

Witherspoon ran into the drawing room and skidded to a halt. Harry Donovan had his wife on the settee, his hands were wrapped around her throat. "You stupid cow, I'll kill you. You've been trying to ruin me since the day we married . . ."

Witherspoon and Barnes dived for Donovan. The inspector grabbed one of Donovan's arms. Barnes got hold of the other one. "Let go, Mr. Donovan," the inspector ordered. "You're going to kill her."

But the enraged man had enormous strength. "That's the whole idea," he ground out between clenched teeth.

"Uh . . . ooh . . ." Mrs. Donovan's guttural cries filled the air, her feet kicked helplessly as the three men wrestled with all their might. Barnes let go of Donovan's arm, made his hand into a fist and punched the man in the side as hard as he could.

Donovan gasped and lightened his grip on his wife's neck just enough so that Witherspoon could pry his fingers loose. Barnes grabbed his shoulders and pulled him off the thrashing woman, hurling him onto the floor. Panting for breath, he fell into a heap on the carpet.

Another police constable, followed by a wailing serving maid, came running into the room. "Hang on to him!" Barnes shouted, pointing at Donovan, who was struggling to get to his feet.

He turned his attention to the inspector, who was bent over Mrs. Donovan. "Is she all right, sir?"

Mrs. Donovan gasped for air, her breath was coming in small, hard pants. She pointed to her throat. "Tried to kill me . . . you saw . . . tried to kill me."

"Dear lady, don't try to speak," Witherspoon soothed. "We saw everything." He looked up at the servants standing in the doorway. The one who'd been screaming was mercifully quiet. "Can one of you please get Mrs. Donovan some water."

Witherspoon looked at Donovan. He was now standing between Barnes and the constable. "Mr. Donovan, what do you have to say for yourself? This is attempted murder."

"He killed Harlan Westover," Mrs. Donovan gasped the words out as she struggled to a sitting postion. "And he tried to kill me."

Donovan's face darkened in rage, he lunged for his wife. "You stupid cow, you've ruined me."

The constables grabbed him and pulled him back. "We'd better get him down to the station," Barnes said.

Witherspoon looked at the enraged man. "Harry Donovan, you're under arrest for the murder of Harlan Westover and the attempted murder of your wife."

Mrs. Jeffries was pacing back and forth in front of the kitchen table where Ruth, Mrs. Goodge, and Betsy were all drinking tea. Smythe and Wiggins were out. She'd sent them to keep watch on the Donovan house as soon as the inspector had left this morning.

"Why are you so nervous?" Betsy asked her.

"Because I'm not sure I was right about this one," she replied.

"We can't help you there," Mrs. Goodge sniffed. "You haven't told us much of anything."

Mrs. Jeffries looked at the cook and smiled apologetically. "I'm sorry, I'm not being deliberately mysterious. It's just that I'm not sure that there's enough evidence to be sure of myself, let alone for the inspector to make an arrest. And if my theory is incorrect, I don't want to poison the well, so to speak." She sighed. "If the inspector doesn't make an arrest, we may very well have to put on our thinking caps and approach this from a completely different point of view. I don't want to prejudice your thinking if I'm completely wrong in my assumptions."

Mrs. Goodge didn't look convinced.

"We've already had one false start," Mrs. Jeffries explained earnestly. "After Wiggins gave us Melcher's bloodstained shirt, I was thinking he was our killer. As a matter of fact, that was the one thing that didn't fit in with my current theory. But this morning Constable Barnes told me that after speaking to Melcher's clerk yesterday, he'd found out that Melcher had a bad nosebleed the day after the board meeting. The fellow bled all over himself. So you see how easy it is to be wrong."

"We understand," Ruth said cheerfully. "And if nothing happens today, I'm sure there's still plenty of evidence about for us to find. This killer won't get away with it, that's for certain."

Mrs. Jeffries wasn't so sure. She had a vague suspicion that throughout history, many murderers had gone unpunished, at least by human justice. She heard the back door open.

"They're back," Betsy leapt to her feet and ran towards the hallway just as the two men appeared. "What happened? Was there an arrest?"

"It were ever so excitin'," Wiggins said. "We did just what

you said, Mrs. Jeffries, we stayed out of sight and kept a close eye on the place. Mind you, we didn't know what we ought to do when all the screamin' started. But just then the inspector and Constable Barnes pulled up in a hansom, and so we didn't 'ave to do anything."

"What on earth happened?" Mrs. Jeffries asked. She motioned for them to sit down and took her own seat at the head of the table.

"There's been an arrest," Smythe said calmly. "Just as you thought, Mrs. Jeffries, Mrs. Donovan's leaving brought things to a 'ead, so to speak."

"Who got arrested?" Mrs. Goodge demanded. "You can fill us in on all the details later, just tell us who?"

"Harry Donovan," Smythe replied. "He was arrested for Westover's murder and the attempted murder of his wife."

"Harry Donovan," Mrs. Jeffries exclaimed. "Are you certain?"

Everyone looked at her in surprise.

"Who did you think was going to be arrested?" Ruth asked curiously.

"Mrs. Donovan," she admitted. "I was sure she was our killer."

"Why would she have wanted to kill Harlan Westover?" Wiggins asked.

"Because she hated her husband and wanted to ruin him." Mrs. Jeffries shook her head. "I was certain she was the one who'd done it. I thought she found the key to the Lynch house amongst her husband's things."

"Why would he have a key?" Ruth interrupted.

"Because he used to own the house," Mrs. Goodge supplied. "And as he used to own the place, he might have accidentally hung on to the key. It's just like Melba's neighbor lettin' her in to her house when she'd locked herself out."

"That's what gave me the idea," Mrs. Jeffries said.

"So that's why you sent Smythe over there to see if the locks had been changed."

"That's right, people don't realize that they have more than one key to a door when they're selling a house. I thought he'd probably tossed it aside and forgotten about it.

We knew that Westover probably locked the door behind him when he came in that day; Mrs. Lynch had her lodgers well trained in that aspect. So I reasoned that whoever had done it, had had a key. That pointed to the Donovans, but I thought it was Mrs. Donovan, not Mr. Donovan."

"What about the stain on his shirt?" Betsy asked. "How would that point to her? She wasn't at the board meeting so anything he might have written wouldn't have pointed to her as the killer."

"True," Mrs. Jeffries said. "But I didn't necessarily think that his note, if indeed he actually wrote a note, would do anything more than give us an idea of what had really happened at the meeting. I never thought it would point to the killer." She shook her head in disgust. "I've been so wrong, so blind."

"I wouldn't say that, Mrs. Jeffries," Smythe said. "You got the inspector and Constable Barnes to the Donovan house in time to save that woman's life. If you hadn't she'd be dead by now. God knows her servants were fairly useless."

"You should of 'eard 'im," Wiggins added. "He were screamin' at the top of 'is lungs that he hated her and she was tryin' to ruin 'im."

"She was going to force him out of the building," Ruth said. "Remember, she'd made him put up the building as collateral for a loan. Obviously, he knew that even with Westover's wonderful engine, the firm wouldn't be able to survive."

"But I still don't see why he'd kill Westover," Mrs. Goodge sounded genuinely puzzled. "He could just as easily have sacked the man if he wanted to be rid of him."

"Probably because Westover was going to do something about that engine being unsafe," Mrs. Jeffries suggested. "We'll have to wait until the inspector gets back to find out all the details. But I must say, I'm very disappointed in myself." With that, she rose from the table and despite protests from the others, she went up to her room to have a good hard think about where she'd gone wrong.

• • •

The inspector came in later that afternoon, just as the household had gathered around the table for their tea. He popped his head into the kitchen. "Hello everyone, may I have tea with you?" His eyes widened in surprise as he saw Ruth Cannonberry with them. "Gracious, I didn't know we had company."

"Hello, Gerald," Ruth gave him a big smile and a wave. "Do come in, your staff very kindly invited me to have tea with them."

Blushing with pleasure, he made his way to the table. "We've made an arrest in our case."

"Of course you have, sir. We knew you would." Mrs. Jeffries smiled cheerfully and poured another cup. "Do sit down and tell us all about it."

He pulled out the chair next to Ruth, gave her another quick smile, and sat down. "Thank you, Mrs. Jeffries," he said as he accepted the steaming cup. "It's difficult to know where to begin."

"Who'd you arrest, sir?" Wiggins asked helpfully, even though he already knew the answer.

"Harry Donovan," Witherspoon replied. "It was most extraordinary. We only went over there because I wanted to ask him a few questions, but when we got there, he was in the process of trying to murder Mrs. Donovan. He doesn't much care for her. Apparently she's loaned the firm a great deal of money and he'd used his office building as collateral."

Mrs. Jeffries was desperate to know where she'd gone wrong. She knew precisely what questions she wanted answered. "Why did Harry Donovan want to kill poor Mr. Westover?"

"Westover had resigned from the firm, he was going to send a cable to the company in South Africa and tell them the engine that was being sent to them wasn't safe."

"That's not a very good reason for murderin' someone," Wiggins said.

"It was reason enough for Harry Donovan," Witherspoon's eyebrows drew together. "He's a bit mad, I think. Apparently, the firm has been in financial straits for years. They don't have a very good reputation. He felt that they couldn't stand any bad news about the company so he murdered Westover to keep him from sending off that cable."

"How did he get into the 'ouse?" Smythe asked. "Did Westover let him in?"

"He had a key," Witherspoon replied. "Apparently, he used to own the Lynch house. He set it up to look like suicide but then made a grave mistake when he left. He dropped the key on his way out. I expect he was in a bit in a panic." Witherspoon went on to give them all the rest of the details about the arrest. They listened carefully, occasionally asking a question or making an admiring comment.

Finally, he said, "Thank goodness Constable Barnes suggested we search Westover's rooms again. If we hadn't we'd not have gone to Donovan's house when we did and poor Mrs. Donovan would be as dead as Harlan Westover."

"You're so very clever, Gerald," Ruth patted him on the arm. "You've caught ever so many killers. I think you ought to be promoted."

Witherspoon blushed like a schoolboy. "I'm not so clever. I couldn't solve any cases without a great deal of help. We owe the solving of this one more to Constable Barnes than to me. He had one good suggestion after another."

"Nevertheless," Mrs. Jeffries added. "Lady Cannonberry is right. With your record of solving homicides, you ought to be a chief inspector by now."

His cheeks turned even redder. "Please, no. You give me too much credit. I like being an inspector. I'd be a terrible chief."

"Nonsense, Gerald, you'd be perfect," Ruth insisted. "Of course, you would have to do a bit more socially . . ."

"Like a dinner party," Mrs. Jeffries interrupted. "You see, Inspector, even Lady Cannonberry agrees a dinner party is in order."

Witherspoon knew when he was beaten. "All right, then. But only if Lady Cannonberry will act as my hostess."

"I'd be honored, Gerald." She smiled graciously and started to rise. "This has been lovely, but I do need to get home now."

"Allow me to escort you across the garden," Witherspoon leapt to his feet.

"That would be wonderful, we can talk about the dinner party. I've all sorts of wonderful ideas about it."

As soon as they were out the back door, everyone turned their attention to Mrs. Jeffries. "From what he said, you were right in your thinkin'." Mrs. Goodge said reassuringly. "You just got the wrong spouse is all."

Mrs. Jeffries sighed. "Do you really think so?"

"Course we do," Smythe said firmly. "You sussed out that Donovan was the only one of all the partners who'd be ruined financially if the firm went under."

"Yes, but I thought that meant that Mrs. Donovan killed Westover to make sure the firm went under. Without Westover, the company didn't stand a chance to survive in the long run."

"And you were right about Donovan havin' a key," Wiggins added.

"True, but I was sure Mrs. Donovan was the one who'd used it." Mrs. Jeffries forced herself to smile. "I know you're all trying to make me feel better. But I made a terrible mistake, and that's that."

"Maybe it was a mistake you were meant to make," Betsy said softly. "It saved a woman's life. *You* saved a woman's life."

Mrs. Jeffries stared at her for a moment and then smiled. "You're right. Perhaps I was meant to make it."

After dinner that evening, Betsy sat down at the table and waited for Smythe. He'd gone to the stables to check on Bow and Arrow, the inspector's horses. The kitchen was empty, and the rest of the household had retired for the evening.

She didn't have to wait long before she heard the back door open and Smythe's heavy tread coming up the hallway. She straightened her spine, bracing herself for a confrontation. She didn't think he'd like what she was going to tell him.

He grinned broadly as he came into the kitchen and saw

her waiting for him. "You shouldn't have waited up for me. But I'm glad you did. I want to talk to you."

"And I want to speak with you as well."

He dropped into the empty seat next to her. "The case is over, love."

"And I promised we'd set a wedding date when it was finished," she reminded him. She swallowed heavily. "And I always keep my promises."

"I know," he said. He watched her carefully. "How do you feel about bein' a June bride?"

"I was thinking more like October," she held her breath, hoping he wouldn't get upset and think she didn't love him. "I've always fancied getting married in the autumn."

"October," he repeated. "All right. Are you sure, though?"

"Quite sure," she slumped in relief. "That's ten months from now. That'll give us plenty of time to plan a wedding. Much better than June, that's too soon."

Smythe gave her a puzzled look. "Too soon. I wasn't thinkin' of June this year, I was thinkin' next year."

"Next year? But that's almost eighteen months from now!" Betsy couldn't believe it. "Don't you want to marry me?"

"Of course I do, lass," he laughed. "I was tryin' to do what you wanted and give us time. But if you're set on October . . ." he broke off as she poked him in the arm.

"You silly man," she leaned over and gave him a quick kiss on the lips. "You knew exactly what you're about. June it is, then. Next June."

Enjoy the rich historical mysteries from Berkley Prime Crime

Margaret Frazer:
Dame Frevisse Medieval Mysteries
Joliffe Mysteries

Bruce Alexander:
Sir John Fielding Mysteries

Kate Kingsbury:
The Manor House Mysteries

Robin Paige:
Victorian and Edwardian Mysteries

Lou Jane Temple:
The Spice Box Mysteries

Victoria Thompson:
The Gaslight Mysteries

Solving crimes through time.

WELL-CRAFTED MYSTERIES
FROM BERKLEY PRIME CRIME

- **Earlene Fowler** Don't miss this Agatha Award–winning quilting series featuring Benni Harper.

- **Monica Ferris** This *USA Today* bestselling Needlecraft Mystery series includes free knitting patterns.

- **Laura Childs** Her Scrapbooking Mystery series offers tips to satisfy the most die-hard crafters.

- **Maggie Sefton** This popular Knitting Mystery series comes with knitting patterns and recipes.

SOLVING CRIME CAN BE AN ART

penguin.com